*For Liz + Charles
with !
...*

A LONG HOT UNHOLY SUMMER

TERESA WAUGH

QUARTET

First published in 2014 by Quartet Books Limited
A member of the Namara Group
27 Goodge Street, London W1T 2LD
Copyright © Teresa Waugh 2014
The right of Teresa Waugh to be identified
as the author of this work has been asserted
by her in accordance with the
Copyright, Designs and Patents Act, 1988
A catalogue record for this book
is available from the British Library
ISBN 978 0 7043 7369 3
Typeset by Josh Bryson
Printed and bound in Great Britain by
T J International Ltd, Padstow, Cornwall

*For my children and in memory of Bron
and of many a long hot summer*

I

A young man with high cheek bones and dark curly hair was sitting in the white van in which he lived. The van was parked outside the station in Toulouse from where, when the mood took him, the young man could observe the endless comings and goings of travellers – young people with backpacks or businessmen clutching briefcases, mackintoshes flapping behind them as they strode purposefully forward, well-dressed women clicking along the pavement in their high heels. All human life was there from the ruffian to the gentleman, the prostitute to the *doctoresse*. He resembled none of them and at times, so unreal did they all seem, that the mere sight of them made him feel nauseous. So pointless were they in their ceaseless activity, as they hurtled, like little silver balls on a bagatelle board, hither and thither, apparently with no specific destination.

He was a clever young man and he knew it, but despite his brains and good looks things had not always gone well for him. Like many lonely people he liked to spend hours communing with his laptop. This is what he was doing in his parked van, looking up only occasionally to glance at the busily passing throng. Today the crowd held no magic for him; there were other things on his mind.

Sometimes he would spend hours playing virtual games – war games which he always won and which he played against unknown people from far-flung parts of the world, most of whom he despised for their stupidity or crudity or for their covert love of real and extreme violence. Then he would enter a chat room, looking for someone a little more intelligent to talk to – a pretty girl with a brain in her head or perhaps an unsung philosopher with whom to discuss his ideas for a new world order.

For some weeks he had been talking to a Ukrainian girl who lived on a farm somewhere in the south of the country. Living, as she did, far from the nearest town, she found her life to be harsh, relentless and lacking in either prospect or adventure. She had wanted to go to university but her unyielding father required her to stay at home and help on the farm, feeding chickens and pigs and milking cows. Digging up turnips in winter. She needed to escape and had at first been in touch with a nice Libyan boy who wanted a blonde girlfriend and who like her sought adventure. He had seemed besotted with her and had even planned to visit her in the Ukraine, perhaps to take her back to his country, but then the revolution had come and he had gone to fight for freedom. Somehow they had lost touch. Perhaps the Libyan boy had discovered enough adventure on his own doorstep.

From the picture she posted on the site, it was clear that she was a pretty girl, but some of her thoughts were so ill-conceived, so vapid that our young man decided to look elsewhere. He had turned to another girl – good-looking, bright and, he thought, malleable. In fact he was rapidly becoming so obsessed with her that he had taken to sitting in his van gazing for hours at her picture and sending her long verbose messages. He told her fantastical tales about himself, imagining that she would be impressed by the idea of him writing a film script or playing the saxophone – activities about which he had idly dreamed as a teenager years ago. But mostly he expounded his philosophy of the meaninglessness of life, the vanity of everything and above all the non-existence of God.

Then he temporarily forgot that there were days when he heard the voice of God commanding him to do the strangest things.

II

Not so far from Toulouse, in an isolated little village huddled on the edge of the *Montaigne Noire*, with magnificent views across the Lauragais Plain to the distant Pyrenean peaks an old woman was claiming that a miracle had been wrought through her prayers to an eighteenth-century Archbishop.

The local television news had shown the old prelate's remains being brought home from a Protestant cemetery overseas where they had lain undisturbed for over two hundred years until his body along with the bodies of a number of other French priests, had been dug up to make way for a new railway line. A certain amount of interest had been awakened by the discovery of the Archbishop's coffin. He had been a distinguished, important man in his day – Bishop of Evreux, Archbishop of Toulouse and finally, the last Archbishop of Narbonne and *Président des Etats du Languedoc* which position had earned him a tiny place in history.

Madame Pellissier had instantly begun to pray to the old boy, begging him for all kinds of blessings. She asked him to intercede that her arthritis might be cured, her sight restored, her back straightened. And lo and behold, she claimed, he had listened. He had indeed interceded for her with the Almighty. Her sight, she swore, had never been so clear, but since she couldn't read and since she had always lived in the same village in the same house, both of which she could describe blindfold, the truth or otherwise of her claim remained difficult to establish.

But not unnaturally Monsieur l'Abbé who nowadays preferred to be called Fafa – his real name being François – was delighted by the old lady's claims. In so many ways the Church was dying on its feet what with the young people lying in bed on Sunday mornings instead of attending Mass as their parents had been wont to do. Those who could occasionally be bothered to go to church generally came to the Saturday evening Mass which in recent years had strangely been allowed to count as being on a Sunday and which meant that they had no need to get out of their beds at an unacceptable hour. The well-off came straight from the tennis court or the swimming pool, the less well-off from the muddy *bassin* where they swam in summer or from chattering under the plane trees that shaded the little village square where the old men played boules.

It particularly hurt Fafa to see, just as he was pronouncing, 'The Mass is ended. Go in peace,' young girls in skimpy skirts rushing in an unseemly manner for the door, hands already fumbling in bags and pockets for a cigarette to be frantically lit as they crossed the threshold of the church. But now here was Mathilde Pellissier, a good, old-fashioned member of his flock, a woman of faith who perhaps was being rewarded with a miracle for her years of religious devotion while the faithless cynics laughed behind her back.

'*Ah, Monsieur l'Abbé,*' she said – for she could never dream of calling a priest by his first name any more than she could approve of one wearing *des blue-jeans. 'Je vous assure, c'est un miracle, un vrai miracle!*' And she crossed herself for fear.

At Mass Monsieur l'Abbé wore his jeans under his soutane. For want of a long mirror he was unaware of the soutane being too short and therefore leaving a good fifteen centimetres of his offending trousers visible to any of his ageing congregation who were still able to see well enough. Sometimes he wore trainers which squeaked on the sweaty stone floor of the ancient little church as he walked up the aisle. But his heart was in the right place and Madame Pellissier was grateful in her solitude for his frequent visits. She was grateful too for the seriousness with which he listened to her claim of a miracle. He would, he assured her, report the matter to the Bishop.

Nobody knew quite how old Madame Pellissier was but she had been a widow for as long as anyone could remember. Her father had been killed at the Second Battle of Ypres in 1915 which made her nearly a hundred at least and her only son had died of meningitis at the age of twelve while his father was in a German prison camp during the Second World War. Pellissier came back from five years of incarceration a broken and a sick man only to die a few years later of a pulmonary embolism. Since then Mathilde had consoled herself with religion, gardening in the small plot across the road from her house and cooking. She kept rabbits and chickens which she sold in the local market and whose necks she cheerfully wrung on demand.

The village in which she lived had changed radically in recent years. There had been a time when it was peopled by women like herself, dressed in black with black aprons over their black dresses. They washed their clothes in the *lavoir* at the bottom of the hill where the stream had been directed through a trough under a tiled roof. They gossiped as they scrubbed, their hands red and rough and raw from the cold water. Most of the men were agricultural workers although one was a blacksmith and Pellissier himself had been the local *châtreur* whose job it was to travel from farm to farm castrating whatever animal or fowl was deemed to require such treatment.

In recent times the village had been more or less colonised by the Dutch and the English, some of whom lived there the whole year round whilst others arrived at Easter and in the summer in four-by-fours crammed with children and lavatory paper and Edam cheese. They squeezed themselves into tiny houses long since abandoned by the peasantry and built extravagant swimming pools, the permanent residents usually being employed by the *estivants* to maintain their houses and their pools throughout the winter. Madame Pellissier confided in the priest that although she didn't like, as she put it, to *catégoriser les gens*, she didn't care for the English.

The priest, in a moment of weakness, remarked that they were better than the Dutch since they left their own inferior cheeses behind and were generally happy to spend their money in the local shops.

But, until from beyond the grave, the Archbishop decided miraculously to cure her sciatica (or was it her sight?) and her photograph appeared on the front page of the local paper, Madame Pellissier's main claim to fame lay in her ability to make the best *cassoulet de Castelnaudary*. She still cooked it – always in the traditional earthenware dish – on the open fire in her kitchen where she left it to simmer all day or even longer.

There were those – mostly foreigners from Toulouse – who chose quite wrongly to add goose to their cassoulet. This, in Mathilde's view, was an aberration. The one and only, true cassoulet should contain nothing but pork, pork skin, sausages and haricot beans and be made in the right region. It was a well-known fact that Parisians returning to the capital after the summer holidays and attempting to make the dish back there, could never succeed. It was all because of the water, Mathilde opined. She had no faith in Parisian water.

Fafa, the priest, was not averse to Mathilde's cooking and frequently visited her at an hour when she would be likely to offer him something to eat.

Her late husband, she would repeatedly tell him as she handed him a steaming plate of cassoulet, loved the dish so much that even as he lay dying he begged for it. But by the end he was so weak that he had had to *pousser le manger* – to push it down. This he did with tears in his eyes. Although having no problem of the kind himself, Fafa expressed great sympathy for the poor dying man.

It was not merely her innocent faith, nor was it just her excellent cooking which drew the priest to Madame Pellissier. As much as anything else it was the loneliness of his chosen profession which led him to seek comfort in her little kitchen smelling of wood smoke and cassoulet, where she tended on him almost as if he were her long lost son. She was forever telling him to wrap up against the cold, to make sure he ate enough or to drive carefully – the *estivants*, she maintained, drove through the village like madmen. *Comme des fous.*

Until only a few years earlier Mathilde had been used to earning a little extra money by making cassoulet for local people who came bearing the ingredients for her to cook on her open fire. Later they would heat the dish in their own ovens until a thick crust was formed on top then boast as they entertained their friends that Mathilde made the best cassoulet in the world. But now she prepared it only occasionally for a favoured few or for herself – with Monsieur l'Abbé in mind, of course.

When Christiane turned up on her way home from the shops one hot summer's day she found the priest, dressed as ever in jeans and trainers with a mock-leather jacket over a sky-blue T-shirt, sitting at the table in Mathilde's smoke-filled kitchen with in front of him a plate piled high with beans and sausages. Beside the plate was a glass which Christiane recognised as an empty mustard pot. It was adorned with a picture of Babar the elephant and filled with what was probably sour, thick purple wine of the kind that leaves a violet moustache on the upper lip of whoever drinks it.

Nothing changed in this kitchen, Christiane thought. Winter or summer *la soupe* would be stewing on the open fire and the priest would be there with his mock leather jacket.

In days gone by Madame Pellissier had often made cassoulet for Christiane whom she had known since she was a little girl and who had come, as she frequently did, to ask how the old lady was. Christiane was not sorry to see the priest. She had long since given up any claim to rigorous Catholicism, but she liked Fafa as much for the fact that he looked after Mathilde as for anything else. It made her very angry when he came in the summer to swim in her swimming pool and the children laughed and sniggered at the sight of his thin white body and emerald green bathing trunks. They seemed to think that priests had no right to bathe.

Fafa leaped to his feet and put out a hand to shake Christiane's. He felt a little awkward having been found tucking into so greedy a meal but she appeared to take no notice. She kissed Mathilde who welcomed her effusively then accepted the old woman's invitation to sit on a wooden upright chair next to the priest. Mathilde remained standing, her old body bent, her gnarled hands pushed into the front pocket of her black apron, and on her face a wide smile that revealed her blackened, crooked teeth.

Would Madame Christiane like *un petit marc*? Mathilde took one hand out of her pocket and, holding it just in front of her face indicated with her thumb and forefinger a measurement of about a centimetre. She always offered Christiane a little Armagnac which she called *marc*, pronouncing the final 'c' with almost violent emphasis. Except at Christmas time Christiane always refused.

Embarrassed by the occasion, the priest hurriedly finished the rest of his cassoulet, surreptitiously wiping his mouth on the back of his hand and, straightening his shoulders, turned to face Christiane. What did she think about the return of the Archbishop's remains and Mathilde's miraculous cure?

According to Christiane who was working on a biography of the Archbishop, he was a perfectly ordinary sinner, not unlike the rest of us, but now that he had at last been laid to rest in the heart of his arch-diocese which he visited so rarely during his lifetime, there was a ludicrous idea being bandied about in certain circles to the effect that he should be a candidate for canonisation.

She had read in the paper about the return of his remains to Narbonne and on account of her own work had since visited the cathedral where the Archbishop now lay in a side chapel; reunited once more with his flock. There had been a fine theatricality about the day so beautifully orchestrated by the city fathers when the old boy's body was carried by barge up the canal for which he had been almost entirely responsible. Tirelessly had he worked, cajoling, persuading, wheedling, anything to ensure that the funds for the great undertaking be made available by Paris. That the Languedoc be not forgotten by the swirling mass of greedy, ambitious courtiers who surrounded the King.

It must have been a moving sight to see the procession winding through the streets to the cathedral, the old man's coffin surrounded by princes of the Church and all the city's dignitaries and followed by distant members of his family as though by a widow and his own children and grandchildren. A huge *tricolore* fluttering in the spring breeze over the landing stage by the canal had proclaimed the importance of the occasion. Which was funny, Christiane thought. The Archbishop would have loathed the *tricolore* with its revolutionary associations. Wouldn't he have preferred golden fleurs-de-lis on a white background? It had been a strangely anachronistic event but at least it momentarily distracted attention from the appalling scandals which were otherwise plaguing the Church at the moment.

Mathilde was throwing her hands in the air and proclaiming her delight. What a splendid thing it was to have brought the old man back to where he belonged and – she put her hands together as though in prayer and waggled them backwards and forwards in front of her face – did Madame Christiane realise that he was a saint. *Un vrai saint, je vous assure.*

The last thing Christiane wished to do was to offend or hurt Madame Pellissier in any way and she wondered what line the priest had taken over Mathilde's claims to having been miraculously cured of her ills, for as far as Christiane could see the old lady was no more active or able than she had been six months earlier. Besides she found it hard to tolerate anything which she regarded as prejudice or blind ignorance – even the innocent ignorance of someone like Mathilde who had had little or no education and whose thinking had been entirely formed by the Church. And did Fafa encourage her in these beliefs? Did he himself believe in miracles performed by long-dead good-living bishops? How could he? It was one thing to stick your colours to the mast of religion for purposes of comfort in distress or in old age, but surely no thinking person could pass through this world without questioning the absurdities that religion threw in your face. She had once heard a priest say that only other religions could cause him to doubt his faith, and she respected him for that.

Faith, in Christiane's view, more perfectly demonstrated the willing suspension of disbelief than did *Alice in Wonderland*, *Le Petit Prince* or any number of science-fiction movies. People chose to believe. That she could understand, but that an educated young man today might encourage people to believe in miracles was quite beyond her.

'Well,' she said hesitantly, 'I gather it was quite an occasion for Narbonne…'

'For Narbonne – and for the Church,' Fafa insisted. He was never quite sure where he stood with Christiane and finding himself caught between her and Mathilde didn't know exactly how to play it. When alone with Mathilde he found it fairly easy to believe in miracles as she did; to believe that through the intercession of one worldly Archbishop she could be cured of her ills. But as soon as he found himself in the company of someone more sophisticated he could never prevent an insidious feeling of doubt from creeping in. Not that he ever seriously doubted what he regarded as the Eternal Verities – but it was just these miracles…

He imagined that Christiane – a woman whom he both liked and admired would have little if any time for such things. And he wished to please Christiane. Was that his problem? Was he too eager to please?

Sensing his discomfort, Christiane turned to Madame Pellissier to congratulate her on feeling better which she might attribute not only to the Archbishop, but to the warmer weather?

Having by now decided to take his leave, the priest kissed Mathilde warmly on both cheeks, assured her that he would pray for her, then shook Christiane by the hand.

She, with a wicked look in her eye, remarked on how happy he must be to discover that miracles were at work in his very parish and urged him to keep her in the picture. 'Because,' she said, as you may know I'm writing a life of the Archbishop and I'd hate to overlook anything.'

'Ah, Madame Christiane,' Mathilde raised both hands and shook them on either side of her face, 'if only you knew *quel saint homme* – what a holy man the Archbishop was…' The irony of Christiane's remarks to the priest had not passed her by.

Before she too took her leave of the old lady, Christiane sat with Mathilde for a while chatting about this and that – the family, the price of melons, the weather – one thing and another.

But as soon as she was in her car her mind turned back to the Archbishop and to the extraordinarily exciting piece of luck that had come her way. It was every biographer's dream.

A carpenter repairing some panelling in the *mairie* of the village where the Archbishop had spent so much of his life had come across a secret cupboard behind a well-disguised sliding panel. And in that secret cupboard, mouldy, half eaten by mites and worn by time were concealed the Archbishop's journals.

The *mairie* housed in a little old building opposite the church where the old boy must frequently have said Mass, had been used by the Archbishop in his day as his private study – somewhere where he could escape from dependent relatives and the social hurly-burly of the château.

For purposes of research Christiane had already visited that village several times, making friends there with, among others, the mayor who immediately informed her of the discovery. The papers had been straight away handed over to the Municipal Archives but she, leaving the children with their father in England, left for France as soon as she possibly could, and there she sat for days pouring over the Archbishop's papers under the watchful eyes of a grey, beady archivist. The damage caused by time and damp infuriated and tantalised her and yet it was a miracle that so much of the journal had survived. She could never have hoped for a more fruitful or exciting find. The old boy had indeed been quite a reprobate.

'Aha,' she repeated to herself as she drove back from Mathilde's. '*Quel saint homme!*'

III

Most of the young people were still in bed when Christiane reached home.

Home was Aigues Nègres, a long low stone-built farmhouse that Christiane and her husband had bought as a ruin some twenty years earlier. It stood in an isolated position down a track off the narrow road that led on up the mountain beyond the village where Mathilde lived, and must have had one of the most extensive views in the whole of France. On either side of it stood a group of small stunted trees planted long ago in a vain attempt to protect the building from the ravages of an inclement Atlantic climate and from the much dreaded and much hated *vent d'Espagne*, the warm wind from the south which had a reputation for sending people mad.

Little by little over the years the house had been transformed from a crumbling, mouse-ridden camping site to a relatively comfortable family home in which to spend the holidays. There was a swimming pool and a ping-pong table and, more recently, a permanent *va-et-vient* of teenagers.

For Christiane Aigues Nègres was home. Although brought up in Bordeaux where for all his working life her father had slaved away as a *petit fonctionnaire*, she had spent much of her childhood with her paternal grandparents in the Languedoc. She was French but her mother was English and when Christiane married an Englishman she moved to the West Country to produce English children. Claud, a university lecturer, specialising in twentieth-century French literature, shared his wife's love of Aigues Nègres to which they hoped one day to retire.

As she carried a tray of peaches from the car, Christiane called out for someone to help her unload the rest of her shopping. She was sometimes horrified to the point of disgust by the amount of food she had to buy each week to satisfy the ravenous appetites of so many young people. Today was Friday and she seemed to have bought even more than usual for the weekend. The least those young people could do, she thought, was to help take it all out of the car.

Her younger daughter, Agnès, appeared from round the corner of the house wearing a sulky look on her face, an over-sized white T-shirt appropriated from her father and pink plastic flip-flops. Her long, shapely brown legs were bare. Christiane could never be sure what it was that intermittently gave rise to that sulky look on the face of one who was traditionally the happy-go-lucky member of the family.

'Everything's gone wrong,' was all Agnès would say as she heaved a bag of vegetables out of the car.

'So where are the others?' Christiane wanted to know.

Agnès shrugged. 'Still in bed.'

Christiane wasn't sure whether to be irritated or pleased. Had they been out of bed they might well have been slopping around in the kitchen having breakfast at what she regarded as lunchtime. This way they could miss out on breakfast altogether.

'Papa's gone to get some mousetraps and pick up his new printer,' Agnès added. 'Be back soon.'

'So what's gone wrong with you?' Christiane asked, hardly expecting a reply.

'Nothing,' came the answer.

'I went to see Mathilde,' Christiane remarked by way of changing the subject whilst beginning to unpack a mountain of cheeses. Her shopping, she noticed, completely covered the surface of the large kitchen table.

'Yum, yum!' said Agnès picking up a large piece of Port Salut and sniffing it. 'Did you get a camembert too?'

'No, but there's Roquefort and Cantal – that should be enough to keep you all happy,' her mother replied.

'So how was Mathilde then?'

'Very excited. She thinks a miracle has cured her arthritis or her blindness or something. Not that she looked much different to me. Monsieur le Curé was there eating cassoulet.'

14

'Yuk! Poor Mathilde,' Agnès opined, 'having that creep hanging around her all the time.'

Christiane remonstrated with her daughter.

'But Mu-u-um…how can you like him? He wears horrible T-shirts and have you seen him naked?'

Naked? Of course she hadn't seen him naked. What was Agnès talking about?

'Well you must have seen him in his bathing trunks? His body's all white…'

Christiane sighed and started to unpack sausages and saucissons and pâtés and all the other delicious things she had bought from her favourite *charcutière*.

By the time lunch was ready Claud had still not returned with his mousetraps and his printer and Isabelle, Christiane's older daughter, was nowhere to be seen.

'Where on earth's Isabelle?' her mother wanted to know.

'Oh,' replied Agnès, sitting down and helping herself to a piece of bread, 'I forgot to say, she went with Papa.'

There was something indefinable about Isabelle's behaviour lately that caused Christiane to feel a certain anxiety on her behalf. Something about her manner. She seemed uncommunicative, almost shifty. Any attempt Christiane made to talk to her had been met with cold disdain.

'What for? If she needed to go shopping she could have come with me. He won't have wanted to hang around in the town – especially in this heat.'

'She said she had something very important to do,' Agnès smirked and glanced across the table at Isabelle's friend, Ellen, who carefully avoided catching her eye.

Seeing her daughter's furtive glance, Christiane looked round the table at the five teenagers sitting there and wondered what on earth they were up to. They all looked as good as gold. When they had finally rolled out of bed, pulled on shorts and T-shirts, failed to brush their hair and stepped outside for a first cigarette of the day, they had all come to the kitchen with smiling faces and good manners. They had laid the table and made the salad dressing; they had remarked on the delicious food and offered to hoover the swimming pool. You couldn't fault them.

'Well we'd better start without them,' Christiane said, pushing a dish of crudités towards Maddy, Claud's dark-eyed niece. Sam and Jake, the two boys, were sitting together at the far end of the table like two mirror images of Tin-Tin Christiane thought, with their hair sticking up in coifs. Even the baggy, three-quarter-length shorts they wore seemed to resemble the plus fours worn by the famous boy detective whose image, if not that of his little white dog, Milou, would have adorned their T-shirts a generation ago. Now, she noted with distaste, they sported either pictures of hideous monsters or flip double entendres.

Like most meals at Aigues Nègres lunch was a noisy affair with everyone seeming to talk at once except for Christiane who, when she wasn't looking at her watch and wondering what on earth had happened to Claud and Isabelle, was thinking of Mathilde and the Archbishop and wondering how the canonisation – or at least the beatification – of the old prelate would fit into her book. It could, she supposed, provide a fine ironic end to the story of his life.

Lunch was over and the teenagers were stacking the dishwasher, pushing each other and giggling as they did so, before Christiane finally heard Claud's car draw up in front of the house.

'Where have you been?' she asked irritably as he came into the kitchen. 'I was beginning to think you must have had an accident or…' Then as he broke in with, 'Isabelle…is she here?' she noticed the frantic look on his face. At the same time the teenagers suddenly disappeared from the kitchen all at once, as if by magic.

'I thought she went with you…'

'She did, but I can't find her.'

'What do you mean, you can't find her?' Suddenly Christiane remembered the furtive look she had intercepted on Agnès's face at lunch. What did those wretched teenagers know with their innocent airs and their Tintin hairdos. 'Agnès,' she screamed. 'Come here, *viens ici…tout de suite…*' And to Claud, 'Anyway why did she need to go with you?'

'She said she wanted to have her hair cut…'

'Have her hair cut? She just had it cut the other day – she's the only one of them that ever does cut her hair…'

Christiane went to the door and yelled again for Agnès, who eventually appeared dragging her feet unwillingly it seemed and staring at the ground as if to disguise a nervous smirk. Her cousin, Maddy, looking strangely cocky, was in attendance. Both girls had long hair almost down to their waists which flopped untidily around their faces and over their shoulders, catching in strands on their clothes. Christiane felt suddenly immensely irritated and wished she could take the garden shears to both their pretty little heads.

'Does either of you know why Isabelle wanted to go to Castel?' Christiane demanded ferociously.

'She said she wanted to have her hair cut.' Agnès was still smirking uncomfortably.

'Don't be so silly,' said her mother.

'I think,' Maddy helpfully interrupted, 'she thought they didn't do it very well last time so…'

Panic was beginning to make Christiane angry and, in any case, she was quite sure that the two girls knew something that they were not saying. She had begun to shake.

'She'll be back later,' Agnès, on whom the severity of the situation seemed suddenly to have dawned, firmly announced. 'Don't worry Mum.'

Christiane looked helplessly at Claud – where had he last seen their daughter? What time was he supposed to have met up with her? Had he any clue as to where she might have gone?

With the stunned expression on his round youthful face, she thought, as he stared uncomprehendingly back at her, he looked more like a teenager himself than a responsible adult. He ran his fingers desperately through his unruly hair, as though to find his daughter there, and pushed his round, steel-rimmed spectacles sharply on to the bridge of his nose before answering.

He had waited for more than an hour, he said, and had asked for her in the shops and at the hairdresser's where of course she hadn't been seen, he'd rung her mobile but it had been switched off and then he'd come home. He thought she might have telephoned.

But she hadn't.

IV

Christiane was enjoying her work and had hoped to spend the afternoon at her desk where photocopied pages from the Archbishop's diary lay waiting to be read.

Last evening I supped at Madame Adélaïde's. Of all the King's daughters Madame Adélaïde is not only the most beautiful but the most cultivated, the most distinguée and assuredly the one most gifted with esprit, thus there is nothing unexpected in her being His Majesty's favourite.

On being shewn into her presence, I discovered Madame to be reclining elegantly on a chaise longue with a book in her hand, looking entirely as if she were about to pose for Monsieur Nattier who has so exquisitely portrayed in turn all the Daughters of France. As I was ushered into her presence, she immediately took it upon herself to lay aside her book.

It was not for me to enquire as to the nature of her reading but nor was I entirely surprised when, raising one eyebrow and looking quizzically up at me from under her thick lashes, the Princess declared, 'This book is not to be read by priests. This book is banned – et Monsieur Dillon, vous ne le lirez pas – you shall not read it.'

Aware as I am of Madame's passion for learning and of her curiosity concerning all things, I immediately supposed her to be in possession of a work by one of the Encyclopédistes. Perhaps she had at last procured a copy of Monsieur de Voltaire's Candide, brought back for her from London, Amsterdam or Geneva. Madame has long been an admirer of that scoundrel Monsieur de Voltaire's writing. A scoundrel indeed, albeit a clever and amusing one.

I was not long in Madame's presence before Monsieur de C was shewn in accompanied by the duchesse de G and the comte de L. By the time supper was served the company had swelled to some twelve or fifteen persons. Soon the conversation turned around Le Franc de Pompignan's recent address to the Académie. His tirade of invective against the Encyclopédistes was much derided by the assembled company with Monsieur de L being of the opinion that the marquis had unwisely stepped into a nest of vipers since Monsieur de Voltaire for one is unlikely to ignore what he must surely regard as the arrogant folly of a lesser mortal. One could not wish to become the object of Monsieur de Voltaire's ridicule for even now, with advancing years, his wit remains as acute as ever it was and his pen as sharp.

'Besides,' Monsieur de L insisted, 'he fears nothing and no one.' Much merriment ensued as Monsieur de L recounted the story of how, as a young man, Voltaire had circulated some viciously satirical verses about the Chevalier de Rohan-Chabot who had had the temerity to accuse him of being a parvenu. Incensed, Rohan-Chabot had Voltaire beaten up, but to no avail.

'En fait, c'est un parvenu!' the duchesse suddenly declared. 'Tout le monde le sait.' Everyone knows. Everyone knows that Monsieur de Voltaire adopted a particule to which he has no right. 'Quel parvenu!'

I found myself looking nervously around the room in the sincere hope that no close friend of Monsieur de Voltaire's might be found among the company there assembled. One who, delighting in mischief, might choose to repeat to him what the duchesse had so heedlessly proclaimed. It is not hard to imagine with what ease Voltaire might lampoon her for, with her heavy jaw and low brow, she is not a handsome woman and, although full of *esprit*, she can on occasion lack the *finesse* so much to be desired in a noblewoman.

I took my leave of Madame Adélaïde at a relatively early hour for I have much to do tomorrow before setting forth on the following day for Hautefontaine and hence to Toulouse where I shall visit the university and inspect the public works for which, with a word in the ear of the duc de Choiseul, we have at last obtained some further financial aid.

It is ever difficult to persuade the great of Paris to part with so much as one sou for the improvement of the lot of the poor in some distant part of the kingdom. Were some of the princes who flaunt their wealth at the court of Versailles to visit the impoverished and dirty town of Toulouse, they might be moved to understand the need that city has of bridges; they might realise too how the banks of the river require to be shored up against flooding thus to allow the citizens to go about their business unhindered by the squalor and disease attendant on frequent inundations.

On my return to the rue du Bac I found Madame de R anxiously awaiting my return, concerned that I should have a good night's sleep in preparation for the journey. She was in no mind to hear about the *souper* chez Madame Adélaïde for no sooner had I donned my nightshirt than she took up her candle and with an unsmiling, *bonne nuit mon cher oncle*, made to retire to her chamber. Despite her youth and the pleasing elegance of her slender figure, my dear niece does at times evoke in me the memory of a stern but pretty little Scottish governess who in my infancy at Saint-Germain was wont to whip me for the very slightest of misdemeanours. I surmise that it is the untimely death of her husband which may have soured a formerly sweet temperament.

Whatsoever her faults I am fond of my niece and delight in the company of her little daughter whom she, I opine, is given to treating somewhat harshly. For me it is a considerable convenience to stay at the house in the rue du Bac which she so fortuitously inherited

*from her late husband along with the property at Hautefontaine in
the Forêt de Compiègne where the hunting is equal, if not superior,
to the hunting at Fontainebleau. I should thank the Almighty daily
upon my knees for this double blessing.*

V

Claud and Christiane had gone back to the town to search
for their missing daughter. The frightened teenagers had been
prevailed upon to tell anything and everything they knew
about Isabelle's movements. Of course she had gone to meet
a boy, or, more worryingly, a man she had met through the
internet.

His name, Agnès said, was Etienne. Not very helpful that
since she didn't know his surname, nor did any of them know
where he lived, or where he came from; they only knew that
he was really fit.

Fit! Fit! For God's sake! Who the hell was this man and
where had he taken Isabelle? Christiane was already imagining
her daughter dead in every ditch between Toulouse and
Calais. She needed to do something, to go somewhere, to
talk, to run, to scream, to drive, to find her child.

'She said,' Agnès proffered, 'that she was only going for
lunch. She'd get a lift back afterwards.'

'Who the hell was going to give her a lift?' Christiane
demanded angrily.

Claud was more circumspect. They would ring their
friends and ask if any of them had seen Isabelle, then they
would go back down to Castel, look for her there and if she
hadn't turned up by a certain time they would have to go to
the police.

Left on their own, with instructions to listen for the
telephone, the teenagers spent the afternoon mooching

around the swimming pool, suddenly afraid of what might have happened to Isabelle. She had seemed so sure of what she was doing, so certain that she would come to no harm, that this boy or man or whatever he was had been sent from heaven to rescue her from the bourgeois narrowness of her parents' home. Mum, she thought, would have to come round to him in the end. Papa might be more difficult. For one thing she wasn't sure if Etienne had a job but she thought he might have a sort of a bit of one. Anyway his ambition was to write a book – he was terribly clever. He might even write a film script.

'We should have told.' Agnès looked as if she was about to cry.

'But we swore not to,' said Jake. 'She'll be all right. Isabelle's no fool. She'll be back by supper time and there'll have been a hell of a fuss about nothing.' His face – as pretty as a girl's – wore no expression as, sitting on the side of the pool with his legs dangling over the edge, he casually flicked the ash from a cigarette into the water and watched it slowly separate and disperse. A tiny bit of ash.

'She'll never come back,' Maddy's black eyes flashed. 'They're not going to find her in the town – she's probably in Toulouse or Paris by now.'

Agnès did begin to cry. Not just to cry but to sob. 'She may be, like, dead,' she wailed. 'Why didn't we stop her?'

'Because he sounded like a nice guy.' Isabelle's friend, Ellen, stood up and, much gratified by her slender, bikini-clad figure, she swayed on her hips and tossed her long, artificially blonde hair away from her round face before turning to glance across at the others. She knew that she had encouraged Isabelle in this crazy adventure but she had been convinced that Etienne was genuine – after all she had seen his photograph hadn't she? He had thick, dark curls and high cheek bones didn't he? Why would someone like that have to lie? He couldn't possibly have had any difficulty in finding a girlfriend. Of course she would never have done anything to hurt Isabelle. In any case they were best friends weren't they? Had been ever since they were little. The fact that she, Ellen, would have a better chance with Jake once Isabelle was out of the way had nothing to do with anything.

That silly baby, Agnès, was still blubbing as if blubbing ever got anyone anywhere and the rest of them were looking so unbearably glum that Ellen decided to go back to the house and try to ring Isabelle's mobile. With her cigarettes and lighter in one hand and her mobile in the other, she tossed her hair out of her eyes again, slipped her feet into her flip-flops and sashayed her way across the hot tiles to the shade of the orange-flowered bignonia hanging over the terrace that ran the length of the house.

As they had all done repeatedly since lunch, she tried to call Isabelle but Isabelle's mobile was still switched off. Their endless frantic texts all remained unanswered. Ellen began to panic. Then, suddenly, the land line burst shrilly into life. She leapt to answer it, but it was only Christiane wanting to know if there was any news and to say that she and Claud were going round to the Préfecture before coming on home.

At supper no one spoke. There was nothing to say. Claud and Christiane had both drunk quite a lot but for once the teenagers held back. Christiane ate nothing, Agnès with puffy eyes played with some salad in between fresh outbursts of tears and both boys shovelled food into their mouths whilst looking as if their hearts would break. Maddy and Ellen sat side by side messing with something or other on their plates and repeatedly flinging their arms around each other's necks so that their faces were hidden by the mingling of their long tangled manes.

Christiane looked at Ellen. She wondered if the child knew something that she was still not telling. Ellen had been around since she and Isabelle were both four or five years old and Christiane had perforce grown fond of her although there always seemed to be something slightly untrustworthy about the girl. Any criticism of her friend infuriated Isabelle who swore that Ellen was the truest, truest friend and that anyway she was very funny.

She didn't look very funny now, Christiane thought. Neither had she looked very funny when two policemen arrived before supper to cross question her and the others and to take away Isabelle's laptop which she had fortunately left behind. This to Christiane meant that her daughter had meant to return.

If that was indeed what she intended, why hadn't she come home? Yet if she meant to stay away, why had she left her precious computer behind? Neither line of speculation brought any consolation to Isabelle's distraught parents.

No one wanted to go to bed but no one knew what to do if they stayed up. Only Christiane spent the evening ringing her sister and her widowed mother in England and anyone else with whom she desperately hoped her daughter might have communicated. Earlier, she had to no avail rung her aunt, Tante Annie, who lived only half an hour away and who had always had a close relationship with Isabelle. Christiane knew that Tante Annie was someone to whom Isabelle would naturally turn in trouble

At eleven o'clock precisely a sudden, electrifying bleep was heard from Ellen's mobile. A text – from Isabelle?

VI

Although it was beautifully cool in the little old damp church, the very flagstones seemed to be sweating as Fafa advanced up the aisle to say Mass on Sunday morning.

Strangely the congregation seemed to be much larger than usual which he cynically attributed to the fact that his flock was seeking refuge from the sweltering heat of the last few days, not unlike Joseph Escrieux's herd of Charolais which Fafa had seen standing swishing their white tails over their broad backs under the scrubby trees in the corner of the old boy's field.

Then he saw Claud and Christiane standing very close together, their upper arms touching, both their faces reflecting the grim misery of their plight. Behind them stood a row of dejected teenagers, heads bowed in sober thought. Of course, Fafa immediately realised, three quarters of the parish must be here, all gaudily dressed in their holiday finery, ready to express their sympathy and – unusually – to pray. To pray for the safe return of the lost girl. He was himself horribly shaken by the news of her disappearance having seen her at her parents' house only two or three days ago.

At the front of the church Mathilde, dressed in her habitual black, a worn black straw hat jammed on her head, knelt in prayer, telling her beads with crooked hands.

If anyone's prayers can bring her back, thought Fafa, they will be Mathilde's. He turned to face the congregation, taking everyone in at a glance. How few of them, he imagined, believed in God and yet when an apparently insurmountable problem arose, they turned as one to the Almighty – *le Tout-Puissant*. He hadn't seen Christiane in church since Christmas and he doubted that he had ever seen Claud there. But then Claud, he knew, was a Protestant.

After saying Mass the previous evening, Fafa had gone to see Mathilde and there, in her kitchen, he had watched the news with cricked neck as a stick-like, well-groomed young woman, her head sombrely tilted to one side had, in muted tones, reported the story of the missing English girl. The old black and white television set with its fuzzy picture was hard enough to see without it being fixed to a shelf in a corner just below the ceiling.

Tears were running down Mathilde's rugged cheeks. Despite the crick in his neck, Fafa too felt like crying. Instead he bent his head and offered up a silent prayer. He had called at Aigues Nègres in the afternoon and, faced by the terrible atmosphere there, had found himself horribly tongue-tied. Far easier a thing it was to pray by the bed of the dying or to console the bereaved than to confront the blind misery of these parents and the scowling uncomprehending gaze of the teenagers. Mathilde's miracles paled into insignificance beside the terrible tragedy which had struck in the midst of their small community.

Never in all her days had Christiane imagined herself as one of those parents appearing on the television, desperate to find a lost child. In fact she had always thought they were wasting their time since no killer or kidnapper was likely to come forward bearing the body of a raped or murdered child. Now she dreaded the prospect of a television appeal, but on discovering that police procedure in France was quite different to that in England, she suddenly felt cheated. No such appeal was to be considered.

Yet, she thought, it was essential to publicise Isabelle's disappearance as widely as possible since someone out there might know something. Isabelle herself might see the television and, being moved by the anguish of her parents, return of her own free will. As it was, she appeared to have left of her own free will. Then there were the two text messages to her sister which could not be discounted.

If only Christiane could believe in those messages. Of course the texts gave Claud and Christiane hope even though there was something about them which struck fear into their hearts. Could one say with any degree of certainty that they definitely came from Isabelle? The police were busy trying to discover their provenance but Agnès was sure they were genuine. But was Agnès whistling in the wind?

The first one had simply read so inadequately: *am okay Is.* And what about 'okay'? Wouldn't Isabelle have written 'ok', especially in a text. The children were always working out newer and shorter ways of sending their messages. Why avoid anything so well-tried as 'ok'? Besides, what about 'Is'? Didn't she usually sign herself 'Iz'?

'Oh Mum,' Agnès had wailed, 'of course it's from her...' and she burst into tears. People always spell things wrong in texts, she managed to explain between sobs.

'But why doesn't she say where she is then?'

'It doesn't matter where she is as long as she's OK,' Agnès burbled. 'Mum, please, please say that you know it's from her...please please...'

But Christiane couldn't know and in any case she was concentrating on the daunting prospect of the television news. What would they say? How would the story be presented? Would there be sufficient urgency in the narrative or would there be no more than a passing, glib reference to a girl who had gone missing?

She wished she were allowed her appeal and imagined speaking in a clear calm voice: 'Isabelle,' she would say, '*si tu nous vois, si tu nous entends, écoute...*' She would speak first in French and then in English. She would say that there would be no recriminations and Isabelle, seeing her, would be moved. But the police were adamant. Such things did not happen in France.

As, surrounded by the teenagers, she and Claud sat there gazing at the television, images of Isabelle were flashed across the screen – pictures of her laughing in a bikini, playing tennis, grinning inanely in a school photograph and a recent one of her standing outside Aigues Nègres with a strangely thoughtful look on her face. There was no doubt about it:

Isabelle was a very pretty girl. With her elfin looks, short brown hair and wide eyes.

She looks like her mother, Claud thought. He could no longer speak because of the lump in his throat.

Christiane sighed and turned off the television. 'Do you think she saw it?' she said.

'Maybe someone who knows her whereabouts did,' Claud replied in a flat tone.

All at once the teenagers rose and one by one silently left the room, leaving Isabelle's miserable parents alone, frozen in their despair. There was nothing they could say to one another which could make any difference to anything or which could in any way allay their fears. Independently, albeit together, each was living through his or her own hell. Sometimes they felt numbed by the awfulness of it all, at other times one or other of them would feel a surge of rage. How on earth could Isabelle have allowed herself to do anything so manifestly stupid? How could she be so selfish? Or Christiane would feel furious with Claud for having taken her to Castel without having been more curious as to what she was up to. But how could he have ever dreamt that she was planning to disappear? Or perhaps she hadn't meant to disappear, then waves of nausea would engulf Christiane and she would begin to shake again.

At other times things would suddenly seem quite normal as Christiane talked about what to have for lunch, asked someone to make the salad dressing or, for an instant, allowed her thoughts to go back to the Archbishop. The teenagers would be pushing each other and joking and someone would be complaining about the heat. Everything was all right after all – everything was the same as it had always been. But it wasn't and the feeling that it was never lasted for long.

It was horrible to see the whole village at mass the next day. All there, believers and non-believers, Dutch, English and German, all come to express their sympathy or – awful though it was to imagine – some perhaps to gawp and indulge their prurient curiosity.

Fafa had made it clear that he was saying Mass specifically to pray for Isabelle's safe return. So warm and kind and so sincere was he that for a moment Christiane allowed herself to believe in the power of prayer. She imagined Mathilde must be praying to that old scoundrel of an Archbishop that he might intercede for them with the Almighty. If that was the case and Isabelle was found alive and well then perhaps she would have to change her attitude. Would she, in contradiction to all her academic training, bring quite a different slant to bear on the biography she was writing and end up by sending the old boy to heaven and herself canonising him. She thought not. But she knew she would do anything – perjure herself, lie, perhaps even kill – to get her daughter back. She could certainly imagine hiring a killer to do away with Etienne, whoever he was. Not that she would know how to go about it.

'Christiane! You're talking of murder!' Claud had said in shocked surprise.

Outside the church as Claud and Christiane did their best to extricate themselves from the crowd of sympathising neighbours, cameras flashed. The press had arrived.

VII

Still Christiane's papers lay untouched on her desk.

Si peut-être un jour, the Archbishop wrote in his clear, carefully slanting hand, *if perhaps one day my journals come to be discovered and read by a student of history then will the small part I have played in the events of the day be recorded for posterity. The secrets of my heart will be revealed and so too will it be recognised how I have striven to aid and enrich the lives of the people of my diocese.*

Through my personal endeavours and intervention, we have now, to my great satisfaction established a Chair of Physics at the ancient university of Toulouse, so distinguished for its Faculties of Theology and of Roman Law yet hitherto ill-served in the field of modern sciences. I have no shame in maintaining that although, in the words of the Scripture, man does not live by bread alone, neither does he live by the Scriptures alone. How wrong it is for the people of this great kingdom to be left in ignorance and poverty of mind merely by virtue of their living in the furthermost corners of that same kingdom. The Almighty has not blessed mankind with intelligence for that intelligence to be allowed to putrify.

Last night after a most fatiguing voyage we arrived at Hautefontaine. The little girl had weathered the journey well despite her mother's repeated injunctions to sit up straight as the berline bumped along painfully over the deeply rutted roads. My niece on the other hand found much to complain about concerning the discomfort of the berline, the manners of the coachman, the inferiority of the horses, not to mention the cleanliness (or lack thereof) at the hostelry where we put up for the night.

For my part, the true inconvenience of such journeys lies in the poor quality of the badly cooked, savourless dishes which the innkeepers at these roadside hostelries see fit to serve to the weary traveller. Watery crayfish soup and over-cooked, dried-out roasts with insipid sauces do nothing to revive a man after a tiresome day on the road. It might be as well in future to send our own chef ahead so that he may prepare for us a more palatable meal. That he might supervise the proper cooking of the roasts and himself concoct a delectable sauce or two, such as a green one and a Spanish one.

Once we reached Hautefontaine, despite the lateness of the hour and weary though I was, I insisted on going to my little house in the village, there in my study to find some much needed solitude whilst my niece oversaw the unpacking of our luggage and scolded the servants.

It is beginning to grow cold in the evenings but a fire had earlier been lit in the chimney so that by the time of my arrival the study was warm and snug. The first thing I habitually do on rediscovering the refuge of this my private room, is lovingly to examine my books which line the walls, to see that no harm has come to them in my absence and to ensure that each is in its proper place. The library in the château is overflowing with books, but this is my own personal library. Here are reference books, ancient texts to which I may refer for my sermons, favourite books from my youth, the *Fables de La Fontaine*, Latin and Greek lexicons, M. Boyer's *Dictionnaire françois-anglois & anglois-françois* which belonged to my father and which has accompanied me from Saint-Germain to Paris and from there to Evreux and is now here in my study at Hautefontaine. Here are also the works of Messieurs, Descartes and Pascal and of many other writers and philosophers whom their various Holinesses have seen fit to include on the *Index Librorum Prohibitorum*. There are besides one or two clandestine volumes of such a nature that I would not care for them to fall into the hands of my niece, or indeed into the hands of one of the servants or any of my parishoners.

I drew such a one from the shelf with the idea that a little light-hearted entertainment might be welcome before I confronted whatever missives might await me on my escritoire.

My *escritoire* is a magnificent piece of furniture that once belonged to my niece's late husband, for a member of whose family it was fashioned in Paris some forty years ago by M. Boulle. It is decorated with the very finest marquetry inlay but, finding it rather over-elaborate in this small room and having recently admired an exquisite *sécretaire* in the *style neuf*, created for Madame Adélaïde by M. Oeben, I am of a mind to order one for my study here and to have the other removed to the château. The more sober, geometric designs of the *style neuf*, I think to myself with a smile, may be better suited to a prince of the Church than are the tortoiseshell and enamel Cupid and Psyche of M. Boulle's inlay…

At this point several pages of the Archbishop's journal become illegible, time and damp having compacted them into a grey wad of nothingness.

VIII

On the Saturday evening Etienne was sitting in a crowded bar just off the Boulevard de Strasbourg in Toulouse, there being no more room on the pavement outside. An untouched glass of beer sat on the small round table in front of him; from the huge television screen fixed to the wall opposite a blonde woman with a voice like a parrot was reading the news. Etienne was barely listening. He was hungry and so for the moment more interested in the thought of the steak-frites to be eaten later at a restaurant just round the corner. The restaurant with the Scottish wallpaper and the best steak in France.

Then all of a sudden there was a hush and everyone turned simultaneously to look at the television as the presenter, lowering her voice to a more suitably sensitive pitch, announced that the police were looking for a fifteen-year-old English girl, reported missing from her parents' holiday home in France. Pictures of a slender young girl filled the screen. They hadn't found the girl. Of course they hadn't.

Etienne picked up the glass in front of him and drained the beer in one go. As he drank someone rose from the next table and accidentally knocked his elbow, causing him to look up into the face of a stylish young woman dressed in tight white jeans and a tight yellow T-shirt. Her hair was tied back in a pony tail that revealed a long neck. Smiling a naturally broad smile, she bent to apologise, then waving an elegant, tanned hand in the direction of the television, she muttered, '*Quel horreur! ...et les pauvres parents...*' Then she did a double-take. Etienne froze.

'Don't I know you? Weren't we *en terminal* together?'

Of course. They'd been at school together. Etienne could hardly forget her and naturally if he hung around in Toulouse he was bound to bump into someone he knew although it is a big city and over the years he had developed a habit of literally keeping his head down, never catching an eye and somehow becoming invisible in a crowd.

In those days, at school, this girl had been so attractive and so clever and so cool that for all his good looks he would never have dared to approach her although friends were always telling him that she fancied him.

He looked at her now, smiling down at him and longed for her. But rather as one might long for an angel.

'Qu'est-ce-que tu deviens?' he asked.

She was a doctor.

'Et toi?'

He never liked being asked what he was up to.

'This and that,' he said.

She waved again in the direction of the television. 'I hope they find her,' she said and then with a quick *'Salut'* and a kiss on both of his cheeks she disappeared.

Shortly afterwards Etienne slank out of the bar and made his way to the restaurant round the corner. As usual people were queuing for tables but he didn't mind. He could wait. He had a worn *Livre de Poche* edition of Sartre's *La Nausée* crammed into the back pocket of his jeans. It was his favourite book. Had been ever since he and that pretty doctor were at school together. It was his bible. At times, like Sartre's Roquentin, he had an overwhelming sense of being superfluous – *de trop*. Like Roquentin he felt waves of nausea at what he saw as the 'contingency' of things. What are all these things? So many things. What are they for? Do they even exist? He sometimes wondered if he even existed himself – *cogito ergo sum* – that had never convinced him. Or perhaps he existed only in someone else's imagination rather than his own. How could he ever know?

In front of him in the queue were a fat man and a fat woman. He vaguely noticed their huge bottoms both encased in fawn-coloured cotton trousers, and pulled his book out of his pocket. He opened it at random but gazing at the familiar words found himself unable to concentrate. He wondered if Isabelle had ever studied Sartre at school. Beautiful Isabelle. Then he thought of her mother and father and wondered what they were like – what they were doing as they waited for her return. Long might they wait. What was she to them or they to her? He felt confused. Then he thought of his own mother. She had died. He had not asked for her to die and yet in some deep part of his psyche there was a consciousness that in some way he had been responsible for killing the one he loved.

Etienne hadn't seen his father for more than ten years. He doubted whether he would even recognise him if he saw him now. He certainly hoped he would not. In any case he never wished to see him again.

For all he knew his father was dead. He'd as likely as not died of drink or perhaps been knifed in a brawl. He had been a brilliant *patissier* in his time, capable of making the finest millefeuilles and the lightest profiteroles in Toulouse but such was his addiction to Armagnac that he was sacked from one job after another until there wasn't a *patissier* in the city who would employ him. He consistently hit, punched and kicked Etienne's mother who was always too frightened to go to the police or to leave either home or her brute of a husband. Home was a three-room HLM in a concrete block where many of the other tenants, like Etienne's father, were unemployed and crime was rife.

Sometimes Etienne, who had also been victim of his father's violent moods, wished that he had killed him himself and so saved his mother from a slow and painful death caused by her brutally inflicted wounds. Instead – a clever boy – he had taken refuge in his books.

But as an only child he felt a heavy burden of responsibility for his parents, as if, in some strange way, it was his presence that brought this cataclysmic violence down on all their heads: the shouting, the bawling, the kicking, the screaming, the smashing followed by the whingeing, cringing, blubbing apologies and then the sound of his mother being raped in the next room – or sometimes right there, in front of him.

How could his mother, the daughter of a gentle Algerian father and brought up in the belief that women should be subservient to their husbands, how could she have supposed at the age of twenty-one or two that marriage to a good-looking, Christian Frenchman would be like living with a wild animal? Her parents had wanted her to marry a nice Muslim boy but she had broken free, rejected her religion, been disowned by her family and paid exorbitantly for it.

Sitting at his table in the restaurant, Etienne tried again to concentrate on Roquentin and turning a page read '*le passé n'existe pas...*'

If the past didn't exist then neither did his mother exist, neither had she ever existed, neither had she suffered, been beaten and brutalised. His head began to swim.

A plate of mouth-watering steak and chips was put in front of him. He wolfed it down and when the waitress offered him more from the dish on the side, he nodded his head. Then staring at the newly replenished plate, he surreptitiously watched the waitress move away before scooping his second helping into a small plastic bag he had brought with him in his pocket. He wouldn't, he knew, be able to get out without paying, not that he liked the need to descend to criminality but it had become a necessity. Besides, how was he to survive if he didn't steal? He couldn't count the cars, motorbikes, mobile phones or laptops that he had helped himself to over the years and then sold for far less than their value but at least he now had a reasonable stash of readies hidden in his van. All he had done this time was to salvage a second meal in a perfectly honourable fashion.

He walked fast down the boulevard, head bent, clutching his bag of soggy food, *La Nausée* restored to his back pocket, and started again to ask himself what the point of it all was. He remembered Roquentin laughing – maniacally perhaps – at the thought of everyone eating. Eating and eating. Eating to stay alive when there was no point whatsoever in living.

As he approached the station where he had left the dilapidated van that now served as home, Etienne felt his stomach suddenly gripped by fear. But why, he wondered, was he afraid? Why feel fear – or any other emotion for that matter – if everything was pointless and nothing at all had any significance and if he was all powerful? His mood he thought had been swinging precariously over the last few days.

He took out his key and, still not quite able to conquer his fear, unlocked the door of the van. Isabelle's mobile lay on the driver's seat. Perhaps he ought to make himself scarce for a while.

IX

Ellen was thoroughly fed up. She could see that Christiane and Claud would be worried about Isabelle but it seemed to her that they really were exaggerating, going around all the time with their miserable faces, thinking that their daughter had been abducted by some sex-maniac. If Isabelle had told them she was leaving, they would have managed to stop her. Why couldn't they calm down and just be angry like any normal parents? Anyway it was perfectly clear that Isabelle was all right. Hadn't she sent those texts to say so? Couldn't they see that she wasn't going to tell them where she was because then they would only come and find her and bring her home.

Etienne sounded like a really nice guy – Claud certainly ought to like him since he was always banging on about literature and dreary old Sartre. He and Isabelle had been talking to each other on the internet for ages so he obviously wasn't a murderer.

As for Isabelle, Ellen was actually rather cross with her; she hadn't told any of them that she was in fact going to decamp. They all thought she was just going to meet Etienne in the town and come back that same evening. Now, by her selfishness she had just gone and wrecked everyone else's holiday. No one could think of anything but Isabelle.

On Sunday afternoon Ellen was sitting next to Jake on the edge of the swimming pool. It was very hot and she was sitting very close to him. He moved away a little.

'It's too hot,' he said then suddenly stood up and dived into the pool. As soon as his head reappeared Ellen said, 'Jake, I think you need to talk.'

'Get stuffed,' Jake muttered under his breath then, tossing his head back, he took a great gulp of air, dived to the bottom of the pool and swam a length under water. It seemed that he had no intention of having a long heart to heart with Ellen who told herself that it was because he was 'in denial' that he wouldn't talk. Denial of what she wasn't quite sure. It was obvious that he had been quite keen on Isabelle but, for heaven's sake, she hadn't treated him very well and, in any case, she was only interested in Etienne. They all knew that.

'You couldn't stop her going,' Ellen said spitefully as Jake pulled himself up out of the pool.

He didn't answer, but picked up a towel, shook it out, spread it on the ground and lay down to dry in the sun. He was on the opposite side of the pool to where Ellen was sitting. She stared across at him where he lay, his head buried in his arms, and wondered if she hated him or not. Then, deciding that she didn't quite, she got up, jumped into the water and swam across to him.

Propping herself up with her arms on the edge of the pool with her chin resting on her folded hands, she said, 'They won't find her until she wants them to. Where are they now, anyway? Claud and Christiane I mean.'

'How do I know?' Jake replied, turning his head to look at Ellen. 'With the police I should think.'

'The police are useless.'

'Why are you so sure that she's all right?' Jake wanted to know. 'No one knows the first thing about this Etienne person. He could be any lunatic. You must have heard of girls going off with men they've met on the internet and then getting raped…'

'You're so bloody negative!' Ellen slipped back into the water. Were they all going to have to spend the rest of the summer wondering if Isabelle had been murdered? She wished she'd just come back so that things could go on as usual, even if it meant Jake mooning hopelessly over her. He was as bad as Claud and Christiane, permanently looking as if he was going to burst into tears. And as for Agnès. She never stopped blubbing and had taken to hanging around her mother all the time like a baby. Ellen began to think about trying to go home early, but she wasn't quite ready to give up on Jake who, when she turned up, might just begin to see Isabelle for what she really was. What a slag!

She was just climbing out of the pool when Agnès came running across the yellowing grass towards the pool, shouting, 'Have you heard?'

Jake instantly leapt to his feet. 'Have they found her?'

No, they hadn't found her but the police had just called to say that the text messages had been sent from somewhere in the Toulouse area. 'Which means that she's not far away!' Agnès sounded triumphant. Then, 'I hope she's all right – surely God wouldn't let anything awful happen to Iz – I mean, I don't think He would.' She suddenly threw her arms around Ellen, saying, 'Ellen please please say that you think she's OK.'

Wriggling free from Agnès's grasp, Ellen tossed her wet hair out of her eyes and merely said, 'I don't see what God has got to do with it. If there is a god, He's not very nice to the people in Africa so I don't see why He'd care particularly about any of us.'

'Didn't you pray for her this morning in church?' Agnès looked at her friend in wide-eyed disbelief.

'We-ell, sort of…' Ellen looked at the ground, then at the pool and then at Jake. 'I bet Jake didn't pray either,' she said.

'As a matter of fact I did,' Jake said. 'I thought that's what we went there for.'

Ellen groaned, 'Well I don't believe in God anyway. He's stupid.'

'He can't be stupid if he doesn't exist,' Jake remarked sharply.

Ellen realised to her annoyance that she had made herself sound stupid.

'Whatever,' she said with a shrug.

Back in the house Claud and Christiane were sitting at the kitchen table with a bottle of wine in front of them going over and over the events of the last two days. Their helplessness was overpowering. They both had a terrible need to do something. But what could they do that they hadn't already done? With little hope of success they had contacted almost everyone they knew in England or in France in case there had been any sign of Isabelle. Of course no one had heard a thing until the terrible news broke. A picture of the town from which she was supposed to have been abducted was shown on both the ITV and the BBC news and the story had reached all the Sunday papers.

Now the press was camped out in the village waiting to ask Christiane how she felt. As if that was a sensible question.

Claud had gone out to confront them, to make a statement that might keep them at bay. He told them as politely as he could manage, that there was no further news but that they would be informed as soon as anything came to light, and asked them to respect the family's privacy. The fact that they had mostly abandoned the habit of knocking on people's doors was something, although the whole family was aware that the minute they stepped outside, there would be long-distance cameras aimed at them from every angle.

'Unimaginable,' Claud said, pouring himself another glass of wine. 'They seem to want us to break down in public and to use words like *devastated*. But, on the other hand, we need them. You have to remember that.'

'I sometimes wonder if we do. It's like having a pack of wolves out there – they'd rather hear that Isabelle's body had been found in a wood than that she'd come home…the more lurid the story, the happier they are.'

Claud wasn't so sure. 'They're just doing their job,' he said. 'We need to keep them on side.'

'Jake keeps texting Iz but he doesn't get a reply…' Christiane bent to bury her head in her arms which were folded on the table in front of her, then heaved what might have been a sigh but was more like a terrible shuddering sob. She sat up again and said, 'I think he's in love with her, poor boy. He's looking utterly miserable.'

'Good lad that,' said Claud, getting up from the table. 'I think I'll go and see what they're all up to

Christiane glanced at her watch. 'I suppose I'll have to be thinking about supper soon.' The idea of eating filled her with horror – the idea of everyone always eating. Eating and eating as if stoking themselves up in preparation for some enormously important future to which they were all destined. In France people thought about food all the time, talking about the *lapin à la moutarde* or the *pintade aux choux* that they were planning to have next Wednesday, whereas back in England you found them stuffing their faces with junk food wherever you looked.

On the train, in the street, on the beach, at the cinema. If Isabelle was dead, she thought, she would never want to eat again. Her life would seem purposeless. Why eat?

But at least eating broke up the day.

The telephone rang and Christiane nearly jumped out of her skin. She half hated the sound of the telephone because she always hoped it would be Isabelle at the end of the line and it never was. Yet when it rang she still felt a surge of excitement.

This time it was a smarmy little creep claiming to work for a British tabloid. 'Hi Christine,' he said, 'my name's Reg.' As if she cared. He wished to express his sympathy over the loss of Christine's lovely bubbly daughter who clearly had everything to live for. As a mum, he opined, she must be devastated – what did Christine feel like when her daughter went missing? A gorgeous girl like Isabelle must have had a lot of boyfriends – did she bring them home? Did she have a special one…? And – this was off the record of course…but, I hope you don't mind my asking, was she a virgin…?

Christiane slammed down the telephone. Reg's oily insincere platitudes made her almost as sick as his prurient, insinuating questioning, not to mention his oafish use of the past tense. Although gripped by fear whenever she thought about Isabelle, which was almost every moment of the day and night, she was convinced that her daughter was still alive. As was Claud.

'Who was that who rang?' Claud asked as she came back into the kitchen, a pathetically hopeful look on his face.

'Some rat from the gutter press…why can't they ever leave us alone?

'What did you say?'

'Nothing. I put the phone down.'

Claud was afraid of Christiane alienating the press. They, he claimed, could be at least as useful as the police in tracing their daughter.

Christiane merely shrugged and changed the subject.

'What are you doing about Julien Green?' she suddenly asked.

'How do you suppose I can think about Julien Green at a time like this?' Claud snapped, turning his back and gazing out of the window at Maddy and Agnès in their bikinis walking slowly across the sun-drenched garden, arms entwined, long hair mingling. One dark, one fair.

He had been hoping to spend the summer putting the finishing touches to a treatise on the novelist's use of a second language, centred around a study of the Franco-American writer, Julien Green. In fact he had, that very morning, managed to shut himself up with his computer for a couple of hours and do some work. But how could he admit to that?

Christiane, too, had attempted to concentrate on the Archbishop's journals, but with little success – anything to distract her from the pain of waiting, but it was impossible to concentrate.

'Those children,' Claud said. 'Still gazing out of the window, must be feeling bloody awful. You'd think that one of them might have stopped her.'

'Oh, don't start blaming the children, for God's sake,' Christiane groaned. Then, 'I tried to think about the Archbishop this morning. But I found he made me feel sick with all his pomp and self-satisfied glory. I had thought I was beginning to get quite fond of him. Anyway, I won't be able to do any work until Iz is back.'

In the silence that followed neither one of them dared to think that she might never come back.

X

Etienne was on his guard. For someone as clever as he, he had made too many elementary mistakes – as if his mind had been blurred by drugs. But he had given up drugs a long time ago. More or less at least. His brain whirred so powerfully and so thrillingly without the aid of artificial stimulants that he could see no point in them. They might be fine for the common herd, the dull and the mediocre whose imaginations lacked fire and subtlety, but he, and there was no doubt about it, was a superior person, a person with an infinitely superior mind who could scale the heights of fantasy and see the truth beyond the clouds. Besides, he could do anything he wanted when he was in a certain mood. These moods were better than any drug-induced high – when they overcame him he knew himself to be all powerful, all-knowing, light-footed and free. There was nothing to compare with such exhilaration. At other times there was always Roquentin to console him, Roquentin, whose vision he shared. To whom he invariably turned when the black clouds engulfed him again.

Etienne's worst mistake was to have sent a picture of himself to Isabelle's laptop, which laptop the idiot girl had left behind only for the police to discover so that, to his dismay, the Monday papers all carried that picture. A picture of the man wanted in connection with the missing girl. And the ruddy doctor he had been at school with would be bound to recognise him from it and go to the police. He should never have hung out in Toulouse for a single moment. There might have been a chance that, had she not just seen him, she would never have put two and two together – not from that fuzzy press photograph after all these years. She might just have thought that it reminded her of someone – someone who had had a very short crew cut in the days when they were at school together. Now he had thick black curls cascading nearly to his shoulders. She'd even had to do a double take when she'd seen him in the café. If only she hadn't been there…if only…

It was that wonderful, thrilling feeling of power, of being able to walk above the common man which had led him to be so careless.

One good thing was that Etienne hadn't used his real name in his communication with Isabelle. Etienne was indeed his second name, but anyone who had ever had anything to do with him, knew him as Victor, a name that he liked on account of its connotations and because he saw himself as victorious in a meaningless world. But Etienne was more anonymous and he was capable of great cunning when he wished to deceive the enemy. Or even to deceive himself since he was aware on occasion of two sides of his mind fighting for control.

Luckily the first thing Etienne had done on Saturday was to go to see Fabien, a crooked old *garagiste* he knew who dealt in stolen goods, who fixed speedometers and ran a few other rackets.

The old boy, a fat man with a dirty cigarette sticking out of the side of his mouth and a belt buckled below the great bulge of his belly, wanted to know what the urgency was. Why did the van have to be sprayed in such a hurry?

'Trouble with the police?' he suggested with a knowing wink and a greasy leer.

Etienne shrugged his shoulders and made an indecipherable noise. He didn't suppose it would be in Fat Fabien's interest to shop him but he wasn't giving anything away. He needed a new couple of number plates, but he could deal with that later. He'd nick them from a car park in the evening, after dark.

Fabien said it would take a couple of hours for the paint to dry but Etienne didn't care; there was nothing to stop him driving around with wet paint. He stood over Fabien, watching meticulously as the fat man messily sprayed the vehicle, not allowing him too close a look inside. All Etienne's possessions were in there; he didn't need Fabien poking his nose around among his things.

He paid for the job in crumpled, dirty notes then jumped smartly into the driving seat. He needed to get away as quickly as possible.

Fabien grunted as he stuffed the money into the back pocket of his necessarily low-slung jeans. It suited him fine if all Etienne wanted was some sort of a botched up, half-cock job. No skin off his nose. He gave the younger man a rather unpleasant, sly, satirical look before turning away and strolling back into the darker recesses of his den. Etienne took his foot off the clutch and accelerated out of the dark garage into the sunlit narrow street, causing an oncoming car to scream to a halt.

'*Espèce de con...*' Fabien muttered to himself on hearing the screech of hot tyres on hot tarmac.

It was not until he went out for a baguette on Monday morning that panic momentarily hit Etienne. There his picture was plastered over the front of the paper on the stand outside the *papéterie*. As soon as he saw it he ducked, shoulders up, head down, and turned to hot foot it straight back to his van which luckily was parked just round the corner. Once back in the relative safety of his vehicle, he took out a Stanley knife and began to hack at his hair. Later he'd shave his head or dye his hair. He'd buy a pair of glasses and some kind of blond dye and let his beard grow. But first of all he'd have to get the hell out of Toulouse. When he'd taken the van to be sprayed he hadn't been too worried about Fat Fabien who, being himself on the wrong side of the law, would naturally want to steer clear of the police. But to withhold evidence about an abduction was something else. Fabien might well think that by shopping Etienne he could curry favour with the police.

What with Fabien and the doctor Etienne realised that he could be in serious trouble. He tried to remember if there had been anyone else around in the garage while he was there. He thought not.

Luckily he'd already fixed the new number plates to the van, but now he needed to have the damn thing sprayed again.

It would probably be easier, he thought, to get to Bordeaux or Limoges perhaps and nick a vehicle there. He desperately needed to be a couple of steps ahead of the police. He would have liked to go down to Spain and nip across from Tarifa to Tangier as he knew he could easily hide out in Morocco, but he daren't risk the frontier police.

He would certainly have to stay in France for the moment although, since he was very very clever, there was no doubt whatsoever in Etienne's mind that he could outwit the police. Besides there was a heroic quality to what he was doing.

Etienne had loved Isabelle from the moment he first saw her picture posted on the internet. For several years he had been searching for her and then, suddenly, there she was. A beautiful girl with a neck like a swan's, cropped mid-brown hair framing her features. She was the girl he had been looking for ceaselessly, the incarnation of female perfection, created for him and for him alone and he would have her. She was made for him and she would be his.

XI

It wasn't just that the priest was feeling hungry. He could almost smell the cassoulet stewing on the smoky open fire as he climbed out of the *deux-chevaux* he had parked just beyond Mathilde's house where the road through the village widened inexplicably He glanced at his watch. It was half past twelve…the lure of the cassoulet. *Seigneur*, he muttered to himself. Was it really so very bad to call on a lonely old lady at lunchtime? He knew he brought her a degree of comfort and he knew that she loved to feed him, but this time, besides a meal, it was comfort for himself that Fafa sought.

But the thought of his own greed continued to gnaw at his conscience as he walked past Mathilde's assortment of geraniums and pansies and Busy Lizzies planted in every imaginable kind of tin and pot and arrayed cheerfully beneath her window. The shutters on the window were closed to keep out the heat of the sun but the smell of cassoulet had now become a reality. Ought he perhaps, on this one occasion, refuse to eat and thus deny the sin of greed? But Mathilde would surely be hurt if he turned down her offer and wouldn't it be an act of great unkindness to rebuff the old lady, to insult her generosity? He thought of all the murderers and adulterers and child abductors in the world. Surely his sin of greed hardly counted in comparison. But then he was not tempted by any of those more grievous sins. Would he be able to resist the temptation if he were? He doubted it since he already knew that he was about to accept with gratitude a steaming plate of cassoulet and perhaps a glass of wine. 'God forgive me,' he whispered in preparation for the sin he had decided to commit.

Having from her door seen the priest's car go by, Mathilde was waiting on the threshold for him, with one hand holding back the curtain of plastic beads designed to keep out the flies.

She ushered him in with an innocent, 'Just in time for a little something to eat.' In fact she had been watching the time and hoping that Monsieur l'Abbé would turn up. The cassoulet was at its best today and besides *le pauvre petit jeune homme* was so pale and thin. He needed looking after and feeding up, living as he did so far from his family.

Fafa's mother – which Mathilde would never know – was a drug-addicted prostitute in Lille. Throughout his childhood he had seen the men come and he had seen the men go. He had been neglected, beaten and chastised, occasionally briefly madly cossetted and wept over. He had been despised and kicked by pimps, sometimes abused. His only brother, several years older than he, had taken to crime at an early age, had been in and out of prison and finally died prematurely of a drug overdose. Fafa had found consolation in the Church.

He often thought with affection of the whiskery old priest in the stained soutane who had taken him under his wing, treated him with kindness and talked to him about the Love of God. He was glad that Father Benôit had died before the scandal concerning child abuse and the Catholic clergy had come to light. The poor man could have landed up in prison himself and yet he had been the one constant in Fafa's life. The one person Fafa could confide in and trust. If it weren't for Father Benôit he would not be where he was now and might instead have gone the way of his older brother. In any case all the old man had done was to sit the little François on his knee and kiss and fondle him a bit. He had never raped him nor used any kind of violence and Fafa had been so grateful to be loved. As the boy grew older he became accustomed to the intimate relationship he shared with the old priest and things continued in much the same vein until Fafa entered the seminary. There had been other boys too but Fafa had always sensed that he was Father Benôit's special favourite.

The last time Fafa saw him was shortly after he had been ordained when the old man was on his death bed. Father Benôit had asked for Fafa's forgiveness and Fafa had held the dying man's frail, bony, paper-white hand as they prayed together.

After that Fafa was sent to the South of France and although he regularly prayed for Father Benôit's soul, he never talked about him or his childhood to anyone. The very thought of a sexual encounter of any kind horrified him; his childhood had taken its toll so that his emotional growth had been stunted. He drew comfort from the Love of God and from the warmth of his friendship with Mathilde, the nurturing mother he would have liked to have had.

That is until this summer.

'*Ah, c'est Monsieur l'Abbé!*' Mathilde affected surprise. 'You've come at just the right moment – the cassoulet is waiting.'

Fafa kissed Mathilde on both cheeks. 'I didn't come for the cassoulet,' he lied.

Mathilde chuckled. She knew better. 'It certainly wasn't for my beautiful eyes,' she said. 'Sit down and I'll give you something to eat. You look as though you need it. Me, I've already eaten.' Mathilde ate very little these days. She often thought that she had eaten so much during her long life that she hardly needed to eat any more so that she cooked the cassoulet from habit, hardly touched it herself and was consequently only too glad when Fafa turned up at meal times.

'They haven't found her yet...' Fafa said as Mathilde put a heaped plate of beans and sausages down on the table in front of him.

'The poor little thing. *Le Bon Dieu,*' she waved her right hand dismissively in the air, crumpling up her face as if in agony, 'what's he doing about it. I pray morning and night. I've prayed to the Holy Virgin...*Sainte Marie Mère de Dieu*...I pray with all my strength and I've prayed to the Archbishop too. He'd do better to find that child alive than to bother with my old bones.'

'Her parents are convinced she's still alive.' For an instant uninvited memories from his childhood flashed across Fafa's mind. 'Perhaps for her sake it might be better that she were not.' How could he have said that? Or even thought it? How for anyone's sake could he even contemplate the death of that beautiful girl who had so unexpectedly awakened his latent sexuality only a week or so ago.

The weather was very hot and Christiane had invited the priest to her pool. Fafa enjoyed swimming and was grateful to Christiane for including him although he never failed to feel awkward when surrounded by a crowd of half-naked teenagers jumping in and out of the pool, splashing and screaming and ducking each other. Even so he enjoyed being there, almost as if he were part of a large happy family. Self-consciousness about his thin white body and thin white legs was, he told himself, but a manifestation of the sin of pride. At least he had a nice new pair of green trunks.

Fafa stayed at the pool that afternoon for about an hour, then, just as he was pulling his jeans over his nice new green trunks that had dried so quickly in the hot sun, he noticed Isabelle standing on the edge of the pool preparing to dive. He had often seen her before but somehow only taken her in as part of a group. Suddenly she looked amazingly beautiful, standing there, a boyish figure, so slim, in a vivid turquoise one-piece bathing suit, her sun-tanned arms held out in front of her. Beautiful in a way of which he had never before been aware. He would always find it impossible to express what he felt as he watched her spring so gracefully into the air and execute a perfect dive, barely disturbing the water as she broke the surface. A moment later, at the far end of the pool, her head appeared, as sleek as a seal's. She shook the water out of her face before turning on her back and languidly swimming to the side, her long slender arms stretching out in turn slowly behind her.

Overcome with confusion, Fafa hurriedly finished dressing and turned to go without so much as a good-bye to anyone. From that moment on he could think of nothing but Isabelle. The temptations of the flesh so commonly succumbed to by his parishioners, so often spoken of in the confessional, hitherto ignored by Fafa, had at last come to taunt him. Was it not as much a sin to yield to temptation in the imagination as to do so in reality? Did not Christ say, 'Whosoever looketh at a woman to lust after her hath committed adultery with her already in his heart'?

Fafa needed to talk to his confessor but he was loathe to do so. How could he be genuinely penitent? How could he promise to think no more about Isabelle or even promise to try not to think about her when to do so was so exquisite a pleasure.

Then she disappeared. Just like that. One Friday lunchtime she went to the town with her father and had not been seen since. Never had Fafa experienced such torture. All the horrors of his childhood now seemed nothing beside Isabelle's possible rape, her possible murder. He felt weak with helplessness since all he could do was to pray, from which activity there appeared to be no come back. To make matters worse, he had suddenly begun to wonder what use, if any, prayer was.

But he still prayed, staying awake at night to beseech the Lord to strengthen his faith, to find Isabelle. Every day he said Mass for her recovery... And every day seemed longer and more painful than the last.

He needed to see Mathilde who would not only comfort him, but who would feed him too. He badly needed food since he felt hot and empty and tense as a stretched out wire, having neither eaten nor slept for the last few days.

The cassoulet was as good as ever. For a while Fafa sat there eating and saying nothing for to be in Mathilde's familiar kitchen with her familiar, soothing presence was a relief in itself. But he needed to tell her something. Something which he had vaguely noticed and which hadn't seemed really important – just curious – when it happened on the afternoon of Isabelle's disappearance, but the memory of which kept recurring to him, again and again over the last few days, always making him feel sick with fear.

XII

A number of illegible pages preceded the following passage from the Archbishop's journal:

…immediately, but was soon awakened by Madame de R slipping into the bed beside me. She extinguished her candle, then, sidling up close to me and placing a gentle hand on my belly she whispered into my ear, 'Tu dors, mon oncle?' I at once reassured her in more ways than one that I was now not only fully awake but more than gratified by her arrival.

It had been some time since my niece came to visit me in my bedchamber and, on account of the ill-temper she not infrequently displays towards me, I was quite concerned lest she had decided to draw a veil over the past and to proceed as if there were nothing between us that did not befit the natural relationship between uncle and niece.

Should that have occurred, where I wonder would I, a still young and lusty man, albeit a prince of the Church have turned for comfort? As for Madame de R, she, poor widow, with her cross-grained, vexatious nature, would not be easy to marry, despite her great wealth of which I, most fortuitously, have indirectly become the beneficiary. Nor would she wish to surrender whatsoever authority over her estates to any man, for hers is a controlling nature and an avaricious one. Only last evening she was minded to bewail the cost incurred by my building of the new dovecote, an elegant edifice I bethought myself to have conceived as an adornment to Hautefontaine and as a suitable dwelling for those symbols of peace that are so welcome an addition to the table.

Earlier she had been scolding the servants for wasting candle-ends and for their lavish consumption of bread. As for soap, she allows them none, claiming that cold water is sufficient for their needs.

So it appears that for the present my niece and I are reconciled; not that such a reconciliation is likely in any way to mitigate Madame de R's bad temper. I therefore made it my business to retire to the privacy of my little house, there to write a sermon and to dwell on the promised pleasures of tomorrow's chase when I shall have the satisfaction of riding my recently acquired bay mare for the first time. She is a fine creature with a pretty head and a fiery spirit. My niece who barely interests herself in the chase remains unaware of this acquisition since I fear she would regard it as an unnecessary extravagance, more particularly so were she to become aware of the price I was obliged to pay for such an animal which…

XIII

The teenagers were beginning to quarrel among themselves. Christiane couldn't bear the sound of their endless bickering so obviously caused by the stress from which everyone was suffering.

Maddy, Claud's niece, wanted to go home and Christiane would willingly have taken her to Toulouse and put her on a plane, but whenever she suggested it, Maddy burst into tears, claiming that if she left she would be letting Agnès down. Agnès for her part was permanently crying. She begged her cousin not to leave, saying that they would be deserting Isabelle and that they all must stay until she was found. Endless telephone calls to Maddy's parents merely resulted in their saying that she must make up her own mind. They wondered if they should fly out to be with Christiane and Claud in their hour of need but were dissuaded. There were enough people in the house, Christiane felt, and there was nothing they could do other than be in telephonic communication. Maddy rang her parents at least twice a day and they rang every evening, desperate for the good news which was hardly forthcoming.

Ellen too wanted to go home, but she would only do so if Jake came with her. She was frightened of travelling alone, she said, what with people like Etienne around. She couldn't imagine why Jake refused to come with her since there was no point at all in their hanging about in France when they couldn't do anything to further the search for Isabelle and they would definitely feel better once they reached home.

Jake asked Christiane what they should do. It occurred to him that she and Claud might prefer them to leave, but Christiane, like Maddy's parents, felt the children should all decide for themselves. She had no intention of putting any pressure on them although she thought it was probably better for Agnès if they stayed. Besides, illogically it seemed to her that with everyone around, Isabelle was more likely to return. It was as if, with them all there, she, Christiane, might just wake up from this terrible dream to discover that everything was normal again; that Isabelle was back, that the children were all laughing around the swimming pool while she and Claud concentrated on their work, played tennis in the cool of the evenings and cooked delicious meals. Once again it would be a joy to wake to the blue morning skies and the promise of a gloriously hot summer's day. No longer would the brilliant burning sun be able to mock them in their misery, mercilessly from on high.

There were ten days left before the house was due to be shut up and they were all supposed to return to England for the Autumn term. But Christiane, like Agnès, knew that she would be unable to leave until she had found Isabelle.

There was not a breath of wind and the thermometer hanging on the terrace under the bignonia registered 30°C. *Le 15 août* had come and gone but still the temperature hovered between 30 and 33° in the shade. It had been consistently hotter than usual this summer and the family, being on holiday, had rejoiced in the endless sunshine, but for the last few days the heat had become unbearable. Christiane began to long for a grey, blustery English summer's day.

She dreamed of stepping out on to the pavement wearing a mackintosh, being splashed by passing cars with water from the gutter, being blown along, clasping in front of her an umbrella which the wind repeatedly turned inside out. When she woke from her dream she was always sweating.

She and Claud were sitting in the kitchen, the habitual bottle of wine on the table in front of them. They felt useless. They remembered the little girl who had disappeared from a holiday resort in Portugal a few years back and they remembered the huge publicity surrounding the case. Christiane remembered too how the press had bullied the wretched parents inferring that they had somehow been responsible for the child's abduction. Even hinting that they might have killed her and hidden the body themselves. It made her sick to think how eagerly and with what prurience they had all – herself included – fallen on the papers at the time. And still that child was missing. And now it was Christiane's and Claud's turn. Now they knew for themselves the hope, the despair, the fear, the desolation, the anger, sometimes the numbness of the long hours of waiting. Christiane sighed lengthily and stared blankly at the table in front of her.

'More wine?' Claud refilled her glass without waiting for an answer.

'I don't understand why they haven't found him yet,' Christiane said wearily for the umpteenth time. The picture of Etienne had been in all the papers. Someone must have seen him, perhaps even someone who knew him.

Naturally the police had been inundated with calls, not only from all over France, but from as far away as Naples and Vilnius too. So many crack-pots all wanting to be part of the action, to have their ten minutes in the limelight. Every one of the wretched calls had to be meticulously followed up, even those that appeared to be obvious hoaxes or the fantastical invention of deranged minds. These calls wasted everyone's time, hindered the progress of the investigation and, besides infuriating the police, they hurt and angered Isabelle's miserable parents. Every hour, every moment wasted felt like a further nail in their daughter's coffin.

Claud was saying nothing. There was nothing left to be said. He and Christiane gazed glumly at one another, each lost in his or her own worst imaginings, speechless in their pain.

When the telephone rang, they both jumped, startled out of their private thoughts. Christiane looked at Claud. Her eyes said, 'You go,' but she didn't speak.

Claud got up and walked slowly towards the telephone. There had been too many disappointments, too many hopes raised only to be immediately dashed. Either that or friends and family rang from England only to have to be told that there was no news. Isabelle was still missing, the elusive Etienne still on the run. Tante Annie rang every day.

'We're thinking of you,' friends said. Or, 'If there's anything I can do?' Some said, 'You're in our prayers,' and others, 'I just feel that it will be all right in the end…' What else could they say? What on earth would either Claud or Christiane have said in their place? Sometimes Christiane wished people wouldn't ring, that they would leave her alone to suffer privately. At others, she wondered why on earth so-and-so hadn't been in touch. Someone she had always supposed to be a good friend.

Claud was talking in French into a cordless phone, walking up and down as he did so, in and out of the kitchen. Christiane felt dead. She supposed he was talking to the police but she couldn't make out what it was about since all he seemed to be saying was, '*Où ça?*' or '*Quand?*' or '*Qui?*'

Was there a flicker of hope then, that some advance had been made? All at once Christiane felt a faint rekindling of the optimism which everything during the last few days had sought to destroy. Suddenly she sensed that Isabelle was alive and well, that she would soon be back among them and that she, Christiane, had been failing her daughter by resorting to despair. She jumped to her feet and hurried out of the kitchen to find Claud just as he was saying, '*Je vous remercie…je vous remercie…*' and switching off the telephone.

'The police…' he said, turning to Christiane. 'Fayard – he says there's a woman who's come forward – some doctor or other who claims she went to school with this Etienne. She saw his picture in the paper. Apparently she was in quite a state when she went to the police because she said she'd seen him in a bar in Toulouse the day after Isabelle disappeared. It was on the television at the time and the television was on in the bar so she said something to him – something about us – about how awful it must be for us, and he seemed quite normal – quite unperturbed – but she remembered him as a boy when it appears he had a different name. Apparently he was always a bit of a loner. Very clever…'

'I don't care how clever he is – what are they doing about it?' Christiane took hold of Claud, both hands gripping his upper arms. She almost shook him. 'What about her – what about Isabelle?'

Claud looked down at his wife; the sight of her familiar friendly face now so drawn and weary made him want to cry. 'Look,' he said. 'This is at least something good. Fayard says it's the first piece of concrete evidence they've had – and, by the way, there's a waitress too. She works round the corner at that steak restaurant – you know the one – well she swears that she served Etienne there that same night…'

'Was there anyone…'

Claud knew what she was going to ask. He gazed at Christiane's tragic face with a sense of overwhelming pity. 'No, Christiane,' he said. 'He was on his own.' His voice broke as he spoke. Did that mean that their daughter was already dead, or did it mean she was imprisoned somewhere? Perhaps – he knew he was grasping at straws – perhaps she had just not wanted to be seen in public. After all her picture had been all over the television and the papers from the moment she disappeared. But why didn't she contact her family? She must know how desperate they were.

XIV

Fat Fabien was standing in his garage with the doors open and his back to the street.

'*Merde alors – merde…*' he muttered repeatedly to himself half under his breath. Then, '*Espèce de salaud…*' Little shit. Fabien was holding a three-day-old newspaper in his hands, staring hard at the picture of the fellow whose van he had so recently sprayed. The paper was crumpled from having spent so long in Fabien's pocket and bedaubed with oil from his grubby, mechanic's hands. Now, as he stared at it for the umpteenth time, a length of ash fell from the cigarette in his mouth and landed on Etienne's photograph. He brushed it off with the back of his hand, leaving an ugly smear across the young man's handsome face. '*Merde,*' he said again as he folded the paper roughly and shoved it back into his pocket.

Fabien didn't know what to do. He hated the police and had no desire to have any unnecessary communication with them, but if that bloke had just murdered someone – then that was another matter. He'd waited a few days in the hope that the police would find Etienne of their own accord, without his help. But so far he appeared to have evaded them and it might help if they knew what coloured van they ought to be looking for.

It was too hot. Fabien was overweight and he hated the heat. He hated the heat, he hated the police and now he hated Etienne too. He mopped the sweat from his brow with an oily rag and went to sit down in what passed for his office, a filthy little windowless cubicle at the back of the garage, furnished with a table, a chair, a computer and messy piles of stained papers. A bare bulb hung from the ceiling on a greasy flex to which were stuck a series of dead flies. Being lit, the bulb merely added to the stifling atmosphere. There was a shelf on the wall stacked with what appeared to be old catalogues and telephone directories and above it a grimy out-of-date calendar depicting a busty girl with pouting lips dressed in a scarlet g-string. There were further piles of papers on the floor and on the table beside the computer was a cracked earthenware dish, probably designed for a small cassoulet, but on this occasion filled to the brim with fag ends. Others had been merely trodden out on the ground.

Fabien decided that he wouldn't be able to do anything until the weather broke. It was too hot. Too hot to move. He kicked angrily at a pile of papers on the floor but the action only made him break into a further sweat. His cigarette had burnt out. He threw it into the cassoulet dish with an oath and went to light another one. Even that action caused him to sweat. Or perhaps he was sweating with fear. If the pigs could connect him in any way to Etienne, would they start accusing him of being an accessory after the fact? After all he had sprayed the bloody van, had even suspected Etienne of something at the time. Perhaps he had better say nothing as the last thing he wanted was to have some sodding police officer pushing his nose into his business. Stuff Etienne.

If the girl was dead – which Fabien presumed she was – it would do her no good for him to go blabbing to the coppers. No, he'd do far better to keep stumm. He scratched his belly and belched at the same time then, because he heard someone moving around in the garage, he heaved himself to his feet and ambled out of his office.

A man in his late thirties was standing there looking at an old red Citroën estate which was up on the ramp with its wheels off and a new, unpainted off-side front door swinging from its hinges. The man was tidily dressed and clean shaven with neatly cut hair and something of a military air about him.

'*Bonjour Monsieur,*' he said, turning smartly towards Fabien and offering a well-manicured hand.

Fabien wiped his hand on the seat of his trousers before offering the stranger his out-turned wrist. It was as though his entire innards were about to drop out of him for if he knew anything, he knew a policeman when he saw one.

'*Eh bien*,' he said. 'What can I do for you?' He noticed the copper's eyes flitting swiftly round the garage and wondered what on earth he was expecting to see.

'Nice car,' the policeman said, nodding in the direction of the dirty old Citroën on the ramp.

Fabien gave a non-committal grunt.

This was getting nowhere and as the policeman had not yet declared his identity, there was no reason why Fabien should treat him differently to any other member of the public. He just wondered what had brought the little shit to the garage. Surely it couldn't be anything to do with the missing girl. Fabien began to sweat again even more profusely than ever.

The policeman gave him a beady look and casually asked if he liked the hot weather. 'For my part, it's a bit too much,' he said, 'unless you're on holiday.' He wandered round to the other side of the ramp, affecting a great interest in the car perched on high. 'What do you charge,' he suddenly said, reappearing by Fabien's side, 'to spray a car like this?'

'I don't do that. It's not worth my while – only new wings – they have to be done.' He nodded in the direction of the Citroën. Haven't sprayed a whole vehicle in years.

'You surprise me,' the policeman said as he flashed his badge. Then, 'Police,' he announced and putting a hand in the pocket of his seersucker jacket pulled out the press photograph of Etienne. 'Have you seen this man?' he asked, holding the picture out for Fabien to see.

There was only the very slightest hesitation before the *garagiste* replied, 'No. No. I've never seen him and I don't know him. Never seen him in my life.'

'Really?' The copper raised one eyebrow in what seemed like mock surprise. 'In that case I'm sorry to have wasted your time,' he said, scanning the floor as he walked away towards the door. For a moment he paused before kicking idly at a black paint stain on the concrete floor by the ramp.

'*Eh alors, au revoir Monsieur,*' he said over his shoulder as he stepped out into the blinding sunlight.

'*Merde alors!*' Fabien spat on the floor. '*Espèce de con,*' he muttered as he turned to go back to his office. '*Espèce de con.*'

XV

'*Mais qu'est-ce qu'il y a, Monsieur l'Abbé?*' Mathilde was horrified to see poor Fafa with his head in his hands, looking ready to cry at any moment. What could be the matter? She placed a crabbed hand on his shoulder.

'*C'est la petite…*' Fafa was so good and so thoughtful that she felt sure he must be weeping for the poor abducted child. For her part, she continued to pray to the Archbishop at intervals all day, begging him to intercede for Isabelle that she might be safely returned to her parents. He had after all listened to her prayers before, why would he not listen now? Fafa too must be praying for her.

The priest looked round at the kindly old woman standing beside him with her hand on his shoulder. 'It's what I saw the other day,' he said. 'I had to go to Castel that afternoon and I was walking along the tow path by the canal…I was preparing my sermon in my head wondering how I could touch the hearts of the congregation. You see, so many of them believe in nothing – I don't even know why they come to church. It's as if they have everything they want so there's no longer any need to turn to the Lord.'

Mathilde shook her old head sadly.

Fafa stood up. '*Comme il fait chaud,*' he said as if the heat were the only thing that mattered. 'It's so hot. It was hot then too. That's why I'd gone down to the canal, I thought it might be cooler by the water – it would be easier to think there.'

'Sit down,' Mathilde urged Fafa, 'and take a little more cassoulet...' Her instinct when confronted by anyone in distress was always to feed them.

But Fafa remained standing. If he had gone to the police then and there, would it have made any difference? Was what he thought he had seen what he had really seen? The police would have mocked him, dismissed him with a shrug or a laugh or a hint of irritability. So confused had Fafa been feeling for the last few days that he had sometimes wondered if the Good Lord had abandoned him in his hour of need.

Mathilde, seeing the angst on the young man's face, urged him to go on, to tell her what had happened, what he had seen, what it was that had so distressed him.

So he told her. He told her hesitantly that he had been coming back along the canal path towards the road where he had left his car when he had noticed ahead of him a young man with dark, longish curly hair. The young man was walking quite fast, almost purposefully with his arm round the waist of a slim girl. The back of the girl reminded him of Isabelle, but he didn't then presume it to be her. In any case he couldn't see the girl properly because of the man's arm and because she was wearing a hat – a baseball cap which she had on back to front, he supposed to protect her neck from the beating rays of the sun.

Fafa didn't tell Mathilde of how he had then thought of Isabelle and of the violent pang of jealousy he had felt at the idea of her beautiful boyish body in the arms of another man. Might the Almighty have mercy upon him! But the girl in front of him wasn't Isabelle of course. Could not be Isabelle. Isabelle was so much on his mind that he was seeing her everywhere and in everything. He could not escape her image. He remembered a line from *Phèdre* which he had studied at school – *tout retrace à mes yeux les charmes que j'évite* – how foolish he had thought it at the time, but now there was nothing that did not remind him of Isabelle.

'What was particularly strange,' Fafa said, 'was that this man, this boy had, looped over his shoulder, a coiled rope. At the time I asked myself why he had one arm round a girl and a rope round the other. But now…' the poor man put his head in his hands, sank back on to the chair where he had been sitting to eat his cassoulet and, with a great shudder, burst into tears.

'It was her,' he managed to articulate between sobs. 'It was Isabelle. I know it was now…and I did nothing – nothing. I have prayed and prayed again but it is as though I no longer know how to pray. In an attempt to control himself he sat up straight, dried his eyes with his fists like a small child then suddenly leant forward and buried his face in his hands as if in prayer.

'Praying's not enough,' Mathilde remarked surprisingly sharply. '*Eh bien*, pray if you wish, but you must go to the police.'

'At first I was just so sure it couldn't have been her,' Fafa said by way of an explanation as to why he hadn't already done so. 'And now it's too late. Nothing I say can help them. And perhaps it wasn't Isabelle – and the rope – why did he have a rope? What was it for, that rope…?'

Mathilde hated to see the priest in such distress. Poor boy, he should have gone to the police as soon as he knew that Isabelle had disappeared, not that she was convinced that that would have changed anything. But he would have felt better. He would not have needed to torture himself so.

'But,' he wailed, 'if only I had thought to look and see if it really was Isabelle – then I could have saved her.' The poor man began to cry again. 'I followed them,' he wept. 'I was going the same way and I saw them – they got into a white van…she got in first…I felt almost sure then that it was Isabelle…*Isabelle…pauvre petite Isabelle…*' he groaned.

Something about the way he expressed those last three words caused Mathilde to wonder. Such a cry from the heart.

'*Monsieur l'Abbé,*' she said. You must go to the police at once and you must pray. Pray to Our Lady, pray to the Archbishop – they will listen to our prayers. I have faith.'

It was as though Mathilde who always showed so much respect for the cloth was suggesting that he, the priest, was losing his faith. Fafa mopped his face with a table napkin smeared with the sauce from the cassoulet, rose to his feet and kissed Mathilde. He felt it was too late for the police to find his information at all useful but he knew that Mathilde was right and that he should report what he had seen. At least he might feel a little better once he had done so.

The police, he knew, would ask him if the girl had appeared to get into the van willingly. This was something that he couldn't decide and about which he had been torturing himself ever since.

And the rope. 'Why the rope?' Mathilde heard him say to himself as he stepped out into the glaring light of the sun. She stepped out after him and turned to look at the thermometer which hung in the shade of the vine that grew over the door. 36°C.

Shaking her right hand up and down in front of her, Mathilde blew out through her lips. '*Boudu-u-u,*' she said to herself as she turned and pushed the bead curtain aside to go back indoors.

XVI

Etienne drove fast. He was on a high so was feeling all-powerful. Despite having hung around for a little too long in the environs of Toulouse, he had cleverly avoided the police and even if that rat Fabien did say anything about spraying the van, well the whole of France was filled with vans like his and Fabien certainly didn't know the number. He had, he thought, been quite careless to begin with but that was all behind him and no one would be able to catch him now. He felt like a free man. He also felt important. Ever since he had recovered from the shock of seeing his picture on the front page of all the newspapers, he had revelled in the knowledge that the whole world knew of him. He was celebrated, famous, clever and good-looking. No one would ever again be able to slight him, sneer at him, treat him as nothing. He had made a mark in the world. He was noticed.

Perhaps he ought to send another text message to Isabelle's parents – from Isabelle of course. It might put their minds at rest, but the only trouble was that if he did, the police might be able to trace his whereabouts. Not that he would stay for long in the same place. He was driving like the wind. It was amazing how fast the old van would go. He'd thought of dumping it and nicking another but the complications were too great and, in any case, he was fond of his old *bagnole*. It had been his home for some time now.

He glanced at his face in the driving mirror. It was a pity he'd had to cut off his curls and dye his hair; he'd been so handsome before.

He'd changed his mind about going north and instead was speeding along the *autoroute des deux mers*, east from Toulouse, brazenly whizzing past Castel, the proud home of cassoulet, leaving, on a slight rise to the left the *cité* of Carcassonne crowned with its fairy-tale turrets, then on through the parched and stony Corbières. For all its excellent qualities Etienne's van had no working air-conditioning and the hot breeze that wafted through the open windows brought with it the delicious pine tree scent of the south. The rugged countryside glimmered in the heat and the gleaming tarmac of the road ahead filled Etienne's heart with expectation. He was making for the sea.

At the motorway exit Etienne joined a crowd of impatient motorists, jostling to join a queue. As, with his ticket in his mouth, he shifted in his seat and fumbled for change in his pocket, he noticed the woman in the Renault Espace next to him. She was thin, tanned and bony with cropped hair and a narrow face. She wore a skimpy white T-shirt. '*Pas mal*,' Etienne thought; not unattractive at all, but bearing no comparison to Isabelle. She turned her head to say something to the gang of small children in the back of the car and as she did so she caught his eye.

Etienne winked. It was a pity about his short yellow hair. The woman stared at him with an expression of surprise; then, before accelerating to join the queue ahead of him, she suddenly turned back and gave him a long hard look. With a jaunty air he raised his right hand, wiggled his fingers in a merry wave and winked again.

What sort of a man, he asked himself, as he edged forwards behind the Renault, what sort of a man can do what I have done and behave as I do? A detached self-confident man, he thought. A brilliant man. Some would say a madman. He gave a hearty chuckle as he pushed his ticket into the machine by the barrier,

What he planned to do next was to go to the coast. It was too hot to do anything else, besides he liked the idea of displaying his brown, muscular body on the beach. He would lie in the sun, possibly take a pedalo out to sea, swagger about a bit. No doubt he would be admired and on a day like this in August, there would be plenty of topless women for him to appreciate as they lazed on their backs in the sun or smeared sun cream all over their bodies. Perhaps he would see the woman in the Renault again as, with all those children, she must have been heading for the beach. He might even chat her up since she had clearly fancied him despite his unfortunate hair, but he had heard it said that fair hair with brown eyes was an attractive combination. Perhaps she wouldn't realise that his hair was dyed.

It did not for an instant occur to Etienne that the woman in the Renault had looked at him as she did for any other reason than that she fancied him. What he did not know was that she was a portrait painter and therefore peculiarly observant about faces. There must have been something particular about his appearance or his expression that had caused her to stare at him as she did.

On reaching the beach, Etienne had to drive round for a while before he could find a parking place which made him so angry that he began to expostulate out loud about the idiots and inferior beings, the pointless individuals who were getting in his way. Eventually he found a place from which a car was just moving out but unfortunately it was in the sun so the van would be unbearably hot by the time he came back to it. He wouldn't dare leave the windows open. Not somewhere like this. You never knew what petty criminals might be about. In any case the air outside was so hot that it would hardly make any difference. Luckily he didn't have a dog to leave in the car. Etienne had never liked dogs although it had sometimes occurred to him that to have one would be to have a friend in his solitary life. But he had no need of friends. Not now.

Having carefully parked, he took off his shirt, threw it into the back, locked the van, pocketed the key in his grubby lemon yellow shorts and sauntered off with a swagger towards the beach.

He stepped on to the hot sand. A small girl clutching round her waist a yellow rubber ring shaped like a duck looked up at Etienne, then whispered something to her bikini-clad mother. She, with one quick glance in his direction, pulled the child by the hand, roughly yanking her arm, and walked smartly away in the opposite direction.

On this occasion Etienne had left his favourite book in the van. During the last few days he had been feeling so full of himself that, for the first time in months, he felt no need of Roquentin's companionship.

XVII

Christiane was sitting at the kitchen table in front of her laptop; she was leafing through a transcript of the Archbishop's journals that lay on the table beside her but it was clear from the vacant expression in her eyes that she was far from engaged in what she was looking at. Suddenly she gave a great sigh. She had been thrilled at the discovery of these papers and so excited at the prospect of writing her book but now all that had turned to dust. At moments like this she felt that she would never write it now; the very thought of the Archbishop and the intrigues of his *Ancien Régime* existence had lost their savour. Then a surge of rage welled up violently and unexpectedly in her – rage directed at Isabelle. Isabelle who by her own folly and selfishness had suddenly ruined all their lives. Turned everything upside down, made everyone miserable.

As her rage subsided, Christiane began to feel guilty. How could she have felt so angry with her daughter whom she loved and who, if she was still alive, must be in direst danger? Then she began to cry. If only they knew…if only they knew. The interminable uncertainty of impotent waiting was unbearable. Leaning over the Archbishop's journal, she buried her head in her arms and sobbed. Would anything be all right ever again?

She had thought that if only she could bring herself to concentrate for even half an hour on the Archbishop, it would at least be a distraction from the awfulness of the situation and from the demented nature of her other thoughts.

Christiane resented the way that Claud had somehow managed over the last two days to do some work. It was difficult to focus on anything, he admitted, but it had to be done and, he claimed, it helped to keep him sane.

Just as she sat up and stopped crying Claud came into the room.

'How's it going?' he asked.

Christiane wanted to scream. Instead she just shouted, 'Oh, for Christ's sake get out…' Then she began to cry again.

Claud left the room. Try as he might, he could only say the wrong thing to Christiane these days. She didn't seem to realise that he was just as miserable and afraid as she. For the first few days after Isabelle disappeared, they had been as one, but as time went by they had begun to get on each other's nerves, seemingly unable to hit the right note with one another.

A single thing did hold them together, which was the firm belief that Isabelle was still alive. Whatever might have happened to her, however awful it might be, it had to be less bad than death.

Claud strolled into the garden, took out a cigarette and fumbled in his shorts pocket for a lighter. He hadn't smoked for years until two days ago when he asked one of the teenagers for a cigarette, then yesterday he'd bought a packet.

'That filthy habit won't bring Isabelle back!' Christiane had snapped. 'And it'll probably kill you…'

Claud drew deeply on his cigarette as he walked across the brown grass towards the swimming pool. He was amazed by the teenagers; they bickered but when the bickering stopped, they seemed remarkably composed. Only Agnès seemed to be almost permanently in tears. But they mostly kept themselves to themselves, had become quiet, helpful, and no doubt pensive. They had even by common accord abandoned their much loved Facebook. Nothing like this could ever have happened to any of them before and it was far too serious a matter to be bandied about in public or to be allowed to float unsupervised in the stratosphere.

All of a sudden as he walked, head down, lost in thought, Claud heard a shriek. He looked up to see all five young people stampeding towards him from the direction of the pool.

'Papa, Papa,' Agnès was yelling. 'Isabelle, Isabelle – it's her…' She waved towards Ellen who was clutching a mobile phone in one hand a pair of sunglasses in the other.

Claud looked at the group of excited children standing in front of him and for a moment simply couldn't begin to take in what they were saying. They were all talking at once and Ellen was waving her mobile in his face.

'A text,' she said, 'from Iz…'

As he took the proffered telephone from Ellen, his heart which had momentarily soared, sank. 'We've had this before,' he said. 'You know the police don't think these texts come from Isabelle…'

He glanced at the tiny screen and read: 'having luvly time, Is.' His stomach turned over. He felt frankly sick.

'What sort of a lunatic sends this kind of message?' he exclaimed angrily.

'But you can't be sure it's not from Isabelle,' Ellen said.

'Yes, I can. She would never send such a stupid message. Besides, look, *Iz* is spelt with an *s* again and as for *lovely* – well perhaps that's texting, but to me it looks like someone who doesn't know how to spell in English…I'll have to ring Fayard.' Claud threw down his half-smoked cigarette, ground it into the dusty earth with the toe of his worn black espadrille and turned to go back to the house.

Agnès burst into tears and her dark-eyed little cousin, Maddy, put her arms around her.

Back in the house, Christiane had begun half-heartedly to read through a few pages of the Archbishop's diary. They made little impression on her, but she was trying. She couldn't just sit there all morning waiting for the telephone to ring, waiting for Isabelle to walk through the door. She looked up in irritation as Claud came back in from the garden. Why couldn't he leave her alone for God's sake?'

In fact nothing Claud could do at the moment seemed right. If he came shopping with her, she wished he hadn't, and if he didn't, she blamed him for leaving her alone to run the gauntlet of the staring pitying glances of shopkeepers and passers-by alike. Everyone knew what she looked like now, but they still had to eat and indeed she still had to occupy her time.

She'd read of the parents of other lost children always claiming that they would leave no stone unturned until they found their daughter or son. She could think of no stones to turn that she or Claud had not already turned. Only the police seemed hopeless, slow and senseless. They knew who Etienne was and what he looked like and yet they couldn't find him. Why – oh why had they not yet found him? They were permanently in contact, permanently asking irrelevant questions, never producing any concrete evidence. Nothing since the woman doctor in Toulouse had reported seeing Etienne on the night Isabelle disappeared except some nonsense about a *garagiste* they'd arrested for perverting the course of justice. They were delighted by that. But that was all. And now it seemed as though Isabelle had been gone a thousand years.

As he came into the kitchen, Claud noticed the look of irritation on his wife's face and wished it were easier to communicate with her.

'Look,' he said, holding out Ellen's mobile. 'This has come...'

Framed in the sunlit doorway behind him, the teenagers stood in a group, expectantly leaning forward, hands on each other's shoulders as if placed there for a theatrical performance.

As Christiane stood up to grab the mobile from Claud's outstretched hand, several photocopied pages of the Archbishop's diary fluttered to the ground. Was there some good news at last?

XVIII

Had she not been immersed in her personal tragedy Christiane would have been enthralled by the pages dated 1767 which lay at her feet on the kitchen floor. By this time the Archbishop had long since been promoted from Toulouse to the see of Narbonne.

To be Archbishop of Narbonne at the time meant being also the *Président des Etats du Languedoc* – to all intents and purposes, viceroy of the Languedoc which was the most independent of French provinces, with the greatest measure of self-government. Thus the Archbishop had become a very rich and powerful man.

Alas, he wrote, the time is drawing near when duty dictates that I abandon the sweet pleasures of Hautefontaine in order to visit my people in the South. Narbonne and indeed Montpellier require my presence and thither I must travel.

It is of some consolation to me that I shall be able, on this occasion, to inspect the plasterwork which I have ordered to adorn the dining-room in the Bishop's Palace at Narbonne. This work will, I trust, be near completion. The palace itself is old and with its fortress-like outer walls and its great stone staircase, nearly wide enough for a coach and four, it is somewhat forbidding; consequently, dare I say it, needing to be modernised, revitalised.

Hence the chequered marble floor and the elegant *boiserie* which I have already had installed, albeit to Madame de R's disapproval.

Although she may revel in my station, my niece is nothing if not censorious of what she regards as the merest frivolity. I have, therefore, not yet allowed her to see my magnificent new chasuble, made from the finest Lyonnais silk embroidered with hares and duck and stags and even the occasional hunting rifle. It is an object of exquisite beauty and outstanding workmanship.

My lily-livered hope is that, with her less than perfect eyesight, Madame de R may not at once perceive the details of this design.

Since I was retained at Versailles for longer than I had intended my *séjour* at Hautefontaine has been perforce curtailed which, however, has not prevented my enjoying numerous excellent days hunting.

The King' himself, or so I am informed by the duc de L., is quite envious of our great hunt which is comparable, some may claim even superior, to the Royal hunt at Fontainebleau. I cannot deny that I am visited by the sin of pride when I view my hounds setting out of a misty autumn morning with the hunt servants all dressed in the livery of my Irish forebears.

The forest of Compiègne being rich with both boar and deer, I am never in any doubt that several fine stags will be brought home by the end of the day.

At present, countless numbers of my Irish cousins, most of whom are dependent on our generosity, are staying at the château. They, together with so many of the *beau monde* from Paris and despite the severity of my dear niece who rules over us all with her iron will, create an atmosphere of great merriment.

This merriment, however, has of necessity become out of place by virtue of the news brought to us this very morning that the strangled, half-clothed body of the sixteen-year-old daughter of one of the laundrywomen has been found in a shallow grave in the forest, barely covered with fallen leaves

Were I not obliged to depart so soon, it would be my solemn duty to officiate at the *funérailles* of this poor creature. My niece, on the other hand, insists that it is as well that we leave now since she is of the opinion that the child brought her misfortune upon herself, that she was a frolicksome lass who may well have deserved her untimely end and that it would therefore be unseemly for her obsequies to be attended by a prince of the Church.

I durst point out to Madame de R that the *moeurs* of many of those at present residing at Hautefontaine are barely any different to what may have been those of this frolicksome young person. She, indeed, may have been a great deal more innocent than many of those who should know better.

Such an expression of my heartfelt sentiments, not to mention, my inferences regarding the morality, not to say hypocrisy of our society, instantly met with the wrath of my niece who has seen fit to remonstrate with the child's mother for not having kept a closer watch over her daughter.

Dear God, I say to myself, if You are indeed there, have mercy on us. Have mercy on us all. We are but miserable sinners.

Before we depart from Hautefontaine it is my intention to offer my sincerest *condoléances* to the family of the murdered girl and to express my regret at not being there to perform the obsequies.

Late this afternoon we were visited by an *inspecteur de police* from Compiègne. It would appear that the young lady in question had been involved in an intrigue with one of my hunt servants, the which scoundrel was nowhere to be found on this inauspicious morning.

It is with a heavy heart indeed that I find one of my servants to be the chief suspect in a murder enquiry. As are most of my hunt servants, the man in question is English, coming from the estates inherited by my brother's wife in the county of Oxfordshire. What a fine marriage my brother made in the eyes of the world! The estate which has come to be his own and which will in due course pass to my dear nephew, Charles, comprises an impressive acreage and a large house of great elegance built some forty years ago by one of England's most distinguished architects. It stands in the centre of what was a favourite hunting ground of the kings of England. And still, it appears, there is excellent sport to be found there.

If indeed young Jacob is proven guilty of the horrendous crime of murder, I shall require to know how such a creature came to be recommended to me and thus dispatched across the Channel to commit his vile crimes here and so dishonour the livery of my forebears. I find myself obliged to question whether this person was in fact escaping the heavy hand of the English law; had he already committed some bestial crime in his native land? These questions will, I trust, be answered in due course...

XIX

As the sun rose over the Golfe de Lyon, proclaiming yet another day of insupportable heat, the beach at Leucate was empty. Yesterday it had been so crowded that there was barely room to fit an extra child between the rows of oiled, sun-baked bodies lounging there. Overnight a hot wind from the south had risen causing a mini-sandstorm that would have covered anything abandoned on the beach the day before – a plastic spade, a bottle of sun-cream, a bathing towel. It had half covered the naked body of a young girl lying face down in the sand, her arms outstretched.

The hot wind from the south, known to some as the *vent d'Espagne*, to others as the *vent d'autan* would eventually bring rain, but it could blow for days before it did so, causing even greater heat and discomfort than the soaring temperatures of the last few weeks.

A muscular, sun-tanned beach boy who came, like the wind, from Spain was destined to find the body. Miguel had lain awake sweating for most of the night, kept from sleep by the heat and the ceaseless buffeting of the *vent d'autan*. How he hated that wind. He got out of bed at first light, pulled on a miniscule pair of skin-tight tangerine-coloured bathing trunks and pushed his feet into some pink flip flops before setting off down to the beach where it was his job to pick up the debris from the day before. Sometimes he was amazed by the things that people carelessly left behind along with their litter – books, watches, mobiles, sunglasses, cameras – even iPads. But he had never before found a body.

At first Miguel didn't know what on earth to do. He spoke little French and had no idea how to contact the emergency services – in any case he'd left his mobile behind. None of the shops or restaurants along the front would be open yet. Stunned by the horror of what he had discovered, the wretched boy stood for some time rooted to the spot as the cruel wind whistled around him, whipping up the sand so that it blew into his hair, his eyes, his nostrils and stung his near-naked body.

He tried to blink, then rubbed his eyes in the hopes that what he had seen was not really there, but only succeeded in filling them with even more sand. He knelt down beside the body and whispered something, He didn't know what, but he hoped the girl would turn over, that the sand would run off her body and she would reply. Then he burst into tears.

Madame Monet was standing in the restaurant of her small hotel, looking out through the glass door at the terrace adorned with the huge tubs of oleanders of which she was so proud. The wind which bent them this way and that had already upset a few chairs and broken whiskery branches off the tamarisks that grew at intervals along the side of the road which ran between the restaurant and the sea.

'*Eh bien,*' she thought to herself, 'there won't be many *clients* wanting to eat outside today.' She supposed she ought not to complain as it had been a good season so far; she couldn't begin to count how many orders of bouillabaisse had been carried steaming from her kitchen. But Madame Monet was a business woman and she hated anything that interfered with her money-making.

She went on looking out at the wind-blown oleanders and the rough sea beyond, her arms crossed on her ample bosom. She was dressed as usual in a low-cut pink tee-shirt and a tight black skirt, with a string of glass beads hanging down into her wrinkled brown cleavage She was one of those women, mostly to be found in France, whose heavy body is supported by pin legs and narrow feet which, in her case, were tip-tilted into a pair of wedge-heeled sandals. Madame Monet's toenails were painted vermilion and her yellow dyed hair was scraped back into a tight pleat. On her sharp little face she wore an expression that seemed to speak only of money. And she knew how to make it.

Chez Monique was a simple, old-fashioned, reasonably priced hotel/restaurant which Madame Monet had taken over from her aging father some years earlier. It was very popular and always crowded throughout the summer – there was even an English family who came to Leucate several times a year for the sole pleasure of eating Madame Monet's bouillabaisse. They always liked to sit on the terrace and were excellent customers who ate a lot and drank a lot – *Listel gris de gris, vin des sables*. Well, they wouldn't be coming today.

Just as Madame Monet was bewailing to herself the ignorance of most foreigners who didn't know the difference between *foie gras* and *pâté de foie gras*, let alone between a *baudroie* and a *Saint-Pierre* or any other fish for that matter, a dark-haired lad dressed in nothing but the skimpiest of bathing trunks suddenly appeared on the terrace. Before she even had time to unlock the door and let him in, Madame Monet could see that he appeared to be in some sort of distress.

Miguel almost fell through the door of the restaurant as soon as it was opened, and into Madame Monet's arms, crying and gesticulating as he did so, pointing towards the beach and gabbling half in Spanish and half in incomprehensible French.

Trying to make some sense of what he was saying, Madame Monet quickly led the wretched boy into her small office away from the prying eyes of any of her guests who might appear for an early breakfast. She didn't know his name, but she'd seen Miguel before and knew that it was his job to clean the beach and later in the day to sell peanuts or help with the hire of pedalos. Occasionally he came to the restaurant to buy an ice cream or a Coca-Cola.

As she pushed Miguel down on an upright chair that looked as though it might have inspired Van Gogh, Madame Monet realised that he was beginning to shake. He had stopped crying but he was shaking, shaking as she had never ever seen anyone shake before. His whole body seemed to be thrashing about like a flounder taken from the sea. It was a wonder that he didn't fall off the chair. Still she couldn't make out what had happened.

She kept hearing words like *chica* and *muerta* but she couldn't be sure that she understood them properly. Eventually, after she had given Miguel some Armagnac to stop the shaking and when he had repeatedly asked for the police – who sound much the same in any language – she picked up the telephone and dialled 17.

'*Mince*,' she said to herself. If, as she now suspected, there really was a body out there, the beach would be closed for goodness knows how long while the police searched for evidence of one kind or another, evidence that had probably already been carried away by the *vent d'autan*. The police activity would be even worse for business than the wind itself.

It was bad enough last year; then it had taken days before everything went back to normal after all the papers in the Midi reported that sharks had unusually been sighted off the coast...but a dead body...that had to be even worse...

Madame Monet was quite right. Once the police arrived the beach was put out of bounds and looked like remaining that way for some time to come. Not that anyone could comfortably sunbathe in a sandstorm.

As the morning wore on, crowds began to gather on the pavement with people eager to pick up the merest scrap of information, but all that anyone knew was that the body of a girl had been discovered. The police guarding the site gave nothing away.

With no information forthcoming rumours began to spread with remarkable rapidity…the dead girl had been strangled – knifed – eviscerated – beaten to death… she was German – Czech – Parisian…it was a *crime passionnel* – suicide – drug related… No one knew anything, but everyone had a theory.

Soon people started coming into Madame Monet's restaurant to get out of the wind, to discover if she knew anything about what had happened and, fortunately, to spend a little money. The fact that Madame Monet was able to report that a girl's body had been found at dawn by a Spanish beach boy caused the rumours and her clientele to swell in equal measure.

The poor beach boy in question had been taken away by the police, dressed as he was in his tangerine bathing trunks, to be interrogated by the powers that be as the prime suspect in a murder case.

Since it took a while to locate a Spanish speaker, he was left for several hours, sitting in a hot stuffy room, still in his skimpy orange trunks.

It wasn't until much later that evening that a smart young policeman, eager for promotion, suddenly had the bright idea that the body on the beach might be the body of *la petite anglaise* – the teenager who'd so recently gone missing.

XX

Claud and Christiane were hurtling along the *autoroute des deux mers* just as Etienne had done only twenty-four hours earlier. Perched on its little hill, Carcassonne, that ludicrous pastiche of a medieval stronghold, looked laughingly down as they raced on, on through the dry, rocky, inhospitable Corbières country. Places that had always seemed so beautiful and so romantic to Christiane had suddenly lost their savour. And the wind – the ruddy wind was driving her mad.

Beside her, grim-faced and silent, Claud was driving. Neither he nor Christiane had anything to say to one another for what was there to say when they were heading for a morgue in order to identify their daughter's murdered body? Anything would be better than what lay ahead – the long agonising days of uncertainty, the endless, endless waiting. Waiting for news, waiting for Isabelle. Christiane remembered cases of other missing children with the press always going on about something they now called 'closure'. She didn't want closure. Not if seeing Isabelle's body on a mortuary slab and burying her was what was meant by closure. She could endure an eternity of waiting if only Isabelle were still alive.

They raced past the exit to Collioure and Perpignan – places whose very names Christiane had always found so alluring, places where she had always been happy – and on towards Narbonne. They were nearly there, but why – why had they driven at such speed when they so dreaded what lay ahead?

As they finally left the autoroute and drew up at the toll, Claud stretched out his arm and covered Christiane's hand with his own. Withdrawing her hand, she turned her head to look out of the window so as to hide the stubborn tears that until this moment had refused to flow. From the moment they had received the terrible news until now, it had seemed as if she herself were dead.

Claud had tried to give her hope by saying that there was as yet no proof that the body on the beach was Isabelle's, but Christiane had lost hope, for how, she would like to know, could there be a different girl so like Isabelle, lying there on the sand, dead, strangled? And hadn't Fayard told them that a young man answering Etienne's description had been spotted in the area? No one had reported him until after the event on account of the fact that he had obviously dyed his hair so it wasn't until the girl's body was discovered that people began to think back and to put two and two together.

There had been a woman with a small child who reported having seen a young man striding on to the beach, who looked – well she couldn't explain how he looked, but he had made her feel uncomfortable. There was something strange about him, something that made her not want to be near him. She had immediately hurried her little girl away. Another woman who had drawn up next to Etienne at the motorway exit had thought that she recognised him when he waved and winked at her, but she couldn't imagine where she might have seen him before until she heard of the body on the beach; then she suddenly realised that he looked like the man whose picture had been in all the papers when the English girl disappeared. Now she was sure it was he.

All this information made Claud feel angry. Why the hell hadn't the police caught the man before? What in God's name had they been doing leaving a dangerous murderer to swan around the south of France? And how long had Isabelle been dead? And what had been going on since she disappeared? He was so angry – so angry and yet the only thing for him do was to leave at once, to go to Narbonne in the morning and identify his daughter's body. Having ushered out Fayard and his sidekick who had come so sensitively to impart the news, he slammed the front door and without a word went to the lavatory and was violently sick.

When she came back from visiting Mathilde he had to tell Christiane what had happened and in doing so, he somehow managed to rekindle a faint ray of hope in his own heart. It just might not be Isabelle's body. It could be someone else's. Someone else whose parents would have to go through what he and Christiane were now going through. He felt almost guilty at wishing such misery on those other wretched people – whoever they might be.

Back at home the teenagers were sitting gravely together in the kitchen. They were smoking because there was no one there to tell them not to do so in the house and, in any case, these were exceptional circumstances. They weren't saying very much as, like Claud and Christiane, they couldn't imagine what there was to say.

Having decided that she needed a drink, Ellen had consumed nearly a whole bottle of rather acid rosé and was definitely the worse for wear, not that the others really cared. Ellen was beginning to get on all their nerves.

Agnès confided in Maddy that she hated Ellen because Ellen was supposed to be Isabelle's best friend and yet she didn't care about Isabelle. She hadn't even cried since Isabelle went missing and now that she was probably dead, all she could do was to think about herself.

Maddy looked soulfully at Agnès. She couldn't imagine what it would be like to have your sister murdered. It seemed awful enough that Isabelle was Maddy's cousin; but what should she say? She had no idea what you were supposed to say under such circumstances. You couldn't pretend it was going to be all right and neither could you say 'Cheer up!' How could any of them ever cheer up again?

Jake, seeing himself as the most grown-up of the teenagers, had taken charge. He was still being beastly to Ellen, but you couldn't blame him for that since she was always pestering him and showing off to him and sucking up to him, whereas to both Maddy and Agnès he was really kind. They were glad he hadn't gone home. And now, in the smoke-filled kitchen, he was a calm and comforting presence although he, as the others all knew, was suffering from a broken heart.

Jake looked across the table at Ellen, drunkenly slouched there. Then he looked at the other two girls sitting side-by-side and glanced at his watch,

'They'll be there by now,' he wanted to say, but nothing came out. He tried again.

'You know what,' he said. 'It's not her. I'm sure it's not.'

Sam stubbed a cigarette out in a saucer and said, 'I bet they'll smell the fags when they get back.' Then folding his arms on the table, he buried his tousled head in them and gave a great shudder.

'It won't matter about the fags,' said Maddy solemnly. 'Nothing will matter any more.'

Then the telephone rang and each and every one of them jumped, startled by the sudden shrillness.

'Who'll answer it?' Sam wanted to know.

Without a word Jake stood up and went towards the telephone. Maddy noticed that his hand was shaking as he picked up the receiver. White-faced, he walked with it slowly, out of the kitchen but was back in an instant.

'It was Claud,' he said as he sat down. 'Wanted to know if we were OK. They've just got to Narbonne. Anyone lend me a fag?'

Sam pushed a crumpled packet towards him across the table. In the numbing silence that had fallen over the group, the slightest noise – the cigarettes sliding across the table, the sound of Jake striking a match, seemed like some cruel intrusion on the young people's collective misery.

All at once there came a terrible scream. It was Ellen. She screamed and screamed, at the same time pounding the table with both her fists.

'Shut up, can't you…' Sam shouted, but kind little Maddy for once left Agnès's side and went to put her arms round Ellen.

'Don't tell me to shut up,' Ellen wailed. 'I know you all think I'm a bitch, but don't you realise she was my best, best friend…nothing will ever be the same again…nothing.'

'And don't say was,' Jake spoke steadily. 'She is, still is your best friend.'

No one really believed him.

'Anyway we're not thinking about you,' Sam snarled. 'What about Agnès – and Claud and Christiane…what about them for God's sake?'

Agnès burst into tears, leaving Maddy unable to decide which of the two girls most needed comforting. Ellen was drunkenly, guiltily, broken-heartedly sobbing for all she was worth, slumped on the table, her head in her arms. No one knew what to do. They could only wait.

The last time Christiane had been to Narbonne was to research the Archbishop. She had spent most of the day in the municipal archives reading about the excellent, civic minded works for which he had been responsible and had then visited the Bishop's Palace where she was amazed and delighted by the exquisite plasterwork with which the old boy had seen fit to decorate his dining-room. There was a hare, like a dead animal in a Dutch painting, hanging in a garland of flowers. There were fish and hounds and trees and hunting horns – an exuberance of all that the Archbishop most loved.

In the cathedral, she sat on the Archbishop's throne where he had sat and admired in a drawer in the sacristy an extraordinary silk chasuble exquisitely embroidered with fish and fowl and stag which he had had made for important occasions. What a curious fellow he was. In the museum she had admired Gamelin's portrait of him at the *Apotheosis of Saint Roch*. There in his vestments is her Archbishop, a tall man with a round, plump face and heavy eyelids, pointing up to where the grey-headed saint, arms outstretched is being borne aloft by a mêlée of angels. But the eye is drawn not so much to the skyed saint as to the figure of the Archbishop, standing there, proudly surrounded by a bevy of kneeling clergy.

All this now seemed to be part of another life, or perhaps of a dream. And yet, back at home, Mathilde and the little priest were busy praying to the old devil for Isabelle's return. If only their blind faith were founded in something other than superstition. If only the present were a dream...if only...

Christiane tried to steel herself for what lay ahead. She couldn't look at Claud. He held her arm as she got out of the car but it meant nothing to her for she was alone in her misery just as she assumed he was alone in his. This was like dying.

Fayard, the policeman whose business it was to be in daily touch with the family, was there. He shook hands with Claud and Christiane before introducing them to a colleague from Narbonne who was to accompany them in a police car to the morgue. On the way Fayard saw fit to break the silence by talking about the wind, the heat; he asked how long the drive had taken them, and whether they had found their way easily through Narbonne.

Claud replied monosyllabically. Neither Christiane nor the policeman at the wheel said a word.

Afterwards Christiane didn't really know how they had got there. Who had been with them, what, if anything had been said. She could just remember the white-coated mortuary assistant neatly – so neatly – folding the sheet back from the face, as if he were tidying a bed. Then her head began to swim and she felt a wave of nausea as her legs crumpled beneath her.

Claud turned to catch his wife before she fell, saying almost inaudibly as he did so, '*Non, ce n'est pas elle.*'

It was not she.

That information was of no help to the Police; if it was not Isabelle, who was it? Etienne had almost certainly been sighted in the vicinity of the body on the night of the murder and the police had been confident that, having found Isabelle, it would not be long before they caught her killer. That would then be that and they would be able to congratulate themselves on a job well done.

XXI

Eva Johanssen had spent the summer inter-railing around Europe with friends. She was eighteen years old and came from Malmö in Sweden. Sometime around the middle of August she fell out with her friends and travelled on alone, down through Austria to Italy and back up to the South of France. She liked the thought of the seaside and decided on a whim – almost everything she ever did depended on a whim – to leave the train at Narbonne from where she hitched a lift down to Leucate with a grey-haired man in his early fifties who was on his way to Spain. As she got out of his car this man told her, 'You are very lucky that it was I who stopped for you. I have a daughter of your age and I would never allow her to do what you are doing. It is dangerous and you should be very careful.'

He had been speaking French, which language Eva barely understood although she could tell from the way he spoke that he was admonishing her in some way. She looked at him sulkily, decided he was annoying, thanked him grudgingly, dragged her backpack out of the car and set off to find a room. She liked the look of this place and might stay for several days.

Having texted her mother in Sweden to say she was fine, but having failed to say exactly where in France she was, Eva set out that evening to look for fun. It was not long before she imagined she had found it, but later that night as she lay on the beach, stoned and half drunk, making love to a nameless man, she suddenly felt his fingers being slipped slyly around her neck. She screamed a fearful scream, but no one heard and in an instant she was dead.

Back in Sweden Eva's mother was telling her friends what a wonderful time Eva was having on her travels with such a nice group of young people; she didn't know that her daughter had been travelling alone for at least ten days, but had she known, she would merely have said that Eva was a sensible girl who could look after herself.

Eva misread her mother just as her mother misread her.

It was not for several days that anyone concerned with the case had any idea as to the identity of the strangled girl and no one in Sweden or elsewhere knew that she was missing – or indeed dead. Nothing that might give the slightest clue as to who she was had been found by her body; the wind and the torrential storms it heralded had wiped away any trace that there might have been. The police were at their wits end. They had scoured the area for anyone who might have seen the girl. No one seemed to have done so, or if they had, they couldn't remember her – there were just so many young people on the beach and in the bars.

The hunt for Etienne continued. It was naturally presumed that he was the killer – for one thing a priest from a village in the *Montagne Noire* had recently come forward to say that on the day of Isabelle's disappearance he had seen her with a man who was carrying a coil of rope. And if Etienne had killed one girl, he would surely kill another if he had not already done so.

When Madame Gautier, a little, bossy woman who wore her spectacles on a long fluorescent pink chain and kept a small *pension* some way from the beach, eventually came forward, she had already been interviewed by the police as part of their routine enquiries. She mistrusted them and dreaded having anything to do with them. In her opinion there was nothing to choose between the police and doctors; all they ever wanted to do – the lot of them – was to ask impertinent questions and give you bad news. In any case she'd had enough of the authorities what with being investigated last year by the *brigade des fraudes* who were convinced that she was fiddling her tax returns. It was only through her innate cunning that she had avoided serious trouble.

As soon as the police turned up at *Les lauriers roses*, Madame Gautier decided to clam up.

'*Non. Je ne l'ai jamais vue.*' She had never seen the girl in question. But she had. The police examined her books and finding no record of anyone answering Eva's description having stayed at *Les lauriers roses*, they went, satisfied, on their way.

It was Monsieur Gautier, a retired greengrocer, who eventually managed to persuade his wife that she must go to the police. 'Scratch your head and pretend you couldn't remember,' he told her. After all Madame Gautier had nothing to be afraid of except being discovered to have withheld evidence and who could tell, but someone might just have seen the dead girl arriving at the *pension*.

Eva hadn't stayed at *Les lauriers roses* because there had been no room, but she had sat in the bar and drunk a Coca-Cola.

Madame Gautier had been difficult to persuade since she was convinced that it would be bad for business for her to be connected in any way with the murdered girl – however innocently. All she could tell the police was that the young woman was on holiday from Sweden, that she had been wearing white shorts and a white T-shirt. Eva had sat at the bar playing with her mobile, apparently texting and then when Madame Gautier explained in her broken English that the place was very crowded and it would be difficult to find a room anywhere, the girl had shrugged her shoulders, picked up her backpack, paid for her drink and left.

It was a start for the police to have discovered that the murdered girl was Swedish. Some days later her backpack would be washed up on a beach further down the coast; in it a few T-shirt, underwear, a pair of shorts, a saturated purse containing a plastic card, a saturated passport and a tube of sun cream.

None of all that was of any consolation to Claud or Christiane. They clung to the hope that Isabelle was still alive but they suffered from nightmares in which she became confused with Eva and in which strangulation always played a part for, despite their hope, reason seemed to dictate that somewhere their daughter lay dead.

Sometimes Claud dreamt that he was strangling his own child, at others that he was running to save her but, with his feet stuck to the ground, he could never reach her. Both he and Christiane took sleeping pills but the pills only worked for a few hours before the nightmares began and then they would wake. They tried staying up later and later but that didn't work as they then fell asleep downstairs only to wake terrified in the small hours. They would have slept in separate rooms to avoid waking one another, but the house was full although Isabelle's bed was empty of course, but then she had shared a room with Ellen.

Christiane kept trying to work – anything to kill the waiting hours – but progress was slow although when she finally read the Archbishop's account of the murdered girl at Hautefontaine, she suddenly felt an extraordinary affinity with the past. Nothing had changed. Nothing had improved. Priests didn't decorate their palaces with bas reliefs of shot hares and rifles any more, they abused children instead. Heedless girls were strangled. That poor laundress had suffered just as she and an unknown woman in Sweden were suffering today – and the boy – the hunt servant? What she wondered had happened to him?

She felt herself warming again to the Archbishop. Self-indulgent old spendthrift that he was, he had shown compassion despite his bullying niece's haughty anger. Funny idea to make him into a miracle-performing saint though, even if he had a good heart, but who was to say that he was any less a saint than someone whose idea of goodness was to sit on a pillar in the desert for thirty-seven years? What on earth did it mean to be or not to be a saint? More of an administrator than a man of God, the Archbishop had genuinely cared for the poor and done much to improve their lot – Christiane liked that about him and could easily forgive him his bas relief and his silken vestments. She felt sorry for him having to console himself with anyone so dreadful as Madame de R.

Claud was in the garden smoking. Having decided that he would give up as soon as all this was over; he'd taken to buying cigarettes regularly, something he hadn't done for at least ten years. But when – when would it all be over and how would Isabelle have been treated? How would she have suffered in the meantime? Whatever the case, she would never be the same again. Whatever had happened to her was likely to affect her for the rest of her life. Perhaps it would never be all over. Never.

Unlike Christiane, Claud had given up any pretence of work. Initially he had tried to do something, but now the mere thought of Julien Green caused him to feel so very weary. Who was Julien Green anyway? Who cared a damn about a little known writer whose works were no longer read by anyone except a minor academic in a minor university who was looking for an esoteric subject for a paper with which he hoped to advance his career? He could no longer think as he had done before of Green, the truly bi-lingual, troubled religious writer, torn between puritanism and lust, who translated his own haunting books from French into English, and of how he, Claud, wished to revive an interest in those works. From now on everything was dross. He no longer cared that Green was the only non-Frenchman to have been made a member of the *Académie française*, nor did he care that at the age of sixteen the young Julien had run away to fight in the trenches in the First World War. Only Green's preoccupation with evil remained of the faintest interest to Claud.

He chucked his cigarette butt on the ground and stamped on it angrily. Because his hands smelt of nicotine which he hated, he plucked a sprig of rosemary from a near-by bush and crushing it between forefinger and thumb, pressed it to his nose. That rosemary bush, he remembered with a pang of nostalgia, had been brought back from a hillside in the Corbières where it had been dug up as a tiny plant several years before.

'Do you realise how big that rosemary's grown?' he asked Christiane as he stepped through the door into the kitchen. 'How long do you think it's been there?' It had been collected on a happy family outing to visit the Cathare castles that dominate the rugged landscape to the south of Carcassonne.

'*Chez pas.*' Christiane shrugged her shoulders without looking up. Who cared about rosemary now?

XXII

'*Merde alors…*' There was something wrong with the van. Etienne who was driving in the fast lane took his hands off the wheel for a moment and the vehicle immediately swerved to the right just as a white BMW overtook him on the inside. He clearly had a puncture and needed to move over on to the hard shoulder or preferably drive to the next *aire de repos* which he reckoned was only a couple of kilometers away in order to change the wheel. The van juddered uncomfortably across the road into the slow lane with speeding, honking drivers narrowly avoiding causing a pile-up. Etienne swore out loud. If he went on to the *aire* he might well wreck the tyre for good but, nevertheless, he decided to risk it.

He looked over his shoulder into the back of the van. He might have a bit of a problem getting the spare tyre out but he would manage. He didn't really want to be seen which meant that it might have been safer to change the tyre by the side of the road where he would be less visible. The *aires* were often crowded at this time of year with families stopping to picnic or to go to the lavatory. But on the other hand he would be safer in an *aire* and less likely to attract the attention of a passing police car.

Of course when he drove into the lay-by, it was crowded with German, British, Dutch cars all heading north at the end of the holidays. A large family of large pink Germans was seated around a wooden table under a gloomy looking conifer, eating. The children were all shouting and so distracting their parents from paying any attention to Etienne who found a parking space near them.

He managed without too much trouble to extract his spare wheel and tools from under the chaos in the back of the van and was just jacking the vehicle up when a police car suddenly appeared beside him and stopped.

A wiry little man with a satirical look on his red, sweaty face got slowly out from the passenger seat, to be followed by the driver, a huge bear-like creature who, as he stood up, put his hands to his waistband and yanked up his trousers. The two gendarmes sauntered over to where Etienne was squatting by the jack and stood rather threateningly on either side of him.

As neither of them said a word for a moment, Etienne affected to be unaware of their presence.

After what he regarded as a satisfactorily intimidating silence Red-Face spoke with a sneer, '*Eh bien jeune homme,* what are you doing there?'

Etienne turned to look up at the policeman to whose patronising tone he took exception.

'I don't think I know you,' he said, 'but since you call me *tu,* I suppose we must have met somewhere…'

'Any more lip,' said the bear-like policeman, 'and you'll regret it.' Then, 'So what was all the hurry about that you found it necessary to drive that heap of scrap metal at a hundred and fifty in the fast lane?'

Etienne knew the policeman was lying since it was impossible for his van to travel quite that fast, but because all he wanted was to get rid of the two bastards as quickly as possible before they began to look too closely at his face and wind their chronically stupid brains into action, he heeded the warning about not giving them any more lip. Like a lamb he opened the driver's door of the van and reached in for the euros with which to pay the exorbitant on-the spot fine that they demanded for his speeding offence.

Red-Face leant over his shoulder as he was looking for the money and peered round at the contents of the van, breathing his stinking breath over Etienne as he did so.

Elbowing Red-Face out of the way, Etienne turned and handed him the money which the policeman barely counted before stuffing it into his pocket.

'*On y va,*' he said, turning to his companion. Then, as he opened the door of the police car, he said to Etienne, 'I don't suppose you want the paperwork – you'd only wipe your arse with it.'

These two lazy, bent policemen hadn't even asked Etienne for his papers – a sure way of putting the wind up any criminal but they were neither so daft, nor so inexperienced that they couldn't tell a crook when they saw one. They both knew instantly that there was something not quite right about the young man with bright yellow hair, changing his wheel in the lay-by but it was hot, almost as hot as it had been before the storm and neither of them could be bothered to give him any more grief. They both knew that he was probably on the run and would do anything to see the back of them and at least they must have scared the shit out of him as well as having annoyed him by fining him for travelling at an impossible speed. There had to be some reason why he hadn't argued with them about that fine. He clearly didn't want trouble.

The two men laughed as they drove away. '*Petit con*,' the red-faced one said, as they themselves raced up the motorway at a hundred and sixty, spreading alarm and causing every driver they passed to feel guilty and question what he or she might be doing wrong.

'Small time crook,' Bear-Like remarked.

'*Un vrai pédé*,' said Red-Face. 'Did you see his dyed hair?'

Bear-Like grunted and pressed his foot down flat on the accelerator. After a moment's silence, he took his right hand off the wheel and scratched a furrowed brow. 'Funny,' he said, 'that reminds me of something. Something to do with dyed hair – oh well, too bad. It'll come back to me later.'

And it did, but not until much later when at two in the morning he stumbled out of bed to go for a pee. As he flushed the lavatory, he decided that it was too late to do anything about it now. It could wait till morning; but then he wondered if there might not be trouble. He should have reported what he'd seen at once and he should have taken the number of the little sod's van – besides there was the small problem of the illegally extracted fine. Might be best to say nothing. He'd talk to Red-Face about it before he did anything drastic, he thought as he climbed back into bed. It simply didn't cross his mind that if he'd had his wits about him, Etienne would be in custody by now and the lives of several girls might have been saved, He was more concerned with saving his own skin.

Within a few moments he was asleep, snoring in unison with the large wife who lay beside him.

Etienne breathed more than a sigh of relief as the pigs drove off. Since he'd been spotted on the beach where they'd found the murdered girl his picture had been in every newspaper again and naturally it had been pointed out that he was likely to have dyed his hair, or grown a beard. Everyone in the country was looking for him and that pair of idiots hadn't had a clue. He didn't think they'd taken the number of the van although they should have done when they fined him but, in his opinion, they hadn't done the paperwork properly and had merely pocketed the fine themselves.

From the way they'd treated him, it was quite clear that they suspected him of something – or perhaps they just didn't like the look of him although they surely wondered at the submissive way in which he had paid up when they knew and he knew and they knew that he knew that he couldn't have been speeding.

Ah well, he'd had a narrow escape. He hadn't liked it when the red-faced one with the stinking breath had looked inside the van, not that he could have seen much, but the van was Etienne's private place. The van was where he kept everything he had; it was where he slept and thought and read and went on his computer – which in fact he'd reluctantly ditched – chucked it in the Canal du Midi at Toulouse just in case – even though it was unconnected to any network. He'd wanted to do violence to that policeman when he poked his head into the van and wondered now just how he had managed to restrain himself.

Before long he had replaced the wheel, tightened the bolts and driven off. He was on his way north but just to be on the safe side he'd have somehow to nick another pair of number plates – and possibly dye his hair red.

Not that anyone was likely to be looking for him where he was going. What he needed, he had decided, was a holiday from all the hassle And with that in mind he was heading for the forest where he would park the van, settle down for a few days and listen to nothing but the song of the birds at dawn and the creaking of the branches of the ancient beech trees through whose canopy the sun's dappled rays would come glinting down. It would be like some sort of honeymoon, he thought.

So as he drove on he felt a great rush of joy, a wave of extraordinary elation. He no longer thought of the policemen as stupid, but of himself as clever – brilliantly clever.

XXIII

When in France Christiane usually saw her father's sister frequently. Tante Annie lived down on the plain in a large, crumbling old farmhouse which somehow managed to be classified as a château, where chickens and Muscovy ducks did their best to wreck the salvia bedecked flower-beds and the rough grass which passed for a *pelouse anglaise* on the garden side of the house. During the war the farmhouse had been occupied by the Germans and only recently one of Annie's grandchildren had discovered an unexploded device in a copse beyond the duck pond.

In front of the house was a courtyard surrounded by *dépendances* in which could be found any old thing from a rusty bicycle to a mangle, a broken-down governess cart, a once-used still or a pile of coal. Rows of upside-down bats slept attached by their tiny feet to a massive beam from which a farmer had once hanged himself.

Here, in genteel decrepitude, Tante Annie led the life of an old-fashioned chatelaine, concerning herself with the lives of her few remaining workers whom she still referred to as *paysans*, and inviting the *curé* to lunch on Sundays. For nearly twenty years she had been mayor of her local village, having replaced her late husband in that role immediately after his death. Christiane was fond of Annie whilst mocking her gently behind her back for all her *vieille* France prejudices and respectability.

Tante Annie's children and grandchildren were usually around during the summer which led to a certain amount of *va-et-vient* between the château and Aigues Nègres. But this year was different as Annie had been away helping to look after the children of one of her daughters who was sick in Touraine. She had only returned to the Languedoc a few days before Isabelle went missing and although she had been in constant touch with Christiane, Christiane had not had the strength to visit her, neither had she really wanted her aunt to come to Aigues Nègres. She felt unable to cope with the extra extreme emotion that such a visit would entail.

In fact, since the awful trip to Narbonne, Christiane had begun to take refuge with Mathilde whose gentle innocence she found comforting. It was peaceful in Mathilde's little house and there was something about the old woman and her insistent dialogue with the Archbishop that almost convinced Christiane, cynical though she was, that there was something to be said for the power of prayer. It had certainly brought solace to Mathilde, lending her the grace and courage with which to suffer life's harsh unyielding vicissitudes. But perhaps, like the rest of us, she had merely been programmed from birth to be just what she was.

Lately it seemed to Christiane that a strange and completely illogical understanding existed between her and Mathilde and the Archbishop – the three of them. It had to do with the girl who had been strangled all those years ago at Hautefontaine and of course Mathilde's blind conviction that the old boy was up there, looking down on them, understanding their suffering through his own experience. Christiane was ready to grasp at any wild superstition, any crazy fantasy. Anything to soothe the pain or to assuage the guilt; for she no longer blamed Claud, but herself, for her daughter's disappearance.

Tante Annie would surely be much less comforting than Mathilde since she herself would be so distraught, but in the end she needed to come and Christiane needed to see her, even if it meant seeing the Bishop as well.

Annie, then, was on her way up the hill accompanied by her brother-in-law, the Bishop who was in the habit of spending his summer holiday at the château, moving seamlessly back into his boyhood bedroom, perfectly indifferent to the spreading damp marks on the ceiling.

As they drove through the village Annie slowed down and pointed to Mathilde's house.

'That,' she said, 'is where she lives – the woman who claims the Archbishop has cured her arthritis.'

The Bishop craned his scrawny neck and squinted over the top of his gold-framed, half-moon spectacles.

'*Tiens*,' was all he could think of to say. 'Hold!' Mathilde's insistence on a miracle presented the Bishop with a problem. He could not ignore her claim which it was his duty to investigate before handing it on to the *Consulta Medica* – the Miracle Police in Rome. For his part, he was profoundly mistrusting of miracles and of the whole process of canonisation which, in his view, whilst intended to nourish the faith of the ignorant, served only as fodder to the enemies of the Church.

As the car wound on up the hill, he turned to Annie, 'Who do you suppose,' he enquired of her, 'took it upon themselves to butcher the carcass of *la pauvre petite Sainte Thérèse* in order for her left tibia – or fibula or whatever – to be dragged around from place to place, supposedly for the edification of the faithful? They've even taken it to that godless land across the Channel.' He waved a dismissive hand. 'The perfidious Albion. What folly!'

Annie nodded her head rather as Indians are wont to do – neither a 'yes' nor a 'no'. She was not comfortable with her brother-in-law's scepticism since the religion to which she had steadfastly and determinedly adhered throughout her life more closely resembled Mathilde's than the Bishop's. She said nothing.

'How many big toes do you suppose Saint Hyacinth had?' the Bishop mused aloud. 'I know of at least six. Or Saint Roch – how many ear lobes did he have?'

Annie had never regarded religion as a suitable subject for humour. '*Eh bien, voici!*' she said, and then, just as she turned into the drive to Aigues Nègres, relieved to be able to change the subject, 'Look! One of the most beautiful views in France.'

At the end of a rutted track, the old stone house so comfortably settled on the hill, its red-brown shutters half-closed against the heat, seemed like a welcoming haven of peace. Behind and below it, the magnificent expanse of the plain shimmered in the late afternoon sunlight.

'A beautiful spot,' the Bishop remarked as he climbed out of the car.

If it had not been for her dejected body language and the strained expression on her face, the flawless picture of a happy home would have been complete when Christiane appeared – a slim, graceful figure framed in the doorway with pots of cheerful red geraniums on either side.

Annie rushed towards her niece, arms outstretched, and as the Bishop stood awkwardly back, waiting for his turn to speak, the two women clasped each other in a great embrace, bursting simultaneously into tears. They cried for a while without saying anything. For, once more, what was there to say?

What had happened was beyond words, and for Annie who, in any case had always had a special feeling for Isabelle, that whimsical child she had loved since she was a small girl, it was almost as if she had a lost a daughter of her own.

Christiane kissed the Bishop on both cheeks and the three of them turned to go into the house.

Claud had gone for a walk and the teenagers were lounging miserably by the pool. It was as if life had always been like this and as if it always would be. Day after day nothing changed. Nothing. Only everyone sank more deeply into despair.

'The hopelessness of the Police,' Annie said. 'What in the name of God have they been doing?' She glanced idly round her as if to find in the familiar room some clue as to the missing child, but instead she sensed an air of desolation hanging over everything. Not having been used for days, the sitting-room had developed an un-lived-in, unloved look. A vase of wilted wild flowers stood precariously on the edge of an occasional table, as the beams of evening sunshine slanting through the windows beneath which lay heaps of unswept-up dead flies, lit up a layer of dust that coated the furniture. Would Isabelle ever return? Would the flowers ever bloom again? Annie felt her eyes filling once more with tears.

Then the telephone rang. Christiane sighed. 'It's never good news,' she said, rising wearily from the sofa.

'We can only pray, *mon enfant*,' she heard the Bishop remark to her retreating figure, just as a crowd of teenagers burst into the room, barring her way to the telephone which continued to ring.

XXIV

An old man died in the neighbouring parish and when Fafa said Mass at his funeral, despite his determination to concentrate, the familiar words poured meaninglessly out of his mouth. He could have recited the Mass backwards with his mind quite elsewhere and lately, of course, his mind had been elsewhere, entirely occupied with Isabelle. The old boy's coffin was carried under the laughing blue sky to the little cemetery on the edge of the village where he was consigned to a shiny marble vault bedecked with gorgeous plastic flowers and on the outside of which there hung a faded photograph of his long dead parents. It was hot. Absent-mindedly Fafa shook hands with the few mourners as they filed out of the cemetery.

Snivelling into a handkerchief, the old man's wife was being comforted by a fat daughter with an arm round her mother's shoulders. Fafa for once could feel no compassion. What was the loss of one old man compared to the loss of Isabelle? The widow, he thought, would just have to accustom herself to her new way of life. After all, she had the fat daughter to console her and a pair of grandchildren and in any case the deceased had, by all accounts, been a bad-tempered old so-and-so at the best of times.

That night in his lonely narrow bed Fafa fantasised – as he had taken to doing – about Isabelle, imagining that the Church had at last given way to pressure from the left to allow married priests. In his private narrative Isabelle was naked in his arms and Isabelle was his wife. He had persuaded himself that to think of himself as married made his lust less sinful.

But then reality asserted its ugly head and he remembered with a shudder and a terrible sob that the object of his desire was missing – presumed murdered. How could he bear the agony? He cursed the Lord for his misery and as he did so he became frighteningly aware of how much he had changed recently. What had come over him that he could even think of cursing the Lord in whom he had always so innocently put his trust? He began to recite the Hail Mary, clenching his fists so hard that his fingernails cut into his palms. He couldn't remember how many Hail Mary's he recited before he eventually fell asleep.

When he woke in the morning it was already hot; the air was breathless and he was feeling washed out and full of sin. Suddenly he didn't want to think about Isabelle so, as he shaved his thin face, he turned his mind to the Bishop.

There was a problem with the Bishop who was staying as he did every summer with his sister-in-law in the plain. Fafa had never met him but now he would have to see him on account of Mathilde who, for her part, was in a high state of excitement at the prospect of a visit from the great man. But Fafa, feeling contaminated by his own thoughts, was in no mood to face distinguished prelates, more especially his Bishop whom he felt might instantly see right through him. Besides the Bishop was somehow connected to Isabelle which in a way made the whole thing even more embarrassing. Fafa began to sweat. The only reasonable thing for him to do would be to go to confession before encountering the Bishop at Mathilde's house, but since the meeting had been arranged for that very morning, there was no time left for confession.

If only the Bishop were not a local figure, it wouldn't be happening like this. The whole thing would have been arranged in a far more impersonal and official manner. Mathilde would probably not even have seen a bishop herself – or not until she had had the opinion of at least three doctors to confirm her miraculous recovery.

It was too hot for breakfast and in any case Fafa was feeling too nervous to eat so, having dressed, he left the Presbytery and walked across the village square to the church. The air was already hot.

Just as he reached the church, a car drew up beside him and he turned to see a smiling round-faced Dutchman who had a holiday home in the village, leaning out of the window of his BMW, waving a newspaper in his direction.

'*Ponshour Monsieur le Curé.*' The Dutchman spoke moderate French with a heavy Germanic accent. 'I see you are in ze news…' He was grinning inanely all over his face.

'*Moi?*' Fafa exclaimed in horror, jabbing an index finger into his thin, tee-shirt clad chest. 'What have I done?' A feeling of terror gripped him as he suddenly imagined his midnight secrets plastered all over the paper and on the very day he was to meet the Bishop.

'You will be a key witness,' said the Dutchman as he climbed out of his car and held the paper out for Fafa to see. He pointed at an article on the front page underneath a picture of Christiane in dark glasses, coming out of a supermarket, her head sinking between her shoulders. 'The missing girl,' he said, 'I think so the police are doing a good job keeping the story on the front page. Soon this bad man he will be caught. Now they are telling us everything they know so this will frighten him and he will be making some mistake.'

He pointed at a paragraph half way down the article where Fafa, described as the local *curé* and close friend of the family, was reported as having seen Isabelle being abducted by a man carrying a coiled rope.

'I think,' said the Dutchman, 'they are soon catching this man. Two persons have been seeing him in the North of France. Perhaps now he is going to Holland.' He laughed heartily at the very idea.

'But the girl? What about the girl?' Fafa had a lump in his throat as he spoke.

'Perhaps she is alive,' said the Dutchman. 'But I think more likely she is dead. Like the girl they found on the beach. She was a silly girl to go with this man.'

Fafa didn't know what to say. He was horrified to think that his name was in the paper. Ridiculously it made him feel that the whole world now knew what he felt about Isabelle and about his secret midnight longing.

'But I see you make your way to the church,' the Dutchman remarked light-heartedly. 'Also I must not stop you to say your prayers,' and with a jolly laugh he climbed back into his car and drove off.

Fafa couldn't imagine how he would get through the next twenty-four hours. He needed to say Mass as a priest is strongly advised to do every day but suddenly he could no longer bear the thought of the oft-repeated, well-known words. Words that seemed for the moment to have lost their meaning for him. Nevertheless, he pushed open the heavy old church door and stepped into the ancient, musty-smelling building. The church was all right, he thought, it enclosed him within its comfortable dank old walls as if to protect him from Dutchmen and newspapers and the evils of the outside world. He breathed a sigh of relief as he closed the creaking door behind him.

And what if Mathilde were right in her belief that praying to the Archbishop for his intercession might truly bring Isabelle back? What nonsense was that! Fafa walked slowly up the aisle then knelt in front of the altar, crossed himself and in a low murmur began to recite the Hail Mary…

'…Holy Mary, Mother of God, pray for us sinners – *priez pour nous pauvres pécheurs…*' Suddenly, involuntarily Fafa was shaken by a great sob welling up from somewhere inside him. It shook him from head to foot and as he sobbed he prostrated himself on the cold stones of the church floor. How could the Holy Mary, Mother of God take pity on him when the only thing he wanted on earth was for Isabelle to be found in order that he, her parish priest, might seduce her. He felt he was losing his mind. Only a short while ago everything had been so clear, so straightforward. He had been content in his modest priesthood, he had loved God and Mathilde and the world in which he lived. His doubts had been minimal and easily laid to rest by prayer, most particularly by recitation of the Hail Mary.

But now... He rose from the floor, straightened his T-shirt, drew a handkerchief from his jeans pocket and mopped his face. He had to go to Mathilde's house to meet the Bishop. Unusually it occurred to him to wonder what on earth he was looking like. Should he have worn something different for the Bishop? He didn't know. After all it was an informal meeting, but still, perhaps he should have put on his one thin suit, or at least a dog-collar? He glanced at his watch. There was no time to do anything about it now and anyway what did it matter? What did anything matter any more?

The Bishop was in a thoroughly good mood. He was amused by the idea of talking to Mathilde about her supposed miracle especially since Christiane had been telling him about the Archbishop's journals, the details of which were of course unknown to the old lady. But, as the Bishop, drove up the hill towards the village, he wondered who was to say that the Archbishop was any more of a sinner than anyone else; he had made himself useful in his day, had cared for the welfare of his people, so if the dead really could intercede with the Almighty which seemed highly improbable, then why not he?

The Bishop's idea of heaven was far less personal and rather more metaphysical. It was not for him to say who was or was not to go there, who might or might not have God's merciful ear. He was not himself tempted by any of his nieces and if he were, perhaps he too would have succumbed. He had long since chosen to forget the tormented passion for his sister-in-law which had gripped him all those years ago. Not that he had done anything about it – because, as it so happened, she had never encouraged him.

As he drew up outside Mathilde's house and switched off the ignition, he smiled to himself. This was certainly a change from the endless complaints about paedophile priests, which had lately taken up a considerable amount of his time. He sighed. Perhaps those sinful priests were unable to help themselves for who at times had not been moved by the soft cheek or delicate neck of an altar boy?

As the years passed the Bishop grew less and less certain of anything. He tenaciously held to his belief in God and the divinity of Christ which belief had become the habit of a lifetime and without which he would be lost, but wherever he looked beyond that certainty he found grey areas with much room for doubt. His consolation lay not just in prayer but in studying and analysing the writings of the Fathers of the Church and of Catholic philosophers down the ages, none of which prevented him from having, like the old Archbishop, a weakness for that scallywag, Voltaire.

Mathilde who had heard the Bishop's car draw up was already holding back the bead curtain for *Monseigneur l'évêque* to do her the honour of crossing her threshold. She had never before received so distinguished a visitor and was at first disappointed to see him dressed in mufti. She had hoped, if not for a mitre and full episcopal regalia, at least for a dog collar and a little purple.

Instead here was a prince of the Church, a thin, caved-in-chested, ascetic-looking man dressed in an open-necked, short-sleeved shirt and grey trousers. But, for all his asceticism, a vein of vanity ran through the Bishop's soul, which prevented him from ever removing his episcopal ring over which Mathilde proudly bowed. She dared not kiss it.

Behind her stood Fafa, weak from nervous tension.

106

XXV

When they crowded into the sitting-room, almost knocking Christiane over as she went to answer the telephone which she couldn't find because as usual someone had failed to replace the handset on the base, the young people were taken aback to find the Bishop and Tante Annie both seated demurely there.

They had come bearing the good news that after so many days of silence another text message had been received from Isabelle. At least they were sure it was from Isabelle this time. 'Iz' was miraculously spelt with a 'z'.

Later the police dismissed that piece of evidence as being of no value; Etienne, they said, had communicated with Isabelle via the net and had surely seen how she signed her name. Of far greater significance was the fact that the message had been sent from somewhere in the department of the Oise which meant that the young man had travelled north. This gave credence to a lorry driver who claimed to have seen someone closely resembling Etienne at a petrol station near Soissons. The police in that department were put on high alert since Etienne must not be allowed to slip through their fingers again as he had done at Leucate.

A criminal psychologist's profile of the wanted man depicted a dangerous murderer, cold-blooded, arrogant and ready to kill again. No more women's lives must be put at risk and the public was warned not to approach anyone they suspected of being Etienne who, it was thought, was beginning to get careless. He would very soon make a mistake that would lead to his arrest but in the meantime there must not be another victim. Men of Etienne's type often revelled in the notoriety brought them by their evil deeds and, with an unshakeable belief in their own cunning and a longing for what they saw as even greater glory, they began to take extravagant risks.

And where, if she is dead, is our daughter's body? Claud and Christiane looked at each other long and hard – and wondered. They were irritated by the gung-ho attitude of the police who seemed to think that they were about to close the net and who firmly believed, without any real evidence, that Etienne had murdered both Isabelle and the girl on the beach. It was as if they no longer cared about Isabelle – about finding her. Fayard high-handedly told Claud that it would all become clear once they had caught the brute responsible for her disappearance.

Days had passed and Claud and Christiane had begun to feel that their whole life had always consisted in this terrible waiting with themselves imprisoned for ever in a particular circle of hell; the police would continue to chase the shadow of Etienne around France, occasionally reporting that this or that lorry driver, *garagiste* or doctor had seen him in Soissons, in Nancy or Bordeaux. Yet the time was rapidly approaching when they ought to be returning to England to the new academic year. But how – how on earth could they just pack up and go? Go without Isabelle? Neither of them could really believe that she was dead and Christiane in particular, having occasionally experienced some kind of second sight, firmly believed that her daughter would turn up in time to return to England. 'I feel it in my bones,' she said. 'I have seen her again and again walking through that door,' and she would point to the door of whichever room she happened to be in at the time. 'I have heard her voice.'

Claud humoured his wife in this belief although he was generally more inclined than she to moments of despair when it seemed impossible not to admit that all the evidence so far had to indicate that Isabelle was indeed dead. Besides he had little time for the supernatural; he thought more often these days about perpetrators of evil, ceaselessly wondering whether or not they were ever aware of what they were doing.

A couple of days ago he'd come in to find Tante Annie and the Bishop ensconced in the sitting-room. He was always pleased to see Annie and usually quite enjoyed talking to the Bishop but this time he was annoyed by him going on about the perfectibility of man and quoting Kierkegaard's belief that all would be saved. Whatever that meant. And who wanted to hear about that at a time like this? It always aggravated him when people talked about the roads Mussolini built or about some violent crook or mass murderer who loved animals or who had a sense of humour. Now he had to be told that some crazy Dane wanted them all saved – Mussolini, Hitler – the lot.

In Claud's view there could be nothing good about Etienne if indeed he was guilty of murder, or guilty, as he certainly was, of abduction. Nothing at all. Nothing anyone did, had done or might do could ever counteract or mitigate the callous cruelty that led them to kill for their own pleasure or convenience. It was no good an emaciated bishop gesticulating with his bejewelled hand and banging on about Kierkegaard and everyone being saved. Saved for what anyway?

Muttering something under his breath, Claud quietly left the room.

Now with this new sighting in Soissons, the police had for some reason decided that they were at last hot on the tail of their quarry. This, combined with the fact that as a result of Fafa's evidence frogmen were dragging the canal and the *bassin* only heightened the tension. As yet just a cat and, mysteriously, a pig had been found.

Because he had driven his daughter, albeit unwittingly, to the fatal rendezvous, Claud was increasingly tortured by a gnawing guilt about which he kept quiet. When Isabelle first disappeared Christiane had angered him by endlessly blaming him, telling him he was crazy to have believed her lies, that he should have smelt a rat. Why would anyone want to go to the hairdresser's in this heat and was he so self-absorbed that he never even looked at his daughter, couldn't he see that she had no need of a haircut? Now he ceaselessly asked those questions of himself.

He went outside to smoke a cigarette under the shade of the bignonia. He could hardly bear the tragic sight of his wife's face nor the fact that in this, their hour of greatest need, they were finding it increasingly difficult to be in harmony with one another. With them both being so much on edge it was only too easy to say something annoying but Claud usually managed to keep his counsel and generally left the room when Christiane snapped at him. She, recognising that she was ready to fly off the handle at a moment's notice, occasionally apologised; reason told her that his misery was as great as hers, but in her heart she felt that hers was greater, deeper, crueler.

'Papa,' Agnès came strolling back from the pool across the brown stubble that passed for lawn, 'I think we ought to look for her ourselves...'

How on earth, Claud wondered. They could hardly set about dragging all the rivers of France.

'The police are useless,' Agnès said. 'You see I know she's alive. I just know it. Perhaps she's with him in the van.' She looked so pretty standing there, without her little cousin for once, a picture of sun-tanned health, the earnest expression on her face enough to move her father to tears.

He felt a lump rise in his throat as he put his arm round her and drew her towards him.

'We think you ought to hire a private detective and – did you know – well someone said that vans and things have a kind of tracker device thing, so why hasn't the van been found yet?'

'Because my darling,' Claud said, 'bad people know how to disconnect such devices. But, you know what – the man who thinks he spotted Etienne…' Claud had to force himself to pronounce Etienne's name, 'he took down the registration number of the van so I think the police will get him soon.' Claud sighed and pulled his daughter even closer to him. 'But that doesn't mean they will have found Isabelle too.'

XXVI

In the North of France the blinding heat which had gripped the whole country throughout the long hot summer was beginning to show signs of abating. Luckily a gentle breeze was blowing as a group of some seven or eight sixteen-year-olds with picnics and plenty of water in their backpacks set out for a day's bicycling in the forest. A few puffy clouds had even gathered in the sky – some of them tinged with grey.

Delphine had only come along in the hopes that Pierre, for whom she nursed a secret passion, might notice her at last. She would not otherwise have joined the party since she was physically quite lazy and, as far as she was concerned, it was really too hot to be riding a bicycle all day. However she prepared a baguette for herself with plenty of butter, a huge slice of *jambon d'York* spread with Grey Poupon mustard, put it in a plastic container along with a large slice of *tarte aux pommes* and decided that the best part of the day would probably be lunchtime. She put her picnic into a small backpack, kissed her mother good-bye and pedalled away to join her friends.

Her mother was delighted to see her setting off to enjoy herself with other young people, doing something sensible rather than hanging around the house all day complaining of the heat and saying she was bored. The forest was a beautiful place where she herself had often walked and, as a girl, bicycled and picnicked with friends. Nothing seemed more desirable than that her daughter should enjoy the same timeless pleasures. She was perfectly unaware of Delphine's passion for Pierre.

Delphine soon discovered that she was going to have some difficulty in keeping up with the others, every one of them so *sportif* in their crash helmets and lycra pants. She had opted for cotton shorts and wore no crash helmet since it seemed to her that a boy could never be attracted to a girl wearing one of those hideous objects. All the same Pierre didn't pay her very much attention since, while she was straining to keep up at the back, he was always at the front of the group with a girl called Laure pedalling as hard as she could to keep pace with him. Delphine began to wish that she had not come. She decided that if Pierre went on talking to Laure when they stopped for lunch, she would eat her baguette and her tart and head for home. She supposed she could find the way on her own.

Although it was relatively cool in the forest under the shade of the great beech trees whose heavy late summer leaves protected the young people from the heat of sun, they were soon hot enough and thirsty enough to want to stop for water and perhaps an early picnic. They needed only to find a pleasant clearing away from the rides that crisscrossed the forest where they could spread themselves out in the dappled sunlight and relax. One or two of the boys had brought bottles of cheap pink wine from the supermarket, with which they were only too ready to ply the girls.

Having wheeled them into the woods, the young people threw their bicycles down, spread themselves out on the dry ground and began to unpack their picnics. Delphine sat alone, a little apart from the others, angrily biting into her baguette. She was feeling miserable, trying not to glance sideways at Laure and Pierre who were lying on their stomachs with their heads close together, shoulders touching, talking in low voices. Without her helmet on Laure was quite pretty, but not as pretty as Delphine – or so Delphine thought as she bitterly tugged at her dark red curls. Besides, she had green eyes. Green eyes that were rapidly filling with tears.

As soon as she had eaten her lunch Delphine stood up and with a vague wave in the direction of the others, announced that she was going home because she didn't feel very well. Laure jumped up from beside Pierre and came across to her; putting an arm round the miserable girl's shoulders, she asked her if she wanted someone to go back with her. Was she all right to go alone?

Irritably Delphine shrugged off the unwanted arm, muttered something about being perfectly all right and walked off through the forest, tears blinding her eyes.

After a while Delphine realised that she didn't know where she was. Why hadn't she paid more attention on the way in? Having reached a track, she had no idea whether to turn right or left, but she was annoyed rather than unduly worried because in the middle of the day at this time of year there would surely be other cyclists or hikers around of whom she could ask directions. Arbitrarily she decided to go to the right, but by the time she had been walking for twenty minutes, slowly pushing her bike without meeting anyone, she begin to feel not only more and more unhappy but uneasy too. She wished her mother would miraculously turn up in her car, put the bicycle in the boot and take her home but, having discovered the battery on her mobile to be empty, she realised there was no way she could call for help.

Not wishing to bicycle for fear of going too far too quickly in the wrong direction, she ambled idly on until, looking suddenly up, she discerned, to her delight, a dot in the distance. The dot grew, nearer and larger until it took the shape of a man. Her immediate troubles, she realised, were now over. The man was walking so she imagined that they could not be too far from what she regarded as civilisation which to her at that moment meant a main road with a signpost.

Advancing with a jaunty, self-confident step the stranger was soon close enough for Delphine to see that he was young and, she thought, very good-looking although it was a pity about his dyed hair.

'*Excusez-moi,*' she addressed him politely as she came face to face with him…

Etienne stopped to look at the childlike girl with the green eyes who seemed to have been crying. What, he wondered, was she doing alone, pushing a bicycle through the forest.

For the last few days he had been camping in his van, parked off the road under the shade of the old beech trees. Sublimely confident in his ability to avoid the police and perfectly convinced that he was untraceable having for so many years been living *Sans Domicile Fixe* – with no fixed abode – he had felt emboldened to take a walk in the middle of the day, even abandoning the baseball cap and dark glasses that he wore when buying food in the supermarket. No one looked at you then and what with the modern self-checkout system, you might as well be invisible.

The weather was good – so much cooler than it had been for weeks – not many people seemed to be about and he needed to think – to think about what his next move might be and walking was conducive to thinking.

The last thing he had been expecting was that he might have the good fortune to meet a solitary girl in need of his help, let alone one so innocently confiding as this one, for Delphine, in her relief at seeing him, had begun, in a garbled way, to tell him about herself. About how she had set out with some friends but the friends had been unkind, anyway she wasn't feeling very well, her mobile wasn't working, she wished her mother would come and pick her up but then she didn't really know where she was and in any case how could she contact her mother without a telephone? She told him where she lived and asked this kindly smiling stranger with the dark brown eyes if he knew how far she was from home and if he knew which way she should go…or perhaps he had a mobile she could borrow.

Etienne had no mobile but if he had he would not have wanted to use it. He knew from the radio that he had been sighted at the garage in Soissons and, for all his self-assurance, he didn't feel any need to help the police who by now knew not only the colour of his van, but the registration number too. He realised that it might be only a matter of days before they took it into their thick heads to search the forest which meant that he probably ought to think of moving on which was a pity since he was quite happy where he was, living a strangely euphoric idyll. Moving on was what he had been thinking about as he walked and then suddenly – here was this silly girl, whimpering and telling him her life story.

As a matter of fact he's far better looking than Pierre, Delphine thought, tossing her pretty little head as Etienne, helping to push her bicycle over the rough ground, led her off into the wood. The quickest way home, he assured her, was to cut through the forest which he knew very well so he could show her the way.

She smiled up at him in gratitude, but just as she was thinking how lucky she was to have met such a kind young man, she felt a sudden twinge of apprehension. There was something distant, something detached and odd, something cunning, she couldn't say precisely what, about the way he looked at her – almost as if she were a thing, not a person. Yet that look was mesmeric – she was unable to turn away from it. And he – he continued to look, greedily, like a starving man might look at a juicy steak. Apprehension turned to fear...her heart began to thump and her mouth went dry, her legs grew weak, her stomach dropped... She opened her mouth to speak but didn't know what to say...

A little later there was no one near to hear her final cry, nor to see her rolled into the shallowest of graves, her pathetic body casually covered with twigs and dried leaves.

The following day her abandoned bicycle was found a couple of kilometres away in a clearing in which the police surmised that a vehicle must have been parked for a day or two. But Etienne's van was no longer there.

'Something nasty about that part of the forest,' a young police officer told his girlfriend that evening. 'It's the atmosphere – there's something evil in it as if any number of murders had been committed there over the centuries.'

XXVII

All hell seemed to break loose with the discovery of the second body. The canal at Castel had been dragged to no avail and then, with the sighting of Etienne in Soissons, the police decided to search the forest of Compiègne on the presumption that, knowing he had been seen, the fugitive would need to go to ground and hide pretty quickly, and where would he be most likely to hide, if not in the forest?

Delphine's mother had reported her daughter missing at half past nine in the evening, having rung the home of one of the girls who had been on the picnic, only to discover that Delphine had left the party at lunchtime, intending to go home. The police moved quickly but they were too late; the body of the murdered girl, barely cold in its pathetic grave, was found by a police dog at half past eight the following morning; further on her bicycle was found but Etienne – the elusive Etienne – had disappeared again.

'*Et la petite anglaise…?*' What had happened to her? How did they know where to look for her? It was suggested that she might even be alive and with Etienne in his van, but that was generally dismissed as being quite out of keeping with his pattern of behaviour. There were a million places in which he could have hidden or dumped a body and, having done so successfully, he had grown careless as such criminals were wont to do. Careless and arrogant. He was probably enjoying the enormous publicity that his crimes now attracted.

Not only were the French papers full of the story, but in Britain, the press seemed to be concerned with nothing else – world affairs, terrorism, the crisis in the Eurozone were all momentarily forgotten in the gleeful reporting of a serial killer who wasn't English for once, but French. In Scandinavia where Etienne was compared to Anders Breivik, the Norwegian mass murderer, criminal psychologists and psychiatrists of every kind were interviewed on the television and in the press. Was Etienne likely to kill again? Did he hate women? Was he mad or was he sane? What was the nature of evil? As if anyone ever knew the answer to anything.

The police were beginning to panic as with every day that passed the press grew shriller and Isabelle's wretched family grew more desperate. They knew that they ought to have caught Etienne by now and that Delphine should never have been killed. But where did you look for a man who had been out of the system for so many years? Had he, they began to ask themselves, killed before? There were unsolved murders from the past that would need looking into – a prostitute in Toulouse two or three years ago and, before that, a nun in Albi – but most importantly, he must be found before there was another tragedy.

Christiane was stunned when Fayard appeared at lunchtime to inform her and Claud that the body of a young girl had been found lightly buried in the forest and that

Etienne was the prime suspect. He hadn't wanted them to hear about it on the news. He looked grey and furrowed. He was supremely conscious of the fact that he and his force were failing these people and yet they had been working day and night on the case.

'*Bien sûr*,' he said. 'We are thinking the murderer it is this Etienne, but we have no proof. Can it be coincidence that he is twice seen in the neighbourhood where a body is found?'

Having refused a seat, he was standing awkwardly in the kitchen, wishing he could light a cigarette. Claud stood beside him whilst Christiane was sitting at the table with a glass of wine in her hand. She looked at the policeman, a compact man with a neat moustache, and wondered if there was anything he could do which he wasn't doing. Wondered what he really thought about the case.

'There is a difference,' she said, 'a huge difference between these murders and Isabelle's disappearance – I mean the texts – what about the texts? Whoever sent them, they came from Iz's mobile.'

Fayard couldn't see any problem with that because if Etienne sent the texts which it was now thought that he did, it was through the kind of bravado that they were beginning to see as part of the pattern of his behaviour. After all the latest one came after the girl was found on the beach.

Christiane began to feel sick. How much more could she and Claud bear? And now with this other family somewhere in the Oise who already knew their daughter was dead, she began to ask herself if it might almost be easier to know the worst. But no, she would cling determinedly to the belief that Isabelle was alive.

The strangest thing, she told Claud later, was that the murdered girl had been found somewhere very near to where the body of the laundress's daughter had been found more than two hundred years ago. In some strange way it had at times consoled her to think about that laundress so that she had even taken to having imaginary conversations with the woman who, unlike everyone else, always managed to say the right thing and to understand just how she was feeling.

'So much for your Archbishop's sanctity,' Claud remarked, 'and his intercession with the Almighty.'

'I know, but Mathilde is such a good woman that I wish, if only for her sake, that they would take the matter seriously and just beatify the old boy but Oncle Hervé doesn't want the matter to go any further.'

'It would be a funny kind of bishop who believed all that rubbish,' said Claud. 'And an even funnier one who was prepared to lie in order to perpetrate it further.'

'I'm sure that plenty of lies have been told about the lives of saints before now. Anyway Mathilde's determined to get two doctors to certify to the miracle and then Oncle Hervé will have to send the claim on to Rome whether he likes it or not.'

'It's unlike you to stick up for that mumbo-jumbo,' said Claud.

'Perhaps it's desperation,' Christian replied wearily. 'Anyway Mathilde still prays to the Archbishop every day and I'm sure that when we get Iz back, she will believe that her prayers helped.'

'When – when – when…' Claud groaned, then for fear of crying, felt in his pocket for his cigarettes and made for the door to the garden.

'Nothing else seems to work,' Christiane addressed his retreating back, 'so we might as well pray.'

She sighed and looked round the kitchen. Everything was in a mess, in fact the whole house was in a mess since no one had the heart to bother about it any longer. Perhaps she would feel better if she installed some kind of order before going shopping which she had to do as the cupboard was almost bare. Various people had offered to shop for her since Isabelle's disappearance but she felt in turns so restless, useless, or claustrophobic that, although she had occasionally accepted, she almost always preferred to run the gauntlet of the paparazzi, not to mention the staring and whispering of strangers. On the way home she would take refuge with Mathilde in whose comforting presence she would often sit for several hours.

The teenagers were in a bad way, bickering again, crying, wanting to go home. It was Claud who had taken to spending time with them, talking to them and trying to keep them occupied. The weather had at last broken and after a night of rain, he took them off into the woods to look unsuccessfully for *cèpes* whereas half the locals were out scouring the verges for snails which they put lovingly into plastic bags. For some people nothing had changed.

When Christiane eventually arrived in the village on her way back from the shops, she found Mathilde settling her collection of snails into a box of flour where they would stay under a heavily weighted lid for a few days until their insides were deemed to have been cleansed.

Christiane loved eating snails and was even up to collecting them herself, cleaning them and cutting off their greater intestines before cooking them, but today she looked at them with disgust.

She flopped down on to an upright chair without even kissing Mathilde and buried her head in her hands.

'Have you heard?' she asked Mathilde

Yes, Mathilde had heard the news. Another murdered girl.

'Normally,' Christiane said, looking up through her fingers, 'at this time we're counting the days before we have to leave, wishing we didn't have to go, wanting to stay for ever, wanting the summer to go on and on…we've always been so happy here – and now this… We don't want to go – we don't want to stay – we don't know what we want…' she heaved a miserable sigh '…we just want Isabelle.'

Bent over her box of snails, Mathilde had her back to Christiane, but she was listening to her every word. She straightened herself up slowly and turned to face Christiane.

'*Moi*,' she said, tapping her chest with both her crooked hands, 'me, I still have faith. You may make fun of me, but how can you think for an instant that *la petite* won't come back. Even if *Monsieur l'abbé – ce petit galopin –* has lost his faith, I will keep praying and hoping – and you will see, she will come…'

Mathilde was annoyed with Fafa. Dismayed by what she regarded as his lack of manliness, she now felt rather as an anxious parent might feel about a wayward and disappointing son. He was, she considered, letting down the Church, letting down his ministry and letting himself down. A wise old woman, it had not escaped her notice that he had fallen for Isabelle and that this new passion had subsumed what had formerly been his love of the Almighty, all of which resulted in his sitting in that chair where Christiane sat now and crying. He'd even lost his appetite for her cassoulet.

She might have begun to lose faith in Fafa for singularly failing in what she regarded as his duty to spread hope and comfort among the flock, but her faith in the Lord and indeed in the Archbishop remained steadfast. No coward soul was hers.

'You know what,' Christiane suddenly lifted her head from her hands, 'I don't know about faith, Mathilde, but you always give me hope and I've been thinking lately about the last text that Agnès received – that day when Tante Annie was here. The police dismissed it once they'd found out that it came from somewhere near Soissons. They automatically thought it was this boy playing mad tricks, but how can they be so sure – how can they be sure about anything? They can't even prove that the same man killed both those girls…'

Mathilde hadn't heard about the latest text which Christiane explained had merely said 'Say I'm OK' and was signed Iz with a 'z' not an 's' which was how Isabelle always signed herself.

'I'm beginning to believe that this time it really did come from her,' Christiane said. 'And why would she say she was all right if she wasn't? I sometimes think that there must have been something wrong with her – something we didn't know about – something we didn't notice – some deep unhappiness which made her want to leave home. Perhaps she really is fine with that boy – perhaps he isn't a murderer – if only we knew…' Here Christiane buried her head in her hands again and began to weep and to weep. If only she knew.

XXVIII

The Bishop had never paid more than passing attention to the events surrounding the return of the old Archbishop's remains to his erstwhile diocese and until the other day he had been quite unaware of Christiane's interest in the matter. Now what with all this fuss about a miracle, he thought that, sceptical though he might be, he would at least like to find out a little more about this eighteenth-century cleric who one way and another had recently provoked so much excitement.

On pain of she knew not what Christiane had allowed him to take the diaries away for a couple of days. She knew he would be fascinated by them and had no doubt that he would treat them with care. If he did lose them – so what? Hadn't she lost her daughter?

So it was that the Bishop sat in a wicker armchair in the garden with the diaries on his lap, looking up occasionally across the bed of scarlet salvias that fringed Annie's rugged lawn, over the field of ripening maize beyond, to where the canal ran behind a distant line of scrubby trees. He really did regard this as home. After all it was the only real home he had ever known, the place where he had grown up with his brothers and sisters, where both his parents had died where he had fallen in love with the adorable Annie who still welcomed him so warmly. Once his lustful passion for Annie had faded, he had retained a deep and lasting affection for her. Perhaps, he fondly thought, it was like the affection an old married couple might have for one another. But then the marriage had never been consummated, he reflected with a slight pang as he turned his mind back to the Archbishop. His life had not been one of pleasure but one of study and duty which he should never regret.

The Archbishop of Narbonne had in his day been a very powerful man, almost Viceroy of the Languedoc, and in this capacity he had wrought wonders for the poor of his diocese, squeezing money out of people in high places who, no doubt, would have preferred to spend it lavishly, if not on war, on frivolity. He saw to it that bridges were built, university chairs created and, without him La Robine, which linked Narbonne to the Canal du Midi, opening that city up to European trade, would never have been built. The good done by this man was so considerable that perhaps in his way he was a saint, but surely not one that the Vatican would approve for he was a worldly, open-minded man who, horror of horrors, recognised not only Anglican marriage, but Anglican orders too, surely a far greater sin than sleeping with his niece.

In any case, the Bishop had little time for the intricacies of canonisation. He felt a deep sympathy for an English cardinal who had in his lifetime expressed a dislike of the process, and who claimed that nothing was to be gained by miracles, but whom, now, the powers that be were attempting to beatify. The Cardinal, though, had the last laugh as when they came to dig him up and move him from where he lay next to a man he loved to a 'holier' place, all they found were the brass handles of his coffin. Or perhaps it was the Almighty who was laughing. The Bishop knew that in the eyes of his Church, he was himself guilty of the sin of pride, but, like the English Cardinal, he would drink to conscience before drinking to the Pope.

He felt as he read the Archbishop's journal that here was a likeable human being, a man who, for all his weaknesses, was fiercely loyal to the Church, who in old age refused to sign the Concordat giving Napoleon too great a control over it, but who still retained his independence of mind and who would surely never have imagined anything so foolish as that he might have some influence with the Lord two hundred or more years after his death. That he might be instrumental in finding a missing girl or in curing an old woman's arthritis.

'*Quelle bêtise!*' the Bishop muttered to himself as he turned his attention back to the journal on his knee.

As for Mathilde, the Bishop felt sorry for her and touched by her simple, sincere faith, but, for all the world, he could not find it in his heart to further her cause, even if she found two doctors to attest to the fact that her arthritis had been cured which he anyway regarded as highly unlikely. Her hands were crabbed, she walked with difficulty – what cure could there have been? Yet, there she was daily on her knees asking the old rogue of an Archbishop to find a lost child. How difficult it was to reconcile such blind faith with any form of rationality, or any form of rationality with a religion of any kind, but he had made the leap into darkness required of faith many years ago and had adhered to his beliefs ever since, although they did not comprehend latter-day miracles.

...thus I am obliged to concede that it was not without a certain vanity, the Bishop read, that I donned my exquisite new chasuble for High Mass in the cathedral this Sunday, a vanity that was soon

to be punished by the remorseless admonition of my dear niece. She had most regrettably made it her business to examine the garment closely whereupon she expressed the opinion that it was quite out of keeping with propriety for it to be embroidered as it is, with stags and hounds and instruments of the chase. She was not to be mollified when I protested that to have ordered such material was not only to have given much desirable employment to the needy, but also to have allowed the artisan to exercise his skills in a novel and useful way that would give him satisfaction in his work and nourish the creative talents with which the Almighty had seen fit to endow him.

I soon retired to my library, there to attend to the many papers concerning the affairs of the diocese which have accumulated during my absence. Poor Madame de R followed me to the very threshold of that room, remorseless in her scolding until I was obliged most unceremoniously to close the door in her face.

It was not very long before I was interrupted by a courier bringing mail from Hautefontaine with the news that the highway police, taking him for a vagrant and beggar, have arrested Jacob, my young hunt servant wanted for the murder of the laundress's hapless child. I have, since leaving Hautefontaine, been not a little haunted by that tragedy.

The miscreant was discovered somewhere in the region of Arras, bedraggled and starving, attempting, no doubt, to make his way to Calais and from thence back to England. His inability properly to converse in the French language soon made him an object of suspicion and now, I fear, all that remains for him is the prospect of the hangman's noose around his neck...

Here the Bishop paused in his reading.

He looked up at the peaceful scene before him; there were a few puffy white clouds in the sky today, butterflies flitted around the salvias whilst the maize in the field beyond rustled gently in the welcome breeze and from somewhere far away could be heard the distinctive *hoop hoop* of a hoopoe. Such an island of peace. An island of peace set in a sea of cruelty. No wonder if men sought comfort in religion.

Naturally the story of the laundress's daughter made the Bishop think of Isabelle. He felt that there ought to be some way of helping to find her, but knew that all he could offer was prayer. He wondered what the Archbishop thought about his servant being hanged and then, with a sudden surge of anger, wished that the same fate might await the young man who had abducted and presumably murdered Isabelle. Much had he seen and experienced during his priesthood, but nothing like the present tragedy had ever touched his family before.

But he had to believe in the possibility of redemption for every human being, be he ne'er so vile, so even this miserable creature must be given a chance to redeem himself, to cleanse himself of his sins before finally being confronted by his Maker. Besides, being a man of moderate leanings, the Bishop had never been one to endorse capital punishment.

As far as eternal punishment was concerned, the Pope had recently abolished Limbo – not exactly a place of punishment, but somewhere to send unbaptised babies. Now it seemed that according to the Church such babies might go straight to heaven – but then again, they might not. Such sophistry was enough to confuse any thinking person. Did the Church now believe that whilst the unrepentant went straight to eternal damnation and everyone else served their time in Purgatory, a few lucky unbaptised babies went directly to heaven to be encompassed by the Everlasting Light that was God – to see God face to face? There to worship Him for eternity? Such simple questions worried the Bishop to such an extent that he could easily understand how mediaeval theologians might have found themselves arguing about the substance of angels.

But it was hardly punishment that really mattered now. What mattered was that the police should apprehend this man who was leaving a trail of murdered girls across the country, all discarded like litter at a picnic, strangled, abandoned, dismissed. A trail that suddenly seemed to stretch right back to the laundress's daughter.

So far the police had come up with very little and the girls' families were left to crawl through the mire of every day, helpless, desperate, terrified, only ever receiving bad news.

The Bishop supposed that just as he prayed for Isabelle and her family, the Archbishop must have prayed for the laundress and her daughter; he may even have prayed for the soul of the hunt servant. Or did he just dismiss the matter from his mind and continue to order extravagant vestments and lavish meals. The Bishop thought not. He closed his eyes and for a moment prayed for the state of the whole world. Further contemplation of the fate of the murdered girls and their families was too painful.

XXIX

Etienne knew he was in trouble. His mood was beginning to swing away from the hyped-up euphoria of self-belief which had sustained him throughout recent weeks as the familiar black clouds of depression gathered ominously around him. He had not wanted to kill that girl. He never meant to kill any girl but what in one man might be mere post-coital melancholy, in him turned to a blinding disgust, a revulsion and hatred of the woman from whom he had taken his pleasure. Then he knew in his mounting anger that there was no alternative but to kill.

The wretched little redhead could hardly have been more than sixteen. A pretty enough little thing who had attracted him strangely by her trusting smile and her earnest belief that he would find a way for her out of the wood. It was all her fault for she certainly ought to have known not to follow him deeper into the forest. She had asked for it and look where it had got her! Indeed look where it had got him!

He had wheeled the bicycle away from the spot where the body lay covered in a mere smattering of dead leaves and where he knew it would soon be found. It was a pity for he was quite happy in the forest and would have liked to stay there a little longer but now the police must be hot on his heels. DNA – his DNA – would soon, beyond reasonable doubt, prove a connection between the girl on the beach and the girl in the forest and now that his van had been recognised and the number registered, he would be apprehended before long and life as he knew it would come to an end. Perhaps he would kill himself first.

He tried to think but the blinding darkness of depression hampered his reason. He felt as though an iron band were being slowly tightened around his head and knew that there was nothing whatsoever he could do to remove it. The self-confident belief in his ability to outwit the police, to lead them a dance, always to triumph, that had sustained him right up until he came across the lost girl meandering hopelessly through the forest had all but dissipated like mist in the morning sun. But there was no sun.

It was all he could do to drop the bicycle casually under a tree before climbing into the van and setting off in the direction of – he knew not where. All he knew was that he must dump the van – and then with what energy he had left find another way out.

It was a while since Etienne had turned to his favourite reading, but now he wondered what his soul-mate, Roqentin, would make of the situation. Roquentin who believed that the past didn't exist. In a way it didn't. It was neither here nor there – the dead were gone, gone in a puff of smoke, to be mourned perhaps but soon forgotten as those who mourned them died. So perhaps he hadn't really killed the girl. Perhaps he hadn't killed the other girl either. Perhaps the police weren't looking for him and the whole drama existed only in his imagination. He wondered again, as he had wondered in the past on occasions when the black mood descended, if he was himself a mere figment of his own imagination.

His hands gripped the steering wheel, turning his knuckles white as a vast wave of nausea engulfed him. Somehow it was the sight of the wheel that made him feel sick – its roundness and blackness, its plasticity. He felt as though it had nothing to do with anything, as though he were sitting in a vacuum, holding this nauseating, pointless object that was in no way connected with the movement of the van which nevertheless moved forward, going nowhere. Or so it seemed to Etienne.

It was night time as the battered, roughly sprayed, black van wound its way through little frequented departmental roads in a vaguely northern direction. Luckily the tank which had been filled at Soissons only a few days earlier was still nearly full but, old banger that it was, the vehicle seemed to drink up fuel at a terrifying rate and although his head was filled with the non-existence of anything outside himself and the pointlessness of everything, Etienne knew that to refill it was to court disaster. It was as though one side of his brain was telling him one thing whilst the other remained practical and reasonable.

All of a sudden he noticed in his driving mirror a pair of headlights rapidly advancing on him from behind, but he had no means of telling what kind of a car was chasing him and could only suppose it to be a police car. Who else would be roaring up this lonely road at this time of night? He put his foot down and the old van rattled as it lurched forward like a tired steeplechaser unable to give that last burst of energy required to finish the race. Etienne cursed out loud and glanced in his mirror to see the offending lights were right on his tail. He could only hope that the narrow road would straighten allowing the unknown driver to prove he was not a policeman, by overtaking and with luck speeding away into the distance.

Gradually the bends in the road became fewer and, as it seemed to Etienne that the road was just wide enough for two cars to pass, he began to drive more slowly, hugging the verge, but, to his dismay, the car behind him slowed down too, keeping a steady twenty metres behind him with its lights on full beam. He did not know for how long or for how many kilometres he crept along, occasionally turning into a side road, with no idea as to where he was going and with the offending headlights always behind him.

Etienne's head was hurting, his heart was pounding. Why was this car so determinedly tailing him? If it was a police car, why had there been no attempt to pull him over? Perhaps, one side of his mind suggested, it existed only in his head like the voices he sometimes heard, but they too could be horribly real. Obliged to listen, he knew they could lead him to do things which at other times would fill him with horror and which when the voices stopped he would regret.

And now the voices were back. Telling him that what he should do was to kill again. To kill. Kill. Kill. Kill…

XXX

Fafa hadn't seen Mathilde for a day or two; in fact not since meeting the Bishop at her house when he had remained quietly and nervously standing in a dark corner of the small kitchen. Mathilde, on the other hand, had been quite voluble, apparently not in the least in awe of her distinguished visitor, giving him the most intimate details of the inconvenience to which her arthritis put her. But, thank the Lord, a miracle had occurred, of that she was in no doubt whatsoever.

The Bishop had appeared strangely at ease with the old woman, sitting at the table with a cup of coffee – although refusing her offer of *marc* – listening to her rather as a kindly doctor might listen until, rising to leave, he took both her arthritic hands in his fine white ones, wrapped his tapering fingers tightly round them, and gave her his blessing. Then turning to shake Fafa's hand, he addressed a few polite words to *le petit curé*, and was gone.

Fafa hung around for a while listening to Mathilde joyfully singing the praises of the Bishop who was not only a true man of God, but *un vrai gentléman* to boot. For once she appeared quite uninterested in her young protégé, so carried away was she by her illustrious visitor and so convinced that he would be able to arrange for the Archbishop's canonisation.

She crossed herself repeatedly and clasped her crooked hands together as if in prayer whilst with tears in her eyes thanking in turn God, the Bishop and the Archbishop, although not necessarily in that order.

Finally she turned to Fafa and with a concerned expression on her face asked him if he was all right and told him to sit down while she fetched something for him to eat. He, like a sulky child, claimed not to be hungry and that in any case he needed to go as he had to see the woman who cleaned the church which was a lie.

Fafa was distraught. How could it be that this passion for the lost girl could induce him to behave so badly? Not only had he taken to neglecting his duty but now he had begun to lie as well. He wondered if he, like the proverbial knight on a white horse that he so little resembled, might set out to find Isabelle and so save her. Might he not succeed where the police had failed? He imagined bringing her triumphantly home and she, in her gratitude, falling in love with him.

His first move was to go back to the canal, to the tow-path where he had seen her disappearing with Etienne. Not that he had any idea what he might find there after all this time. Nor could he imagine how anything he found could possibly help him since it was well known that Etienne was hiding out somewhere in the North of France. But undeterred and unable to concentrate on anything else he spent a whole day wandering up and down by the canal, staring at the ground in the hopes of finding some lost object, something that might be a clue to what had happened. From the bank he gazed into the murky waters of the canal which had already been dragged by the police, hoping not to see a body and, despite the heat, shivered.

He looked up from the water and tried to envisage Etienne and Isabelle as he had seen them that day, walking away from him in the blinding sunshine. He could see the girl's baseball cap worn back to front to shade her neck and felt sick as he remembered for the thousandth time that if she had not worn it like that he would surely have realised that it was she and so could have saved her.

Then he remembered the rope and wondered if the police had bothered to ask themselves why the man had been carrying a coiled rope over his shoulder. After all, if the press reports were right, neither of the dead girls had been strangled with a rope. What could the rope have been for? It had looked very clean, with a blue thread running through it as if it were new.

At the *quincaillerie* Fafa waited impatiently behind a man ordering different sizes of nails and screws, a woman who wanted a new ball cock and another who was just gossiping with one of the salesmen about the weather and how badly the maize crop needed water. The farmers had the sprinklers going all day, but it was never enough.

As he waited in the dim light of the musty old shop he looked around him at piles of plastic buckets crammed one into another, at shining garden tools hanging from the wall and at step-ladders of all sizes propped up in a corner. There was always something appealing about an ironmonger's shop, stuffed with so many different useful things, tempting you to buy a new pair of scissors, a ball of string or a guillotine for a mouse. And there at the back of the shop he suddenly saw a stand on which were displayed reels of nylon rope in various thicknesses. Fafa walked over to the stand and round it. Sure enough there in front of his nose was a large reel of rope, identical, or so it seemed to him, to the one which he had seen Etienne carrying. Of course that rope could have been on sale at any number of ironmonger's throughout the land. But still a shiny white rope with a thread of blue running through it... What if it had been bought here just before Etienne met Isabelle and what significance would there be in that?

Eventually just as the man buying nails and screws was leaving the shop and Fafa was about to take his turn at the counter, the gossiping woman turned to go and spotted the priest.

'*Ah, Monsieur l'Abbé!*' she cried.

Fafa's heart sank as he recognised a woman who was well known in his parish as a trouble stirrer. She rarely came to Mass but, when she did, he noticed that she was always ready to point the finger at others. As he shook her hand and bad her good-day, the shop door opened and an old man with white hair took his place at the counter. Fafa's impatience was mounting especially since he sensed that this woman was likely to waylay him for a while.

What, she wanted to know, was he doing in the town? Had he come specifically to buy something at the ironmonger's and what was it he needed there? She certainly never thought to find Monsieur l'Abbé in the ironmonger's shop – and at such an amusing idea she burst into a peel of laughter... Next she wanted to know what news there was of the missing girl?

She had heard that Monsieur l'Abbé knew her quite well – knew the family too…how were they bearing up? Did he think the girl was dead? She did. And so did her husband who thought the murderer ought to be hanged. Even the guillotine would be too good for people like that…

Fafa was beginning to sweat; the queue at the counter was getting longer and longer as this wretched woman nattered on; in the end he probably waited for nearly a quarter of an hour before finally managing to talk to a salesman.

'*Qu'est-ce que vous voulez, Monsieur?* What do you suppose? So many people come in here every day – how can I remember them all? That rope, we've probably sold metres of it in the last week alone.'

The salesman's thin grey hair flopped over his worried brow as he spoke and his metal-rimmed spectacles appeared to slip further down his narrow nose. He waved his arms around despairingly, flapping the loose sleeves of his brown overall so that they reminded Fafa of the wings of some great predatory bird, and with a weary expression explained that only the other day the police had been in the shop asking about the same wretched rope. What was it with that rope? It was just ordinary nylon rope. Very strong at that.

Fafa was beginning to feel a fool. Even if the man could remember selling the rope to Etienne, how would that help and what would it prove?

'Perhaps,' he ventured, 'one of the other assistants might remember something…'

The salesman shrugged his shoulders. 'You can ask them,' he said, 'but I doubt it, and he looked at Fafa as if to enquire what business it was of his anyway.' When the police came in he had imagined that it was all about the missing girl. But what on earth was up with this *petit monsieur*, suddenly appearing and acting as though he were a detective. In fact he presumed him to be a priest since a customer had been heard to address the skinny young man as Monsieur l'Abbé. There was definitely something peculiar going on.

Mortified and despairing, Fafa left the shop. What had he hoped to achieve other than to draw attention to himself and to make a fool of himself? Out in the street he mopped his brow with his handkerchief and surreptitiously wiped away a tear at the same time. His mind was in a turmoil and he felt desperately in need of help but who could he turn to when all he wanted to talk about was Isabelle? He durst not turn to his confessor; the humiliation would be too great and he would be required, he knew, to pray, to put all evil thoughts out of his mind and to offer his suffering up to the Lord. This he was not yet prepared to do. He wanted to go on sinning, the awareness of which desire in itself only added to his torment.

Neither dared he go to Mathilde whose small house had for so long provided him with a haven. She was a wise old woman and he feared she could read his thoughts, that she might already have done so. Besides he still retained some sense of duty and hated the idea of letting the Church down in the eyes of one such faithful parishioner.

For her part Mathilde, having long since suspected Etienne of a weakness for Isabelle, merely pitied him for it, but then, in a way such a thing was only to be expected, after all, he was just a young man, open, like anyone else to temptation. But she imagined that the poor child's disappearance had confused him and made it so much harder for him to deal with his love – if love it was. She was worried at not having seen him for a couple of days, as if he were hiding something from her which only made her all the more suspicious, but she prayed for him and prayed that he might draw comfort from his own prayers.

'*Eh bien*,' she said out loud to herself as she wrung the neck of a chicken for *Monsieur le Maire*'s Sunday lunch. '*La vie est dure*…hard on us all.'

XXXI

Christiane could no longer feel anything, or so it seemed to her at times. She remembered that there had been a storm at some stage, but now it was hot again, unbearably so. The geraniums in their pots needed watering but she was long past caring about the wretched flowers that she had so lovingly tended until Isabelle went.

She was sitting, as had become her wont, at the kitchen table with a bottle of wine in front of her. She knew she was drinking too much, but she didn't care; at least she hadn't taken up smoking like Claud who seemed to have a permanent cigarette in his hand these days, making the house smell with the smoke lingering like a low cloud in the hot air but she'd given up asking him to go outside every time he lit up. What the hell did it matter if the house stank? She didn't really think they would all suddenly die of cancer. In any case most of the young were already ruining their health with tobacco.

At the far end of the table Agnès was slouched in a chair, chewing a strand of her hair which she held in one hand whilst turning her mobile over and over with the other. She had elected to stay behind with her parents when the others had set off to bicycle along the canal tow-path, taking a picnic lunch. They had all begun to get on her nerves – even Maddy and she was glad that they would soon be going home, leaving her to her own devices.

'You know what, Mum,' she suddenly said, 'I – er – well I did answer Iz's message. I know I wasn't meant to…'

Christiane pricked up her ears and looked sharply at her daughter. Like Agnès, she had been upset by the police asking for the mysterious text which might or might not have come from Isabelle to be ignored. They had some theory that if it were answered it would warn Etienne that they were hot

136

on his heels. It was also considered that if the message did genuinely come from Isabelle and she were still alive it might put her in considerable danger so Agnès had promised her father that she would do as the police wanted but so great was the temptation to contact her sister that after a couple of days she had succumbed and sent a long garbled text to Isabelle's mobile, proclaiming her love and begging her sister to come home. 'No 1s x,' she wrote.

'So?' Christiane raised her eyebrows. Her heart began to pound as she remembered Fayard's warning that a reply might cost Isabelle her life.

At that moment Claud came in from the garden dressed in his bathing trunks with a garishly striped towel round his neck.

'How could you bear to go swimming?' Christiane remarked.

'Anything to pass the time and to escape from this mockery of an existence,' he replied angrily. 'The alternative is to sit and drink all day, waiting for the telephone to ring with more bad news.' He looked at his wife's anguished face and quietly added, 'Sorry.' There was something in her expression which warned him that more bad news might already have been received.

He turned to look at Agnès who, having stopped chewing her hair and fiddling with her mobile, was sitting, white and still as if turned to stone with two large tears trickling down her cheeks.

'What in God's name has happened?'

'Well.' Agnès spoke so quietly it was almost impossible to hear what she was saying. 'My text – she didn't answer...'

Claud and Christiane looked at one another in horror then looked at Agnès, both of them for a moment speechless.

'Why the hell didn't you do what you were told?' Claud suddenly barked. 'After you promised me – you promised...'

He realised he was shaking, shaking from head to foot. 'You knew why, didn't you – why we were asked not to answer…?'

Agnès had collapsed in a sobbing heap.

'It doesn't matter,' Christiane said lamely as though she were talking about a broken plate. 'I don't think it will have made any difference.'

Claud looked from one to the other. He couldn't decide which of the two he most pitied. How in God's name was this hell ever going to end, he asked himself as he pulled out a chair and sat down beside his daughter and placed a hand gently on her heaving shoulder.

'Crying won't help,' he said. And then the telephone rang. The ruddy telephone. It was Fayard to say that he was on his way round to see them. Again he and Christiane looked miserably at one another. Whenever Fayard was on the way they both dreaded the worst. What cataclysmic news was he bearing?

Christiane poured herself another glass of wine and Claud lit a cigarette. They said nothing but the three of them sat there in silence, each immersed in his or her own agony – and waited. With her head still buried in her arms, her hair spread over her shoulders and over the table like a great unruly mop, Agnès had stopped crying.

It wasn't long before the policeman turned up, a purposeful, grim expression on his face. He shook hands all round, declined any form of hospitality, refusing as he so often did even to sit down and began to explain that there had been an important development.

'*Très important*,' he repeated emphatically wagging his right index finger by the side of his square, close-cropped head.

Surely this was not how they were to discover that their daughter was dead. Surely no one with such dreadful news to impart would stand there wagging their finger in that ridiculous fashion…

138

'It's the mobile,' he said.

At the mention of the mobile Claud and Christiane both held their breath whilst, hidden by her hair, Agnès screwed her eyes up tight and clenched both her fists and her jaw.'

'We have found your daughter's mobile,' Fayard continued. 'I cannot at this moment tell you what that means or exactly where it will lead us, but as always we will do our very best to keep you informed.'

The telephone had been unearthed by a police dog scouring the forest where Delphine's body had been found. It lay, more or less hidden by a pile of rotting leaves near where the murdered girl's bicycle had been thrown down and where there was evidence of a vehicle having been recently parked.

'We have of course examined the mobile and taken note of any calls or texts made to or from it.' Fayard sounded clipped and cold. '*Et Mademoiselle,*' he looked down at the top of Agnès's head as one might look at someone's child crying in a supermarket, 'I would warn you that whatever advice the police may give you is given not merely to assist them in their enquiries but also for the sake of your sister's safety.'

Agnès said nothing. She didn't even look up.

'But your sister didn't reply,' Fayard continued, 'because her telephone was no longer in her possession.'

His words hung in the air, their portent striking a chill into all their hearts.

'However, we do not yet know if your message was ever received. Neither do we know if the mobile was lost or deliberately discarded. I myself tend towards the former hypothesis; nevertheless, you must understand that if this man suspects Isabelle of contacting her family, there is no accounting for what he might do. I do not need to warn you that this man is dangerous.' As Fayard who had necessarily hardened himself over the years looked round the kitchen at the stricken faces of the lost girl's parents and glanced down

139

again at her sister's shaggy head, he was suddenly moved by compassion. 'We still hope to find her alive,' he said.

All three wondered if he meant it.

XXXII

Etienne's van was discovered a day later by some children bathing in a river. Abandoned and empty of his few possessions, it was found half submerged in water behind an empty house whose garden ran down to the banks of the Oise. The house had been broken into and there was further evidence of an intruder. Someone appeared to have been nosing around in there. The sniffer dogs were quickly put to work but despite the fact that they appeared confused, running round and round in circles, it seemed obvious that Etienne's days on the run were numbered.

Most importantly, although it was half filled with muddy water, the dogs managed to scent the recent presence of Isabelle in the van but they gave no indication of it having at any stage harboured a corpse. Neither was there any scent of Isabelle in the house. The police scratched their heads in puzzlement and began to search the large garden for any signs of a newly dug grave, but found nothing. They decided to drag the river.

So as to confuse the police dogs which he knew would be hot on his trail, Etienne had, with the instinct and cunning of a wild animal, swum down river before crossing to the other bank, but he felt that time was not on his side. His attempt to ditch the van had gone sorely awry. Assuming the river to be much deeper than it was, he had hoped to submerge the vehicle completely so that it would not be found in a hurry since there was no good reason for the police to look for it where it was. As it turned out the dogs would now be able to pick up his scent although he hoped they would be distracted by the fact that he had walked into the village at dead of night. He did not think the police would instantly suppose him to have crossed the river.

The car that had followed him in the night and which he had finally so cleverly shaken off was not a police car. Of that he was convinced; some useless yob with nothing better to do had probably thought it amusing to put the frighteners on him, no doubt sensing from the way he drove that he was on the run. In the end that car had been a blessing since the thrill of the chase had unexpectedly helped to shift Etienne's black mood so that with relief he felt his spirits beginning to soar again.

When in the small hours he came to the edge of a village where a large Swiss-style chalet of a house stood with all its shutters tightly closed and barred, he slowed down and peered closely at it. It had to be empty and he had to be in luck. Just beyond the house he could see by the light of the moon a gateway leading into a rough drive and, on the spur of the moment, he decided to risk it and drive in. This might be somewhere where he could lie low if only for a few hours. Perhaps longer.

He parked his van round the back of the house, locked it and switched off the lights. After a short stroll around the garden he discovered to his amazement that it led down to a wide stretch of a fast flowing river. Nothing could be more convenient. He made his way back to the house and managed to break in relatively easily by forcing a rotting shutter. He soon realised that the house had been recently occupied – there was milk in the fridge as well as a large piece of Cantal cheese to both of which he helped himself. Pots of geraniums and herbs stood on the terrace and some children's bathing suits lay thrown on the back of a garden chair as if waiting for their owners to return at any moment and go for a swim.

He had better not hang around as there was no knowing how soon the family would be back. But he needed somewhere to hide for the moment and – best of all – there was the unexpected bonus of the river to which in the witching hours before dawn he drove the van.

He was convinced that, had it been properly submerged, he would have had plenty of time to make a getaway and this time he would have hastened south, down through Spain and somehow made his way across to Morocco, leaving his murderous trail in his wake. But things had not turned out that way. And he had one huge problem. What was he to do about Isabelle? Lying in the back of the van, with duck tape around her mouth, her hands tied behind her back with shiny white nylon rope through which ran an appealing thread of blue and her ankles bound in the same fashion, she should have sunk with the vehicle, she should be drowned, dead, forgotten – out of the way.

It distressed him to have to kill the beautiful girl who had been his constant delightful companion for so short a while – a while which had come to feel like a lifetime. In fact he had thought that he might not be able to do so, but the way he had chosen to rid himself of the girl who had become an encumbrance in order to save his own skin was the only way possible at the moment since it did not involve his actually doing the deed – or so he argued to himself. Her death was to be merely incidental.

The uncomprehending, fearful expression in her eyes as, looking into his, the reality of his intentions began to dawn on her, had moved him profoundly. But there was nothing else for it – she had to go. To disappear. Alive she was a constant threat to him as well as an inconvenience.

Another thing which troubled Etienne was the loss of Isabelle's telephone. He had searched the van for it, wanting to make sure that it went, along with its owner, to a watery grave. He feared that it must have been dropped at some stage when he was parked in the forest and if, as they surely would, the police were to find it, it would no doubt give them something further to go on as to his whereabouts. It had made him very angry to discover Isabelle, against his specific instructions, sending a message to her sister and in a fit of blind rage he wrenched the mobile from her, twisting her arm painfully as he did so. It was too dangerous to use it now and all he needed was to find somewhere clever to dispose of it. The bottom of the Oise was as good a place as any, but he had not seen the offending article since leaving the forest and feared that it might be lying, easily visible in the grass near where his vehicle had been parked.

After roaming round the village in the dark, Etienne walked back in the moonlight down the sandy path that ran through the garden to the bank of the river, thoroughly satisfied with what he again regarded as his own brilliance. It was a beautiful balmy night with a star-studded sky and, as his mood momentarily soared, it seemed to him as if all was indeed right with the world. That was until he saw the top of the van rising ominously from the dark water.

He had not cared to stand by and watch, expecting on his return to the river bank to see only the rippling surface of the water but even as he now saw the roof of the van, and despite it being only half under water, he imagined Isabelle to have drowned. He had left her lying down and it seemed impossible that she could have struggled to a sitting position, so it was as though he were seeing a ghost when, having heard a strangled groan, he found her, hands and feet still bound, with her head and shoulders sticking out above the water.

He might have killed her there and then. Held her under the water. Held her there until she died, the obstinate bitch. But he found himself unequal to the task; besides it didn't suit him for the police to find her there in the van, so he cut the rope loose, ripped off the duck tape and told her to swim for it. He was a strong swimmer and he warned her that should she try to escape he would have no choice but to hold her under and drown her.

He chortled and asked her if she knew about crocodiles and how they pulled their victims under the water and held them there until their lungs filled with water before storing them in their larders to eat at a later date.

'There's a lot,' he said 'that we can learn from nature.'

So together they swam down river for a few hundred yards until Etienne, deciding that they were out of the village, grabbed Isabelle by the arm and yanked her up the bank. Once on the bank, he took a piece of rope that he had brought with him wound round his waist and tied Isabelle's right wrist to his left one.

Thus they set off through the night, across fields and through copses, manacled painfully to one another with Isabelle daring not to speak whilst Etienne, mad from the adrenaline rushing through his body, marched on, dragging the wretched girl through nettles and brambles, knowing not where he was heading, madly devising means of ridding himself of her tiresome presence.

Since to be seen would unquestionably mean being recognised, Etienne realised that he needed to find a hiding place before dawn broke. They were walking round the edge of a field of recently harvested corn across which in the half-light could be seen the outline of some farm buildings.

'*Dépêche-toi,*' he pulled the weary Isabelle behind him, persistently urging her to hurry.

She, terrified and exhausted, stumbled along as fast as she was able, her damp T-shirt and shorts clinging to her slender body, her ankles and legs running with blood, lacerated by stubble and brambles.

Overhead dark clouds were gathering and far off could be heard a first rumble of thunder. Etienne hoped it would rain and rain heavily. A thorough downpour would wash away any traces of his flight. Then what he needed was to find the perfect place in which to perform what he saw as his final heroic act, and it must be somewhere where he could easily dispose of a body. A suitable resting place for this, the loveliest of lovely girls. Time was against him.

XXXIII

When she heard that Etienne's van had been found with evidence of Isabelle being, until so recently, still alive, Christiane felt a surge of joy which turned almost immediately to a mixture of terror and frantic despair as she began once again to imagine the horror of her daughter's existence since her abduction. Then she was struck by the awful thought that although no body had been found and Isabelle had apparently been in the van only twenty-four hours before, she might yet be dead. Where had she been taken and how had she been taken there? And indeed was she really still alive.

Claud, suddenly full of optimism, would have nothing of it. In fact he had reached a point where he was unable to bear or face up to any more bad news and so argued to himself and to Christiane that if Etienne, the prime suspect in the murder of two other girls, had not yet killed Isabelle, there must be in his twisted mind a very good reason for not having done so and therefore he was unlikely to kill her now. He persuaded himself that it could only be a matter of days before the two were found and darling Isabelle was returned to the bosom of her loving family.

The evening before they heard the news about the van, Claud's sister, Rose, had arrived from Norfolk to accompany the teenagers back home. She'd hired a car at the airport and reached Aigues Nègres in time for a late supper. Maddy fell weeping into her mother's arms. She couldn't wait now to go home although, like the others, she had the feeling that she was abandoning not only Agnès but Isabelle too.

Then, the next day the news came which immediately gave rise to a tremendous amount of hope, excitement, speculation and feverish, restless impatience.

For the most part the teenagers felt like Claud that the nightmare would soon be over. Jake, with his heart still beating for Isabelle, suddenly didn't want to go home with Rose although he knew he had to go back to school and there was no question of his parents letting him stay in France any longer. He, who had been the leader of the gang, retreated into a moody sulk, barely answering when he was spoken to.

As for Ellen, she had had enough of other people's problems. No one thought about her and what it was like for her to lose her best friend and be snubbed by Jake. It had been a horrible summer and now she wanted time to herself to think about how she felt. All the same it was strange to be going home without Isabelle.

In the afternoon Tante Annie and the Bishop turned up bringing a cassoulet Annie had ordered from Mathilde.

'Save you cooking,' she said as she put the large round earthenware dish down on the kitchen table.

Christiane kissed her aunt and thanked her. She had little appetite these days and as for cassoulet – well it was a bit hot for cassoulet, but someone would want to eat it.

'You haven't seen the little *abbé* lately have you?' Annie asked.

'*Pourquoi?*' Christiane wanted to know.

'Well, we stopped at Mathilde's to pick that up,' Annie waved vaguely in the direction of the cassoulet. 'The poor woman's worried to death. He hasn't been to see her for days which is unusual and besides, he's put a notice up in the church to say there won't be a Mass on Saturday evening.'

The Bishop gave a long sigh. '*Et dire que je suis en vacances,*' he said wistfully. 'To think that I'm on holiday and I was hoping to leave the problems of the clergy behind for a while. There have been enough of them recently to last me a lifetime,' he remarked before adding with a wry smile, '*voilà! C'est la vie!*' In a way the little priest's mysterious disappearance provided some light relief after the endless cases of rapacious sex with which he had had to deal over the last few years. He could hardly remember how many priests had come up before him to be questioned about their iniquitous behaviour – how many had been sent to the other end of the country to pursue their activities with impunity elsewhere. This had always made him feel uncomfortable although he understood the need of the Church to protect its own. Lately, having come to believe that the law should deal with such miscreants, just as it should deal with the brute who had abducted Isabelle, he had taken more draconian measures.

'Are you suggesting that the *abbé*'s absence has something to do with Isabelle?' Claud wanted to know. 'I can't see how it could.'

'Nor can I,' said Annie, 'although Mathilde says he hasn't been the same since she disappeared.' She pulled a chair away from the kitchen table and went to sit down, waving a dismissive hand in the direction of the glass and bottle of rosé Claud was holding out towards her.

'*Non, non, non,*' she said, '*l'après-midi – je ne bois jamais…*'

On the other hand, the Bishop, ascetic though he might be, was tempted to accept the occasional afternoon tipple. After all he was on holiday and he was worried. What on earth was he supposed to do about the missing priest and how could he think about him at a time like this when all their thoughts were concentrated on retrieving Isabelle alive as soon as possible? It broke his heart to see the look on Christiane's face, the sunken cheeks, the deadness in her eyes. How could he be expected to think about one little priest who hadn't particularly impressed him on the single occasion of their meeting?

'So what if he's gone and killed himself?'

All heads turned at once to look at Maddy who was leaning over the back of her mother's chair with her arms around her. With dark eyes and turned-up noses, their two round faces side by side looked ridiculously alike.

'What nonsense are you talking?' Claud asked sharply. Like the Bishop, he felt he had other things on his mind and had no time just now for the parish priest.

'It's just,' Maddy spoke slowly as she straightened herself up and stood with her hands still on her mother's shoulders, 'well, it's just something – something about him and Iz…'

'What on earth are you talking about?' Rose turned her head to look piercingly up at her daughter.

'You see the other day – just before Iz went – he was here. Christiane's always asking him to come and swim – no one else wants him… You don't expect to see a priest in a swimming pool…'

'Don't be silly,' Rose reprimanded her daughter, 'just tell us what happened.'

It seemed that sharp little Maddy had noticed Fafa looking at Isabelle as she dived into the pool.

'He just sort of stood there,' she said, 'gawping. It was disgusting. He had like a weird look on his face. Then he left suddenly without saying good-bye to anyone.'

No one could see what any of this had to do with Isabelle's disappearance but nevertheless Maddy had captured their attention.

'Did you mention this to anyone at the time?' Claud wanted to know.

'Only Agnès, but she didn't believe me. Anyway then it was like – you know – Iz and everything happened and I sort of forgot – well until now.' She gave a sly look in the direction of Jake who was slumped silently in a chair in the corner of the kitchen and added, 'Everyone fancies Iz.'

'What is all this about?' Annie barked. 'You children imagine things. That priest, he's a very nice man. I expect he's ill and no one has bothered to go round to the Presbytery and check – poor man!'

Having taken the smallest sip of rosé, the Bishop carefully replaced his glass on the table. 'I don't think the notice in the church said anything about his being sick,' he said. Something about the situation was making him feel anxious. He wasn't sure what to do. He could ask Fafa's confessor if he had seen him but beyond that, there was no one. Fafa had no family and the closest person to him seemed to be Mathilde. If she didn't know what had happened, the Bishop felt sure there must be trouble brewing. How long could they wait before calling in the police or did they, on account of what Maddy had said, need to do so immediately? Yet how could there really be any connection between Isabelle's disappearance and that of the *curé*?

Claud was irritated by the distraction. 'It's all a fuss about nothing,' he said, 'he'll turn up on Sunday and that'll be that.'

'I just wonder,' the Bishop remarked quietly, 'by whose authority he cancelled the Saturday evening Mass.'

'Who gives a damn about that!' Claud snapped.

The Bishop said nothing but merely looked up at Claud over his half-moon glasses and stared hard at him.

Claud apologised but he was at the end of his tether. Why the hell were they going on about this ridiculous little priest when Isabelle was still missing and in danger of her life?

Wanting to hear no more about Fafa, the news of whose disappearance seemed to have given rise to a certain amount of unpleasantness, Tante Annie turned to Christiane.

149

'Have you heard any more from the police?' she asked.

'Not since I spoke to you this morning.'

'We will continue to pray, my child,' the Bishop said, partly to annoy Claud.

XXXIV

A coil of white rope with a blue thread running through it. Fafa could think of nothing else. It obsessed him night and day and he was quite convinced that it had been bought from the shop he had visited in the town, probably from the very shopkeeper who had been so dismissive of him. Besides it had been bought by a man with the single calculated intention of using it to capture and imprison a beautiful girl just as someone might keep an exquisite exotic bird in a tiny cage, having pinioned it first lest it escape. Of course it didn't really matter where the rope came from. What mattered was that Isabelle's captor who had killed and would kill again was in possession of a sinister coil of nylon string.

Fafa remembered Isabelle in her turquoise bathing suit as she was when he saw her that day diving into the pool at Aigues Nègres, and in his mind likened her to a kingfisher. How could anyone bear to imprison a kingfisher? Yet he had to admit that in his fantasy world Isabelle was often imprisoned secretly in the Presbytery – there hidden away for his personal pleasure. Then he tried to pray, but the image of the white rope always intruded on his prayers; then he managed to convince himself that his only path to redemption lay in his finding Isabelle and saving her from the monster who had her trapped. He felt sure that she was still alive, but how on earth was he going to find a girl lost somewhere in France when the police had so far manifestly failed and when the whole country was on the lookout for her and her gaoler?

He knew that he shouldn't have left the village without telling anyone, not even Mathilde, and he knew that he would be in trouble with his superiors for cancelling the Saturday Mass. He also knew that he would not be back to celebrate Mass on Sunday but he was quite incapable of looking into the future and imagining the outcome of such disobedience, so driven was he by the need to find Isabelle and the belief that he would be able to do so. He wondered if perhaps he was going a little mad, but told himself that this was not the case because if he succeeded in his mission it would be because God had guided him, in which case he would regain his faith, thank the Lord and perform with a sincere heart whatever penance was required of him. If he failed, then he might as well lose all faith for God would have failed him.

Sitting opposite him on the train to Paris was an elderly priest whose prominent Adam's apple stuck out uncomfortably over a narrow worn dog collar and in whose rheumy old eyes Fafa detected a weary look of despair – or perhaps defeat. Strangely the old man was reading a tattered copy of *Crime and Punishment* whilst frequently looking up to gaze vacantly out of the window at the scorched countryside as it flashed by. Fafa felt uncomfortable, as though this man who, in any case, appeared not to have noticed him, could somehow tell, despite his T-shirt and leather jacket, that he too was a priest. He half wanted to move to another carriage but the train was crowded and besides he felt curiously mesmerised by his fellow passenger. Would he, Fafa, end up looking like that man? Had that old man lost his faith? Had he spent his life serving a religion in the essential truth of which he had come to doubt? Fafa felt like crying.

At Limoges the old priest closed his book and rose to take a small rucksack from the luggage rack above his head, then, catching Fafa's eye, he nodded in the young man's direction and went to leave the train. From the window Fafa watched him as he walked unsteadily along the platform and disappeared into the crowd. Had he imagined it, or was it possible that the old man had not only nodded, but winked as he left the carriage?

Fafa settled back in his seat and closed his eyes. At Paris he would cross the city and take a train to Soissons for he was convinced that it was somewhere near there that he would eventually find Isabelle. Exactly how he would set about it, he was not yet sure. Once again he tried to pray. The words of the Hail Mary flitted repeatedly through his mind without making any sense. Then because it seemed so much easier, he found himself praying to the old Archbishop who after all was a man of the world and therefore probably more approachable than the Mother of God in whom he had previously trusted so completely. Perhaps in his time the Archbishop too had had his doubts and would more readily understand Fafa in his predicament and so, willingly intercede for him with the Almighty. Perhaps even the Archbishop had fallen hopelessly in love – who knew? Besides Mathilde always urged him to turn to the Archbishop and Mathilde was one of the goodest people he knew, certainly the one with the most unshakeable faith.

Eventually Fafa fell asleep and he slept fitfully all the way to Paris, waking only as the train slid into the Gare de Montparnasse, one minute late. Coming to with a start he couldn't at first think where he was or what he was doing as everyone around him scrambled to their feet and struggled to reach their luggage. Having barely been to Paris before, he was horribly daunted by the crowded platform with everyone rushing with angry faces, madly, blindly in every direction. He didn't know how to find the metro and was in any case frightened of losing himself in it, nor could he see anyone who looked approachable enough to be asked for help. With a wave of self-pity, he wished he was sitting in Mathilde's innocent house eating cassoulet. He wished he was saying his evening Mass in the musty old village church. What on earth had come over him? He began to cry as he wandered aimlessly through the crowds so that large tears rolled down his cheeks, blurring his vision.

For a while he stood still, as if turned to granite, in the midst of the bustling, hurrying, busy crowd in which every individual seemed to be thinking of nothing beyond him or herself. Thinking of Mathilde made him suddenly wonder whether or not he would ever see her again as it suddenly struck him that the punishment for his disobedience might be to be sent to a far off parish in Normandy or the Jura where he would know no one. No one at all.

Coming gradually out of his trance he began to walk slowly down the platform, vaguely looking about him for any indication of where to go; then, deciding that he was hungry he stopped at a bar and bought a baguette before wandering out of the station on to the forecourt where he found a bench on which was sitting a large, blowsy woman with frizzy dyed-red hair. Her ample aged breasts were bursting out of a grubby red T-shirt down the front of which she dropped the ash of a cigarette held between puffy little white fingers. Her black nail varnish was badly chipped. She reminded him sadly of his mother which was partly why Fafa decided to sit down next to her for a while, there to collect his thoughts and eat his baguette. The woman greeted him with a long sideways look, a sly smile and a shrug of her plump shoulders. Her coarse presence was strangely comforting.

'Up from the provinces?' she enquired casually.

How could she tell? As he bit into his baguette he grunted a reluctant acknowledgement.

The woman turned away and drew on her cigarette, which caused her to start coughing a hacking chesty cough. As soon as she stopped coughing she took another drag of her cigarette.

'You remind me of my mother,' Fafa suddenly said.

'Pauv' type!' His companion gave a rich throaty laugh. Poor sod indeed, but where was he going and what was he doing in Paris?

All of a sudden Fafa found himself confiding in this woman whose name, she said, was Pierrette. He didn't tell her that he was a priest but he told her — he wasn't quite sure why — about his childhood, which unhappy story found an echo in her; he told her that he had never been in love before but that now he had fallen for the most beautiful girl in the world and that this girl had run away with another man who, Fafa thought, was keeping her against her will. He didn't say that the girl in question was the one whose picture had been in all the papers and who was in the hands of a serial killer for whom the whole country was on the lookout.

Pierrette looked at Fafa with pity. What an innocent — and at his age too. She offered him a cigarette which, after a moment's hesitation, he refused. He hadn't smoked a cigarette since he was twelve years old and hadn't much liked it then, yet he was tempted. Now that everything had gone wrong, nothing seemed to have any meaning. Nothing really mattered except for Isabelle. Isabelle whom he must find.

Glancing shyly up at Pierrette's raddled painted face, he asked, 'What do you think I should do? After all you are a woman of the world — perhaps you could advise me...'

She gave another throaty laugh which only gave rise to a further fit of coughing. Eventually, gulping, she collected herself and said, 'Go home young man. Go back to where you came from and forget the girl. You'll find another.'

At which point Fafa was about to admit to being a priest, but instead he merely said, 'Thank you,' put out his hand to shake Pierrette's and rose to go. He had to get across Paris and couldn't waste any more time. 'May God bless you,' he said to her surprise as he walked away.

Funny fellow, she thought, as gazing absently at his retreating figure she lit another cigarette.

XXXV

As the painful light of dawn was slowly breaking over the fields and forests of northern France, Etienne, with Isabelle still tied to his wrist, stumbled into a great barn situated alongside a pair of smaller ones, to the back of an apparently lonely farmhouse. There was a tractor in the barn and at the far end, beside a wooden home-made ladder which led to an upper floor, in a stall partitioned off from the rest of the barn with metal hurdles tied together with rope, was a large Charollais bull. The bull gazed lazily at the two intruders, its breath steamy in the cold morning air before turning its back and continuing to munch at a pile of hay.

It seemed to Etienne that, as things were, he had no alternative but to stay in this barn and hope not to be discovered. A dog had briefly barked in the farmyard and as he rapidly untied the rope round his and Isabelle's wrist and pushed her forward with instructions to get up the ladder, he heard a cock crow.

The tractor could easily be moved without anyone needing to climb to the upper floor, but the unexpected presence of the bull was quite another thing. What if it needed to be fed with hay stored in the loft? Etienne didn't fancy the idea of an angry farmer with a pitchfork handing him over to the police.

He followed Isabelle up the ladder, looked around him to discover, as he had half expected, that the space was used for storing hay of which there was a considerable amount. Taking Isabelle roughly by the arm he dragged her over the bales to the furthest corner of the building and shoved her down into a gap between two of them then sat down beside her. He needed to find another suitable hiding place for himself, but first of all he needed to put the frighteners on the girl so as to make sure that she kept quiet if anyone came into the barn.

'If you so much as squeak,' he told her, 'you're done for. I no longer need you and if there's any trouble I can and will silence you in an instant.' He put his hands gently around her neck and in the distance a cock crew again – a high-pitched *cocorico – cocorico* – joyfully announcing the arrival of another day. Isabelle shuddered and shrank deeper into her hole between the bales. Why? She asked herself, why am I so enslaved? And she shuddered again.

Etienne looked at her. She was a very very pretty girl. He wondered about sex with her. He hadn't touched her yet and he knew that if he did he would be obliged, as was his way, immediately to strangle her and he had no intention of leaving her dead body to be discovered in this loft. Besides he had never taken Isabelle for the purposes of sex. She was an idol, a Madonna, a perfectly pure ideal woman to be cherished and adored. It was a shame that he was going to have to kill her; perhaps when the time came it would make it easier if he had sex with her, thereby making a whore of her and reducing her to the level of most women.

If they were to continue to be on the run they needed strength and at present they had neither food nor water although Etienne had noticed an outside tap by the barn door. He wondered if he dared go down and look for a container – any old jar or tin – which they could use for a drink but he was aware that farmers rose early and besides he didn't want to leave Isabelle alone for an instant. He hoped she wouldn't be able to escape since he had taken the precaution of tying her wrists together and without the use of her hands she would have difficulty in negotiating the ladder. Unfortunately he no longer had enough rope to tie her feet too. In fact he had very little of anything. He was hungry, very thirsty and at the mercy of his wits though due to the adrenalin coursing through his body and the persistent upward swing of his mood, he was strangely untired. Isabelle he hoped would soon fall asleep jammed down as she was between the bales.

Through all the long night, ever since Etienne had pulled her out of his half-submerged van, while she swam beside him in the river and was dragged, stumbling through fields and copses, over hedges and over ditches, until she was forced up the rickety ladder and pushed down among the bales, Isabelle had not spoken one word. She was concentrating on keeping alive and for the time being she thought that the best way of surviving was to do precisely what Etienne told her. She loved him and, not knowing that since she had been with him he had killed two girls, she clung to the hope that his threats were empty, designed merely to keep her quiet. In some peculiar way shock had obliterated the realisation that he had already surely tried to drown her.

Her clothes were damp; she was hungry, thirsty, cold and exhausted but still alert enough to be perpetually on the look-out for a means of escape. She thought that if she pretended to fall asleep, crushed uncomfortably as she was among the bales, Etienne might risk leaving her in order to find food and drink since it was clear they could go no further without some kind of sustenance. Perhaps he would then be caught and she be found or perhaps she would be able to struggle out of her hiding place and somehow, despite the wretched rope around her wrists, get down the ladder. That hardly seemed impossible.

And yet with one part of her mind she feared escaping almost as much as she feared staying with Etienne. She had grown so fond of him over the weeks and until now had somehow seen him as her protector who cared for her and loved her. He hadn't touched her except to tie her up and cover her with an old coat whenever he left the van which he always explained was for her own good. She was afraid that without her to protect him he would be taken away by the police and sent to prison. She didn't want that for him. She had gone away with him willingly – why should he be punished?

In her confused state of mind, she had forgotten the moment when, shortly after first getting into the van, she had realised that Etienne was not going to drive her home but was heading in the opposite direction back towards Toulouse. She had forgotten the fear that gripped her then. She had forgotten that earlier, when she and Etienne were walking by the canal, she had caught sight of the parish priest. She hadn't wanted to see him and hoped he hadn't seen her. She had forgotten too, how later she had rued the fact that she had not called out to him, how she had cried and longed for the comforting security of Aigues Nègres, of her boring old parents, of her younger sister and her infuriating little cousin, Maddy. Then she would have given anything to have been back with Ellen and Jake and Sam, with everything being as ordinary and dull as possible. She had thought herself so clever going off to meet Etienne who seemed such a nice kind, straightforward guy, clever and grown-up.

On the way back to Toulouse, terrified of being raped and murdered, she had thought of nothing but escape but the van was centrally locked and she had no means of jumping

158

from it. Now she would be quite unable to explain exactly how or why or when her feelings had changed, but they had, and although he threatened to kill her, from which threat she needed to escape, she was mesmerised by him and wished him no harm. On the contrary, she knew she would lie to defend him. Surely he loved her too, if not why had he taken her away and why had he looked after her so carefully until now? She remembered being surprised and angry, yet strangely touched by a bag of soggy steak and chips which he had brought her on that first – or second – day. She hadn't been able to understand then why he wouldn't let her come to the restaurant with him. Now it all seemed oddly normal. In so short a time her life had been turned upside down and she had come to accept it. Her family had received text messages to the effect that she was all right so she supposed they ought not to be too worried.

Occasionally her mind went into a different gear and then she longed to escape, to go home, she cried for her parents and for what she had done to them, she wept over her own folly and prayed as she had never prayed before. She swore to God that she would never trust her own judgement again if only He would save her. Then Etienne would look at her and all at once she would be in thrall to him again.

'Try to go to sleep,' Etienne told her. 'We won't be able to stay here for long and you'll need to keep up with me.'

He lay down beside her and she closed her eyes but despite her weariness she felt restless and knew she wouldn't be able to sleep. Occasional sounds from the farmyard indicating that the outside world was waking up made her feel jumpy and she sensed Etienne's body tensing beside her. A man's voice shouted angrily at a dog; then a little further off a woman's voice called to the man.

The man shouted back something about a market and then children were heard yelling and laughing.

After a while there was a slamming of car doors, an engine started and a vehicle could be heard driving away; then everything was quiet again. Etienne began to think of going to look for water. If the whole family had gone to the market he might even have a chance of stealing into the house and finding something to eat. For a little while he lay still, listening. He could hear the bull moving around in its pen below but nothing else so he stood up and was about to move towards the ladder when he suddenly heard children's voices. They were quite near. In the barn beneath him.

There was a clanking noise as if the children who were laughing might be climbing on the hurdles enclosing the bull which suddenly bellowed causing a child to shriek.

'*On y va,*' a small voice piped.

There was more clanking followed by a noise as if someone were climbing the ladder.

'Come on,' the same small voice.

'*On n'a pas l'droit…*' an even smaller voice.

'No one will know unless you tell…come on…' And up they came.

XXXVI

Having been left in the village while Annie went on to Aigues Nègres, the Bishop paid an unexpected call on Mathilde. He was both worried and extremely annoyed by the little priest's disappearance and needed to find out all he could about him before taking any drastic steps. He didn't want another scandal for the Church, however minor, and he was sure that if Fafa's disappearance was reported to the police, it would be in the hands of the press in no time with the very fact that he came from the same parish as the missing girl only adding to the malicious rumour and wild speculation that already abounded.

Possibly Fafa had left some clue, however indirect, as to the reason for his absence which, if he didn't return sharpish, would affect not only this parish but the five other parishes that it was his duty to visit in turn. The Bishop felt that if he reappeared in the next day or two with anything faintly resembling a reasonable excuse, his misdemeanour could be covered up and everything would be able to go on as normal. But if not, then that would probably mean losing yet one more French priest.

The Church in France was in a parlous state with many old buildings standing empty while the number of young Frenchmen wishing to enter the priesthood had dwindled to almost nothing over the last decade so that where France had been wont to send men out to the ministry in India and Africa, it was now to Burkina Faso and the Congo that the Church turned to service its own European parishes.

The Bishop was reminded of more than one African priest in his own diocese who despaired, not so much of the climate, as of the emptiness of the churches, of congregations consisting in a handful of grey-haired old women with one or two bent old men thrown in. They missed the warmth, enthusiasm and hearty singing of the faithful flock back home. And home they no doubt longed to go.

For all the recent advertising campaigns designed to tempt young men into the celibate life of the Church, nothing much had changed. And now here was this silly young man abandoning his duty and causing everyone unnecessary trouble by taking it into his head to disappear. A man who, so far as the Bishop could see, had given absolutely no cause for complaint to any of his parishioners until now.

The weather was still hot although not nearly so hot as it had been, nor anything like so unbearable. When the Bishop arrived Mathilde was picking tomatoes in her garden across the road. She heard Annie's car draw up but by the time she

161

had hobbled back to her house, Annie had gone and there was the Bishop standing by her door, gazing rather helplessly at the bead curtain.

'*Ah Monseigneur...*' Mathilde almost dropped the corners of her apron in which she was carrying her tomatoes, so surprised and agitated was she by the sight of her unexpected visitor.

But the Bishop soon put her at her ease and as she poured him a cup of bitter, thrice-brewed coffee, curious as to the reason for his unannounced arrival, she began to tell him how worried she had been about Fafa, how she prayed for him to return. She prayed to Our Lady and she prayed to the Archbishop in whom she had developed such faith.

'Ah, the Archbishop,' the Bishop muttered half under his breath. It crossed his mind that in those days the Church had been in just such another parlous condition. 'You have great faith in the Archbishop,' he said.

'*Ah oui Monseigneur*,' Mathilde shook her gnarled hands on either side of her head. '*C'est un saint homme*' – a holy man. 'He has prayed for me and now I ask him to intercede for *la petite Isabelle...Monsieur l'Abbé* too,' she assured him, 'was praying to the Archbishop.'

The Bishop kept his council whilst thinking that if the little priest knew what was good for him, he would do well to ask that good-living old so-and-so to guide his feet back home to his parish, to Mathilde and his sadly diminishing flock.

'Did he,' the Bishop asked, 'ever give you any cause to suspect that he might suddenly go away? Did he say what was worrying him? Did he ever express his doubts or give the slightest hint – which you might have missed at the time – as to his destination?'

He was drawing a blank. Mathilde felt as protective of Fafa as she would have done of her own son and so hesitated to say what she really thought which was that, having fallen for Isabelle, Fafa had become unbalanced. That, she supposed, might get him into terrible trouble with the Bishop so she merely said that he had been upset by the girl's disappearance. But then so had everyone else. She assured him that the woman who looked after the church and the Presbytery knew nothing more since she hadn't even spoken to Monsieur l'Abbé for several days before he left.

The Bishop, with his elbow on the table, rubbed his tapering fingers across his furrowed brow before looking up over his spectacles to refuse a second cup of sour coffee. Feeling that there was no more to be said, he rose to go and was about to say good-bye to Mathilde when someone suddenly called her from the road.

'*Madame Mathilde...*' There was a rattling of the bead curtain and a postman poked his head into the kitchen. '*Madame Mathilde – le courrier...*you have a postcard...'

The fact that Mathilde rarely received any post might have explained the excitement, although it did occur to the Bishop that the postman's behaviour was rather odd. But then such behaviour was perhaps normal in the lost corners of France where everyone knew everyone else's business. Mathilde took a card from the postman's outstretched hand and without looking at it, put it on her kitchen table whilst the postman, instead of turning to go, hovered round the doorway, apparently trying to think of something to say whilst looking past the Bishop at the old lady in her kitchen.

He mentioned the weather, then, more boldly, the lost girl. Had anything further been heard about her? He knew that Mathilde was connected to the family – and what a terrible thing it was to be sure. The man who had abducted her deserved the guillotine. Nothing less.

The Bishop who planned to walk the couple of kilometres up the hill to Aigues Nègres wanted to leave but somehow felt that he had to see the postman off first. What on earth was the wretched man going on about, standing there gabbling, thrusting his head into the house, with the engine of his van ticking over all the time in the background?

'And perhaps you know,' the postman addressed the Bishop, little realising that he was talking to a prince of the Church, 'that *Monsieur le curé* has disappeared too. I don't suppose that he's been abducted though,' he gave a vulgar laugh. '*Eh bien*,' he said, hesitantly shifting from foot to foot, 'I suppose I'd better be on my way.' Then as he turned reluctantly back towards his van, 'I don't know what the world's coming to with all these people going missing?'

As he finally drove off and the Bishop was once more going to take his leave, Mathilde, having picked up the postcard in one hand whilst shaking the other in the air, said with a sigh, 'That postman – it's always the same – he knows everybody's business. He will have read this card…' She waved the card unceremoniously in front of the Bishop's face.

'It's from him,' she said, 'from *Monsieur l'Abbé…tenez…*' and with a trembling hand she held the card out for him to take.

'What on earth is he doing in Soissons?' the Bishop exclaimed as he looked down at a crudely-coloured photograph of the cathedral in that town. 'And how did he get there?' Feeling that she must know more than she claimed, he pressed Mathilde for further information, but she, poor woman, was nearly in tears and, as she assured him, could tell him nothing more.

It had escaped the notice of neither of them that Soissons was the town in which Etienne had last been seen and around which the search for Isabelle had centred until the discovery of the van in the river not so many miles from there.

Scrawled in an immature hand, the message on the back of the postcard merely read, 'Pray for me. May God bless you, Fafa.'

XXXVII

Claud was furious when he heard about the priest. What the hell, he wanted to know, did that little idiot think he was doing by muddying the waters and drawing attention to himself? It was hardly surprising if the wildest and most improbable rumours were already being spread about Fafa's relationship to Isabelle and her family.

The Bishop too was appalled but since no one knew anything about *le petit abbé*'s movements beyond the fact that he had been sending postcards from Soissons a day or two earlier, he had no idea what to do apart from contacting priests in that part of France, which he could do easily enough through the Church network. There was no point in involving the police who would undoubtedly point out that Fafa was an adult man and it was no concern of theirs where he did or did not choose to go. Indeed there was nothing – outside his duty to the Church – to stop Fafa from going wherever he pleased.

Every day that dawned Christiane wondered how much more she could bear; for her Fafa's disappearance and the discovery that he was on Isabelle's trail was no more than a mild distraction. Maddy, she decided, was a sharp little thing and clever to have noticed the priest's attraction to Isabelle – but what did it change? Nothing.

Fayard was back and forth every day, trying to reassure the family that everything possible was being done to solve the crime. Nearer and nearer were they to discovering Etienne's whereabouts; he would not escape them for long now and once the police found him, they would find Isabelle.

Listening to the man, Christiane felt sick. Was he inferring that Etienne, when arrested, would immediately admit to killing her daughter and that he would kindly show them where he had dumped her poor body, or did Fayard really believe

165

that Isabelle was still alive? She dared not ask and neither did it seem that Fayard dared say. To be realistic, no one had any idea whether or not the poor child was dead. In their private thoughts they each and every one wavered constantly.

It had seemed a relief when Rose arrived to take the teenagers back home but once they had gone, Christiane thought she might miss them. Feeding them and shopping for them had given her something to do but now with only Agnès and Claud, it would be possible to survive on scraps and tins from the cupboard. No one was hungry anyway. As Rose drove away and Christiane turned to go back into the house she loved so much she felt a monstrous emptiness hanging over it. She began to wander from room to room, standing for a while in each and every one and gazing vacantly at the dusty untidiness that had developed over the days and weeks since her daughter went missing. A desolation, like the desolation in all their hearts encompassed the once cheerful, happy house. Outside, the water in the swimming pool had turned green. No one seemed to care.

There had been a question of Agnès going home with her aunt and the other teenagers but Christiane was relieved that she hadn't wanted to go. For Agnès, as for her parents, life had shockingly come to a halt; how could she go back to school without her sister – without even knowing where her sister was, or if she were alive. Nothing in the future counted. Only the dreadful present. Her parents were fully aware of the fact that at some time, whatever the outcome of this hateful summer, she would have to go back to school and get on with her life, just as they would have to go back to work to earn a living. But at the moment they could look no further than the morrow on which day, they continued to pin their hopes; the day on which their beloved daughter would surely walk through the door. Then, just as when Persephone returned from the underworld, the flowers would bloom again.

Maddy had departed in tears, clinging first to Agnès in despair at leaving her and then to her mother, in despair at the awfulness of everything, incredulous at the world's wickedness, unable to comprehend how her happy life had suddenly been turned to dust. Overwhelmed by the quintessential loneliness of childhood, she no longer knew what to think, what to say or what to feel.

As for the others, they were all equally lost. On kissing Christiane good-bye and trying to thank her for having him to stay, Jake was unable to control the tears that streamed down his cheeks and when he opened his mouth to speak, his voice was almost too faint to be heard.

Christiane hugged him, tousled his hair and thanked him for being such a kind and helpful fellow.

'Try not to worry,' she said fatuously. 'I have a feeling that we'll have her back very soon now.' As she spoke, she believed what she was saying but as soon as the words were out of her mouth, she wondered how she had dared to utter them.

As they all climbed into the rented Renault Espace, with Rose asking the teenagers if they had forgotten anything and whether or not they were all sure that they had their passports, Christiane suddenly felt like screaming. This was such a mockery of all their previous summers. How could she merrily say, 'Don't worry, we can bring anything you have left behind' – or, 'See you soon – lovely having you'? How could anything normal ever happen or be said again when it was Isabelle not a sponge bag or a mobile who was left behind?

So the Renault bumped its way down the track towards the road leaving the three of them, together and alone, each locked in his or her own wretchedness.

Agnès, stunned by her misery, wandered away from her parents to the far end of the garden and went to sit by the algae-green pool. At this moment she hated her mother and father, both of whom she deemed to be responsible in some way for the whole horrible summer. She hated Ellen too and wished that Maddy had stayed after all even though she had been getting on Agnès's nerves lately by sucking up to Sam and sitting on his knee. She was desolate and utterly alone with the awful burden of knowing that she and the others should have told on Isabelle in the first place. Was it her fault? Was she complicit in her sister's death? The idea was too horrible for contemplation.

In any case, it was really all because of Ellen who wanted Jake to herself – the bitch – Ellen only ever thought about Ellen, about what Ellen wanted and about how interesting and pretty she was when, according to Agnès's present mood, she was hideous with that blob of a nose and, anyway, her eyes were too close together. No wonder Jake didn't fancy her.

Much as she wanted to hold Ellen responsible for what had happened, much as she concentrated on Ellen's failings, she was quite unable to banish the thought of her own guilt, which kept pushing its way back into her mind the way a nightmare from which the sleeper has just woken recurs as its victim slips uneasily back to sleep.

Agnès could hear her father calling her from the house. Was it lunchtime or something? She wasn't hungry. She pretended not to hear. She gazed into the murky waters of the pool and decided that it would serve her parents right if she fell in and drowned. If they had failed to look after Isabelle, how could they deserve another child – they might lose her too in their careless way – not even notice her absence. Her father was an idiot, taking Isabelle to Castel without finding out what she was doing there and then just leaving her – and she – how had she the right to live after what she had done to her sister?

What, she wondered as she continued staring mesmerised into the oily water, would it feel like to drown? Someone had said that it wasn't painful so perhaps – if the water was warm – it was like falling gently asleep wrapped in a swan's down duvet. Asleep and – who knows – dreaming of happier times – floating somewhere in the stratosphere with Isabelle who was probably dead by now anyway. Why did her parents go on insisting that she must be alive and that she would be back any day? Did they know nothing about anything? Life at home with her miserable parents, with her persistent guilt and without Isabelle was unthinkable. Unthinkable. Her father had stopped calling as she locked her hands behind her back and, without a moment's hesitation, fell forward head first into the deep end of the swimming pool. The algae-thick waters closed over her as she sank and, but for their rippling surface, no passer-by would have been aware of a body in the pool.

Standing in the sitting-room, and gazing mournfully out of the window at the mockingly bright sunlit garden, her arms hanging limply by her side Christiane called after Claud, 'Do leave her alone.'

Hearing her voice, but not having caught what she said, Claud came to find his wife.

'I was looking for Agnès,' he said.

'I'd leave her. She probably wants to be alone.'

Claud looked at his watch. 'Wouldn't it be better if she had some lunch?' he said. 'Perhaps we all ought to have something to eat.'

'I can't bear the thought of eating anything,' Christiane said and suddenly began to cry. Sometimes she felt so dead inside that nothing, nothing at all could have moved her to tears, hence there was no knowing at what moment she would ever start to cry, break down and sob or just allow herself to weep silently, her face drenched in tears.

'You need to eat something,' Claud said, putting a tentative arm around her shoulder. He thought there were some vegetables with which he could make some soup. Some comforting soup.

'Soup…' Christiane mumbled through her tears. 'If only there were some comfort…anything…anything we could catch hold of…anything to give us hope…' And with that she buried her face in her hands and still standing there in the middle of the room began to wail in agony.

Claud left the room. He needed to find Agnès and to cry and to make some soup. He blew his nose as he stepped out into the garden wondering why Agnès hadn't come when he called. He didn't agree with Christiane that she should be left on her own. Not just now with her friends having just left.

'Agnès,' he shouted. 'Agnès…' He never knew what gave rise to the note of desperation in his voice, nor what caused him suddenly to break into a run and hurtle across the garden towards the pool.

XXXVIII

Etienne's busy mind began to race, to consider the situation from every angle. He didn't want to kill the children although it might have to come to that; he would prefer to enlist their help, possibly send them to get hold of something to eat, but he needed to go carefully and he needed to be sure that he and Isabelle could make their getaway before the boys had time to tell anyone anything.

Knowing from what he had overheard that they were not supposed to be in the barn, he hoped he might frighten them into silence, and since they were there, he presumed no adults were around. In that respect he already had a hold on them before their tousled heads even appeared over the top of the ladder.

Then two little boys clambered into the loft, one after the other. They did not immediately see either Etienne or Isabelle, the first little boy being occupied in helping his younger brother over the top of the ladder on to the floor, but as Etienne rose languidly to his feet and they heard him cough, the two children jumped visibly and turned to look at the ragged, unshaven man with the funny-coloured hair who stood at the far end of the loft. As they looked, they thought they saw another person's head disappearing suddenly behind a bale.

They knew perfectly well that they were not allowed in the barn with the bull and now, here they were in the forbidden loft with strangers to witnesses their rank disobedience. Confronted by such an unexpected problem, neither of them immediately knew what to say, nor did it occur to either of them that the strangers had no more right to be there than they did; they were far more concerned with the terrifying thought of their father's wrath were he to discover their misdemeanour.

The man walked towards them. There was something vaguely threatening about him which seemed to mesmerise them so that they didn't turn and run.

'Who's supposed to be looking after you?' Etienne wanted to know. 'Where are your parents?'

The older child opened his mouth to speak but the little one broke in first with a peculiarly polite '*Bonjour Monsieur*' then, 'Please, please don't tell on us – we're not allowed...'

The bigger boy pushed his brother aside, telling him to shut up before turning to Etienne and explaining that their parents had gone to the market and would be away until lunchtime and that they were being looked after by Mamie. Their grandmother was very old and cross these days which was one reason why she hardly ever came out of her bedroom and anyway she had arthritis and couldn't walk properly so it took her about an hour to get down the stairs. 'She's like this,' he said, suddenly bending double and pretending to be an old person hobbling about on a stick which made the littler boy stifle a giggle.

He straightened himself up again, remarking in a more serious tone, 'My father says she's *neurasthénique* which means she doesn't like children. I don't think she likes adults much either, but she loves money.'

All of this was music to Etienne's ears. The coast was clear with the boys who couldn't be more than about five and seven years old appearing to present no great problem. As to the *neurasthénique* old woman in the attic, she could go to hell while he manipulated the children into providing him with food, not to mention one or two other things which he had in mind and which might come in handy for his immediate plans.

'This is my girlfriend,' he said, turning to Isabelle and yanking her up roughly by the arm. '*Lève-toi,*' he said rudely.

He had quickly weighed in his mind the pros and cons of allowing the children to see Isabelle. They were too young, he thought, to know anything about the police hunt although they had probably seen something about it on the television, but they surely would not put two and two together. Besides he had a feeling that one or other of them might have seen Isabelle ducking as they came up the ladder which was more likely to make them suspicious. The best thing would be to brazen his way out.

'I'm Jacques,' he said, 'and this is Delphine.' He thought it quite funny to call Isabelle after the girl he'd killed in the forest. 'So you two – what are you called?'

'I'm Georges and he's Paul,' the older boy replied, prodding his little brother in the chest with a grubby forefinger.

Nice looking kids, Etienne thought. They were very alike, standing there in their baggy shorts and T-shirts with their round faces, turned-up noses and thick brown hair, except the smaller one had a humorous look to his face whilst the older one was more solemn, as if he bore great responsibility.

'Shall we go down?' Etienne asked, indicating the top of the ladder.

Most of Isabelle's clothes had dried out which was something, but she was cold, weary, stiff, hungry, nauseous and very very frightened. It still seemed to her that for the time being her only option was to do exactly what Etienne told her to do until something – she knew not what – happened that would allow her to escape. She was not sure that he really meant to carry out his threat to kill her but her gut feeling now was that he did, although, she thought, he loved her.

And she was almost as scared for him as she was for herself. She didn't know why she didn't want him to be caught nor did she know why the idea of never seeing him again horrified her so. He had taken to being brutal and rough, quite unlike the early days when he had treated her with such respect and seemed to care for her, but she presumed it was because he himself must be afraid. When this was over, everything would be all right again, she told herself then immediately wondered what on earth she meant by that.

She thought for a moment about her parents but could face neither the idea of their unhappiness nor of her own guilt.

Etienne was dragging her towards the ladder with the two little boys going ahead. 'Do what I say,' he whispered into her ear, 'or else.' Then, after a pause, 'You wouldn't want me to hurt those kids, now would you?'

She began to shake. 'No,' she whispered, 'please, please not the children…'

Her legs were so weak that she wondered if she would make it down the ladder. When those two children appeared, it had occurred to her that their arrival heralded some kind of denouement… Then when she heard Etienne talking to them, she knew that he was in control and that nothing much had changed. He was clever.

She wished he hadn't yanked her arm so rudely, making her shoulder hurt, but then he had looked down at her with his dark hypnotic eyes and once more she had been overwhelmed by the sweeping, all-encompassing passion that engulfed and possessed her whenever she looked into his eyes. She would for the moment do as she was told.

At the foot of the ladder they all four glanced uneasily at the snorting bull before walking out of the barn into the blinding sunlight. It was a beautiful day, sunny, but not too hot with a light breeze that sent a few puffy clouds like children's drawings scudding across the sky.

There was something ominous, almost sinister about the picture-book farmyard in which they found themselves; a harem of chickens pecked in the dust watched over by a magnificent red and black cockerel whilst large, ugly Muscovy ducks swam on a small pond fringed with lush arum lily leaves. A pair of snow white geese stretching their elegant necks ran hissing their way towards them as they skirted the pond, and headed for the house – a low stone farmhouse with a tiled roof and grey shutters still closed against the summer heat.

A huge German shepherd followed them across the yard, slavering at the mouth and wagging its tail aimlessly.

'He's all right,' Georges said, whacking the dog on the nose with his small hand. 'Papa says he's a useless guard dog...' Then, '*Va-t-en...*' And the dog slunk off.

Etienne smiled. The dog certainly hadn't given Isabelle and him any trouble when they arrived in the night. Which was just as well.

Once they were in the kitchen Etienne, satisfied that he had frightened her into submission, dropped Isabelle's hand which he had been holding tightly ever since they left the barn. He needed now to think of other things.

The two boys were wonderfully malleable, offering bread and cheese and Orangina and apparently quite satisfied with Etienne's explanation as to how he and Isabelle had been obliged to shelter in the barn. He wove some story about running out of petrol, walking for miles and an angry father who refused to get out of bed and come to their rescue.

Georges's solemn little face looked understanding. His father was sometimes very angry too. 'Actually,' he said, 'he'd be furious if he knew we'd been in the barn. Please don't tell him…'

Etienne reassured him that he had no intention of doing so particularly since he planned to be far away by the time the farmer came back from the market.

It wasn't until Etienne began cross-examining the boys about where his father kept his shotgun – all farmers surely have a shotgun – that the mood in the kitchen suddenly changed. Georges was old enough to sense that something was amiss, not that he knew quite what and Isabelle, remembering Etienne's threatening to kill, stiffened with fear and her mouth went dry.

'Etienne,' she whispered.

'*Tais-toi*,' he said. 'Shut up and do what I say.'

Georges wondering why 'Delphine' had called the man Etienne, and why, if she was his girlfriend, he was being so mean to her, said nothing but stood there quite still, his startled eyes open wide. He dared not show 'Jacques' where his father kept his gun.

'It's in the storeroom,' Paul's small voice piped up as he ran to a door on the other side of the kitchen and stretched up to reach the latch. 'In here.'

At the same time there suddenly came a shout from somewhere upstairs, '*Les enfants*…what's going on down there? Come upstairs…*tout de suite*.'

Jesus Christ! He'd forgotten about the grandmother – how long would it really take for her to get down those stairs – or to ring the police – or did he have to kill her too…? In no time Etienne was at the door to the storeroom, pushing Paul to the floor as he rushed past to grab the shotgun which stood conveniently in a corner next to a bag of cartridges that hung from a hook on the whitewashed wall.

Like the madman that he was, he charged back into the kitchen, pointing the gun in every direction just in time to see Isabelle disappearing out of the back door. He stepped over Paul who sat crying on the floor and ran out behind her into the yard. 'Stop or I'll shoot!' he yelled. 'And I'll shoot the children too.'

XXXIX

Poor Fafa didn't know what he was doing, where he was going or what had happened to him. He knew he had sent Mathilde a postcard of the cathedral at Soissons – it was a lovely picture and he hoped that somehow it would stop her worrying about him. The knowledge that she must not only be anxious on his behalf, but disappointed in him too, gnawed at him and made him feel guiltier than anything else. She had after all cared for him, almost mothered him and was without doubt his closest friend in the parish. Now that he had let her down he had no more friends. Not only did he have no more friends but he had nowhere to go, no one it seemed to turn to, and nothing but the prospect of leaving the Church or submitting to its draconian discipline. If he left, what then would become of him? At least the Church could be expected to look after its own.

Everything which had happened in the two days since he left home had become confused in his mind. It seemed to him that some mental aberration had occurred, leading him as though blinded by alcohol or drugs to suppose that he could in any way help to find the missing girl.

How, he wondered, had he got to Soissons and what had he imagined he could achieve there? Why Soissons? He no longer knew. After sleeping rough in doorways all he could vaguely remember was sending that card to Mathilde and sitting weeping in a dark corner of the beautiful cathedral.

Back once more in the cathedral he tried to pray but for some time now prayer had completely eluded him perhaps because, having begun to doubt its efficacy, he no longer really wanted to pray. Soul, when least thou wanst to pray then is the greatest need that thou shouldst pray – the words recalled from childhood, from the old priest who had befriended him then, echoed repeatedly through his mind.

He thought of Isabelle and wondered for the first time how old she was. Was she under age, this girl for whom he had developed so errant a passion? It had never entered his head that he might be falling into the category of all those terrible priests who had brought the Church into such disrepute. And what if she were under age? How did that alter anything? He had only dreamt about her. Perhaps she was only a month under age – or two. How could a few days or a few weeks alter the nature of his sin?

He sat with his head in his hands and thought back to confessions he had heard over the years; he had listened to admissions of greed, vanity, malice, sloth – lust. Presuming that a few Hail Marys and the fact of having confessed would make it easy for the sinner to mend his ways, how simple and straightforward he had found it then to grant absolution. He had never, he now knew, had the faintest understanding of the true nature of temptation, or of its possible compelling force. Poor wretches who returned time after time to admit to adultery, drunkenness, violence, idleness, deceit – how little he had comprehended the dark impulses that drove them on to their own destruction.

But what, Fafa wondered, was he to do now with very little money and nowhere to go? Hearing footsteps and sensing a presence, he looked up to see an elderly man with white hair and a white handlebar moustache approaching with a meaningful look on his face. He was sitting in the south transept under the soaring arches of one of the finest Gothic buildings in France and, as he looked up, a beam of early evening light shining at an angle through the great windows above him, formed a geometric pattern on the floor at his feet. He looked at it, turning away from the approaching man with whom he had no desire to engage in conversation.

'*Excusez-moi, Monsieur*,' the man said, obliging Fafa to look up, 'I am the verger and it's getting late. I have to lock the church.' He had a huge key in one hand and as he spoke he shot his cuff to look at the watch on his left wrist.

Incapable of thinking of anything but his own problems, Fafa gazed blankly up at the verger, as if unable to take in what he was saying.

'Are you all right?' the old man asked, leaning anxiously towards the pale, demented looking young man who he knew had been sitting all day in the cathedral. It was not unusual for him to find strange, lonely men or women taking refuge in the great building – tramps or bag ladies, people with mental problems, broken hearts, guilty consciences – or those who quite simply had nowhere to go.

'Yes – yes…' Fafa eventually replied as he looked into the verger's kindly grey eyes. 'Thank you – I'm all right…' And as he spoke he burst into tears.

That evening the light flooding in through the high Gothic windows had long since faded before the verger finally locked the cathedral and climbed into his ancient yellow *deux-chevaux* to drive at his usual forty kilometres an hour to the bungalow on the outskirts of the town to which with his dear late wife he had retired some years earlier.

Beside him in the car sat Fafa who had found himself on the spur of the moment telling Monsieur Duval everything about Isabelle and her family, about how he, a priest, had lost his senses, lost his faith, lost his judgement, lost his self-respect, probably lost his job. He told him about Mathilde who had always been kind to him and how he had let her down, let everyone down, let the Church down, let himself down and now, having run off on this mad wild goose chase – for how could he have ever hoped to find Isabelle – he had no one to turn to and nowhere to go.

Duval, the old verger, not doubting Fafa's story for an instant, took pity on him; he saw him as a weeping lost soul who at the moment needed nothing so urgently as he needed a good meal and a bed to sleep in so, with that in mind, he decided to take the poor fellow home, to feed him and put him up for the night. The next day they would talk again and then when he was feeling stronger, Fafa might be persuaded to seek out a priest, go to confession, return home and find his own confessor.

Over the years Duval, who had once owned a modest restaurant behind the cathedral, had with his kindly face and gentle manner attracted many confidences from the desperate and the down-at-heart – alcoholics weeping into their soup and solitary diners as well as those he met later, lurking and lonely, seeking solace in the fine church of which he now took care. As they trundled their way through the old town back to Duval's bungalow, Fafa sat in silence, exhausted from having talked so much – for he had done all the talking whilst Duval listened, barely uttering a word.

When Fafa woke the following morning he had no idea where he was. The events of the last few days were still cloudy in his mind but as he gradually became more fully awake, he remembered sitting in a car with an old man who had brought him presumably to this house, fed him and given him wine to drink. Rather nice wine, he seemed to recall, and rather a lot of it.

Once in bed he had immediately sunk into oblivion only to wake with little idea of quite why he had come home with this man or why the man – whose name was Dupont… Dubois…Duval, he thought – had taken an interest in him in the first place. Little by little as he lay in bed staring up at the ceiling with his hands behind his head, the exquisite image of the south transept of the cathedral in which he had sat for so long presented itself to his mind. That beautiful building – Dear God! He withdrew his hands from behind his head, crossed himself and began to pray.

'*Je vous salue Marie pleine de grâce…*' Just as the familiar words began to echo through his brain there was a knock at the door.

'*Bonjour mon ami.*' Coffee it appeared was ready in the kitchen and Duval was just going out – two steps up the road to the baker's shop for a baguette. He'd be back in five minutes.

As he dressed, shaved and automatically prayed, Fafa began to feel a little better. This Monsieur Duval who was so kind to him, who had come to him from nowhere – sent to him in a church by God, or so it seemed – reminded him of Mathilde and of the old priest he had known as a boy. No one else had ever been kind to him in the same way. They had looked after him, not as a duty, but as if they truly minded about him, expressing through their actions what he believed to be the love of God. For the first time in days he sent up a genuine prayer of gratitude to his Maker and instantly felt the wholer for it. Perhaps there was yet hope.

By the time the two men sat down to breakfast Fafa had managed to call more clearly to mind the events of the previous day, of how in the dying light of the vast cathedral he had unburdened his soul to this kind stranger who had not only fed and lodged him, but had shown him no disapproval whatsoever.

'Jesus taught us that man does not live by bread alone,' Duval said as he cut into the fresh baguette, 'that may be so, but to my mind there's no doubt that good food nourishes the soul as well as the body – I learnt that when I had a restaurant.'

Duval was putting no pressure on Fafa. He made no reference to their conversation of the night before nor did he remark on the circumstances of the young man being in his house. Rather, he talked about this and that, about his restaurant, his late wife, his home-made plum jam, the job he had at the cathedral, Gothic architecture, French cooking which in his opinion had gone seriously downhill in recent years. He pointed out of the window to a plum tree in his garden. 'I planted it,' he said, seven years ago. 'It bears wonderful fruit – every year.' He went on and on talking.

Strange, Fafa thought, for one who had said so little the day before. It was rather like listening to the radio; nothing obliged you to concentrate or to reply, but he knew that soon something would have to be said about the situation, some decisions would have to be made; Duval was only waiting for him, Fafa, to broach the subject of what to do next.

With a heavy sigh he supposed that ultimately arrangements would somehow be made to send him back to his parish to face the music. Yet he knew that he would have to agree to go. He once more felt the urge to cry as a new wave of despair swept over him.

XL

Naturally Isabelle stopped running. Dead in her tracks. Then she slowly turned to see Etienne not more than ten metres away, framed by the farmhouse door, with the gun pointed straight at her. She had no idea whether or not it was loaded, whether he had found any cartridges and if he had whether he had had time to load the gun, but as she stood there transfixed, she saw him break it and slide a cartridge into each of the two barrels before lifting it, cocking it and aiming it at her face.

'*Etienne*,' she whispered, '*qu'est-ce que tu fais…?* Please put the gun down and let us just go…please…please put the gun down…' As she spoke she instinctively raised her hands in surrender.

From inside the house came a terrific noise of crying and shouting and banging. The old woman must be on her way downstairs. She might well be neurasthenic but from the cursing and swearing that could be heard, she was clearly no coward and, shaken out of her apathy, was on her way to confront the intruders.

Etienne had to think quickly: did he have time to go back into the house and finish them off – all three of them? If he did that would give Isabelle a chance to run in which case the party would be over. He had given false names so could not be identified by the children or for that matter by the grandmother who had not seen either him or Isabelle. He reckoned that his best chance of escape was to grab Isabelle by the arm and make a dash for it, besides it distressed him the way his plans were repeatedly being thwarted – for instance he had not wanted things to happen this way. Had not wanted to leave a bloody trail of children and old women in his wake. It was too messy and would undoubtedly lead to his being swiftly apprehended. He was not yet ready to surrender.

He dropped the barrel of the gun and in a moment had grabbed Isabelle by the arm and was dragging her down the track towards the road. He was growing desperate but he was again on a tremendous high which made him know that he would win through in the end.

With his mind turning faster than ever, he was aware that the old woman would have lost no time in calling the police, but he was also aware of the fact that as they were some way from a town the police would take a while to come; he needed a vehicle and he needed some sort of disguise. He and Isabelle were too well known now not to be easily recognised if they dared show their faces in public. So when, just as they ran out from the farm track into the road, Etienne saw across the *départementale* a tractor with its engine turning and the driver standing behind it, struggling with a gate, his belief in himself grew greater than ever. Beyond the gate, stampeding downhill towards the farmer were a dozen or so frisky, nut-brown bullocks.

It didn't for one instant occur to him that this was an extraordinary piece of luck, rather he considered himself to be entirely and supernaturally responsible for so fortuitous a circumstance, the friskiness of the cattle being merely an extension of his own exuberance. He quickened his pace, dragging Isabelle across the road with him and, just as the farmer turned, having successfully latched the gate, he hit him a reverberating crack on the head with the butt of the gun.

Isabelle let out a sharp gasp as she watched the wretched man fall to the ground.

'*Tais-toi et dépêche-toi,*' Etienne yelled in his exhilaration as he ripped the beret from the farmer's bleeding head and jammed it down over his own multi-coloured hair; then, 'Help me, *salope* – we've no time to lose…' He had begun to unbutton the man's blue overalls and was pulling at one trouser-leg. 'Get the other one,' he screamed.

Isabelle had no idea whether or not the farmer was dead but as she bent over him to do as she was bid a surge of such nausea overwhelmed her so that retching viciously she vomited bile over the man's feet.

'*Salope!*' Etienne shouted again as he struggled to get into the stolen dungarees whilst at the same time pushing her so roughly that she fell across the body on the ground. Then, as a car passed on the lonely road, '*Merde! Les flics!*'

But it wasn't the police; they weren't to get there for some time and whoever it was drove absent-mindedly on, barely aware of a young man and a girl standing by a tractor on the side of the road. What was so unusual about that?

Sitting up on the tractor, dressed in his French blue dungarees, crowned with a blood-stained beret, Etienne felt like a colossus, a man who could do anything, rule the world, conquer China, fly to Mars, break the sound barrier – anything. Behind him in the trailer lay Isabelle. He had ordered her to stay down, hide herself and had in fact seen to it that she was well covered by the empty sacks of animal fodder which happened to be in the truck.

Underneath the pile of sacks Isabelle was shaking, shaking from head to foot so uncontrollably that she thought she would never stop. Nothing in all the time she had been with Etienne had been nearly as awful as this. Too shocked to cry, she still felt sick and, despite the sunny day, horribly cold.

She could only think of the farmer's poor body, lying in a pool of blood, dressed only in underpants and a T-shirt. He was quite young and, if he was dead – was he dead? She didn't know – if he was dead would she be held responsible because she was with Etienne? She didn't know. If someone found him quickly would they be able to save him? She didn't know because she didn't know whether or not he was alive. And if he was, had he been brain-damaged by the blow to his head? She didn't know.

In order to be rid of the horrid image of the bludgeoned farmer she tried to think about her family, her father anxiously pacing up and down, running his fingers through his untidy hair, talking and talking about some boring old

American writer that only he cared about – poor Papa. Then she pictured her mother in the kitchen at Aigues Nègres unpacking the shopping – peaches, melons, saucissons, *pâté de campagne, tarte aux fraises, confit de canard*, camembert, Roquefort, langoustines – it was like the game they used to play on long car journeys when they were little whereby one by one they concocted a list of things they had bought at Harrods' stores. She could see her sister with her long brown legs helping to unpack the cheeses and Jake in the background offering to lend a hand – God – what had she done to them all? She knew that it was hopeless to go on thinking about them as she had done ceaselessly in the early days because doing so had become too painful, so she decided instead to go through the alphabet, counting the names of cheeses – Abbaye – something she couldn't remember what – never mind – brie, camembert, Danish Blue…but still the sight of the bleeding man slumped in the grass by the side of the road forced itself upon her mind and still she shook, and was shaken as the trailer rattled along behind the tractor which Etienne was managing to drive quite fast.

She wondered where they were going, half longing for the police to catch up with them but terrified lest their arrival provoke Etienne into more violence and terrified for her own life. It was unbearable to contemplate her parents receiving the news of her death; until now she had persuaded herself that because of the emails Etienne and she had sent, her family must believe her to be still alive. Besides she had not once feared for her life in the early days when Etienne was so kind, so admiring, so thoughtful, so plausible in his reasons for hiding her in the back of the van with her hands tied whenever he left her alone – but now – what with the daily threats, the gun, the farmer, the little boys – had he really thought of shooting them? She suspected that he had. How she wished he would stop this agonising roller-coaster of a ride, look at her with those dark brown eyes and promise her that it was all a dream, that everything was going to be all right, that the farmer was only bruised, that she could go home to her family, that they would meet again soon… Quite incapable of analysing her own feelings, she sort of didn't want him in prison. Surely it wasn't his fault to be the way he was – all he needed was help – someone to understand him. Again she thought of those brown eyes but this time she saw madness in them as he shouted at her *salope – salope*…and waved a gun in her face. She wished she could talk to him, ask for some explanation, but she dared not raise her head.

Etienne was delighted by the turn of events as he drove his tractor like Jehu past fields of uncut maize, through straggling villages, over bridges and level crossings with the trailer clattering and bumping along behind him. He had never realised quite what a splendid view you had of the countryside from a tractor. He felt like singing but knew that as soon as the farmer's body was discovered the police would be on his trail since it wouldn't be long before someone told them that a tractor was missing. He needed to be careful as to where and how he abandoned it and would probably then need as discreetly as possible to steal another car in order to make his way back to the forest. He had it in mind that having already searched the forest so recently, the police would hardly expect him to go back there so soon.

But for the moment he was blissfully happy, planning the last triumphant act in his fevered mind.

XLI

What the hell had happened? Where the hell was Agnès? As he pounded across the dry brown grass, Claud yelled breathlessly, repeatedly calling his daughter's name, instinctively terrified at the thought of what she might have done. 'Agnès…Agnès…' Then as he reached the swimming pool he suddenly saw her, just as her head surfaced and she, spluttering, choking and flailing about with her arms, went under again.

He had never ever moved so fast as then when he took a flying jump into the pool and in a moment managed to catch hold of his daughter who was by now totally submerged. She thrashed frantically about as he raised her to the surface and struggled to swim with her back to the edge. As he tried to lift her from the water he was horrified by how heavy and cumbersome she seemed – Agnès – his slim little featherweight daughter.

At last he laid her gently down on her front and turned her head to one side in the hopes that she would vomit any water she had swallowed. To his immense relief she almost immediately and with a great heave expelled what seemed like a vast quantity of dirty liquid over the edge of the pool, back into its oily depths and instantly began to cry. Claud noticed that despite the heat she was blue like a small child who has spent too long in the sea.

'Come on,' he said. 'Let's get you back indoors.'

As he lifted her carefully in his arms and started back towards the house he could feel her shaking. She had her hands linked behind his neck and between the crying and shaking she kept apologising, saying she was sorry – so so sorry…

All he knew as he carried her into the kitchen was that he must get her to hospital as quickly as possible. He had little knowledge of first aid but what he did know was that even the slightest drop of water in the lungs could be very dangerous, although since she was conscious and talking, he allowed himself to hope that nothing too serious was the matter – that he had arrived in the nick of time.

In any case it seemed to him extremely unlikely that someone who could swim like Agnès would be able wilfully to drown in a pool since it must be instinctive to swim, to get to the surface, to breathe. She must have known that herself and was probably desperately seeking attention or crying out for help. But how could she do such a thing at a time like this?

Jerked into action by the extraordinary sight of Claud coming through the door bearing a half-drowned Ophelia, Christiane took no time in stripping Agnès of her wet shorts and T-shirt, providing her with dry clothes, wrapping her in a blanket and bundling her into the car.

As they drove to the hospital at break-neck speed Claud suddenly felt a surge of anger.

'What the bloody hell did you think you were doing?' he blurted out furiously as he swerved round a bend and sent the car skidding across the narrow road.

'Claud – for God's sake…' Christiane exclaimed as Agnès, lying on the back seat, burst into a fresh flood of tears.

They were a while at the hospital but when at last she was discharged her lungs having been declared to be in excellent condition, Agnès was dismissed with a weary shrug by a busy impatient nurse, her hair pulled tightly back in a chignon, a permanent frown etched deep between her eyebrows. Mademoiselle should find something better to do than to waste everyone's valuable time – did she not realise that the hospital was for people who were genuinely sick?

As her father hustled her back to the car, she was crying again.

'That woman was horrible,' she said. 'I hate her.'

'She had a point,' Christiane remarked, exhausted.

Like Claud, Christiane's reaction to her daughter's behaviour had suddenly turned to anger although she knew that a cry for help invariably meant that help was needed and it was certainly true that little attention had been given Agnès since her sister disappeared. The teenagers had been left very much to look after one another.

They drove away from the hospital in silence, each absorbed in his or her own angry thoughts, Christiane's wrath suddenly directed away from Agnès on to Isabelle who had not only caused everyone such untold misery but who appeared as well to have broken the bonds that had until now bound the four of them so closely together.

They were passing the village where Annie lived, down in the plain near the canal. Christiane sighed. 'Let's call on Tante Annie,' she suddenly said. The thought of returning to the claustrophobia of Aigues Nègres, just the three of them, all seething with resentment of one another, all waiting for something to happen – something – anything – was unbearable. Besides she had had enough of running the gamut of the press every time she went in or out, with never any good news for or from them.

As they turned into Annie's drive, Agnès took it upon herself to announce, 'If we don't get her back soon, I'll do it again. And next time I'll do it properly. If she's dead, then I want to be dead too…'

Christiane turned on her daughter sitting behind her in the car. 'Shut up!' she yelled. 'Just don't be so stupid…you'll do nothing of the sort.' She knew as she spoke that she was hardly dealing with the problem rationally but how – how could she ever be calm or rational again? How dared Agnès assume so blithely that Isabelle was dead and how dared she want to die – what about her? Did Agnès imagine that she, Christiane, wanted to live if her children were all dead – raped – murdered – disappeared into nowhere?

They drew up in front the dilapidated château and as Christiane and Agnès got out of the car, Claud bent over the steering wheel and buried his head in his arms with a heart-rending groan. Christiane glanced back at him, 'Poor darling,' she said, putting a hand gently on his shoulder before turning to put her other arm round her daughter's shoulders. 'I'm sorry,' she whispered and kissed the child's face then felt Agnès stiffen as she shrugged her way out of her mother's embrace.

Claud climbed out of the car, pulled himself up straight and said, 'We'd better go in and find Annie.'

Annie and the Bishop were in the garden, sitting side by side in a pair of worn old wickerwork armchairs, set uneasily on the bumpy stretch of gravel that served as a terrace. They presented a picture of old-fashioned domestic bliss with the Bishop reading a book whilst she fanned herself idly with a copy of the local newspaper as she gazed across the brown grass to the fields beyond. In the dull heat haze the only bright colour was provided by four shiny green, glazed earthenware flowerpots filled with vermilion geraniums, lush despite the summer's drought. Delighted to be startled out of her reverie and spritely as ever, Annie jumped to her feet to welcome her niece.

The Bishop too stood up as the three of them approached, then hurried off to fetch more dilapidated chairs. Annie announced, 'You poor things…I suppose you must have seen this?' She held the newspaper with which she had been fanning herself out in front of her.

Claud took the paper, glanced at the front page and groaned as his eye was drawn to an article linking the missing girl with the missing priest, even suggesting that the police were now looking into the possibility that the two had run away together, having devised an elaborate plot to mislead everyone into thinking that she had been abducted by a serial killer.

'You'd better not read it,' he said to Christiane as he sat down on one of the Bishop's proffered chairs. 'It would just

190

make you angry. I thought it was only the British press that peddled such rubbish.'

'Who knows how they came up with that idea?' the Bishop wondered. 'None of it will do your little priest any good if he ever turns up. There'll be plenty of people ready to believe such nonsense which will make it impossible for him to hold his head up in the parish. He'll have to be sent somewhere else I'm afraid.'

Christiane didn't care where he went. She'd always quite liked him and been friendly to him, inviting him to an occasional meal and to the swimming pool in the summer but now she'd heard enough of him.

'At least he won't be coming to our pool again.' Agnès who had been sitting silently beside her aunt, twisting the ends of a long strand of hair round and round in her fingers, spoke in a sullen voice.

Annie gave her a sharp look, then, '*Pauvre petite,*' taking one of the child's hands in her own.

'I'm rather more interested in a different cleric at the moment,' the Bishop remarked, turning to Christiane. 'I have to return to my diocese any day now and I have been thinking a good deal about your Archbishop – I rather doubt,' he looked over the top of his spectacles and raised his eyebrows, 'that he is creditably in line for sainthood although I have to admit that I find him an intriguing character. I do hope that you will eventually be able to return to your researches as I should love to read the outcome.'

Christiane looked as though someone had just thrown a bowl of cold water in her face. She felt as if nothing so normal had been said to her for days; certainly no one had mentioned the Archbishop in the context of her work so that she had almost become accustomed to his being no more than a focus for Mathilde's prayers.

'Yes,' she said after a pause, 'yes, I don't know what I'll do. I haven't thought about him at all lately.'

The Bishop was hardly surprised. 'But,' he said, 'I'd be fascinated to know his story – what happened when the Revolution came for instance?'

With Claud having suddenly disappeared to wander on his own round the garden and Annie having taken Agnès into the house to fetch fruit juice and biscuits, Christiane found herself alone with the Bishop.

And now it suddenly felt like an enormous relief to be obliged to make an effort and have a proper conversation which had no bearing on her terrible suffering – no bearing on her lost daughter – no bearing on the fact that her second daughter was threatening suicide and throwing herself into swimming pools. For a little while it was as though she had taken some kind of analgesic which quite obliterated her pain as she found herself telling the Bishop the romantic story of the old Archbishop whose Irish father had fought for James II and come with that King to his court in exile at St Germain-en-Laye. The youngest of ten children, the Archbishop had gone into the Church whilst two of his brothers were killed fighting for the French against the English, one at Fontenoy and one at Laufeld. There was no doubt that he was a worldly man who enjoyed the privileges of wealth and status. He'd been present at Louis XV's deathbed, then with the Revolution had fled the country with his niece who was reputed to be his lover…

At this point, catching the Bishop's eye and thinking that she always addressed him as 'uncle', it crossed Christiane's mind that he must have been quite good-looking in his youth and then, like a teenager, she blushed. Burying her head in her hands and hoping that he hadn't noticed she mumbled on about the Archbishop eventually settling in London, dining with the Prince Regent, refusing to sign Napoleon's

Concordat with the Pope which, apart from anything else abolished his archbishopric, and living off his rich relations.

'I have letters of his,' she said, 'mostly to a nephew…'

'I'd love to have a look at them some time,' the Bishop said. 'It's an interesting story and I hope you will be able to get back to it…'

Christiane looked up to see Claud coming across what passed for grass. He raised his eyebrows at the sight of his wife and the Bishop, leaning towards one another, their heads together, obviously deeply engrossed in conversation.

'What are you two talking about?' he wondered.

The question brought Christiane back with a jolt to the horrible reality of their situation. 'Just the Archbishop,' she said, almost ashamed. 'Oncle Hervé is interested in him,' she added as if making some kind of excuse.

'Not many archbishops like him around today, I suppose…' Claud remarked with a wry smile as he drew up a chair and sat down. 'So what's happened to the others?'

'They've been rather a long time,' Christiane said, wishing that, left alone with her aunt, Agnès might benefit from Annie's kindly understanding wisdom – or was that too much to hope for? Just then the two of them reappeared from the house bearing trays with glasses and fruit juice. Agnès looked a little less sulky than before, her mother thought; someone had listened to her at last.

'Come and see us tomorrow,' Christiane turned to say good-bye to the Bishop, 'and I'll let you have a look at some of those letters. I've got all the photocopies here.'

Supper was an especially gloomy affair at Aigues Nègres that evening.

The three of them sat in silence, playing with a bit of ham and salad, crumbling bread which they didn't eat, each exhausted by the day's emotion, each missing Claud's sister and the departed teenagers, wishing they were still there to help fill the vacuum. Each conscious of a shared misery yet unable to comfort one another, all feeling as though they had been abandoned in some hellish eternal pit.

'I'll give Fayard a call after supper,' Claud said – for something to say.

XLII

My dear nephew,

It is with great pleasure that I have received your generous gift together with your news from Oxfordshire and your kind enquiry after my wellbeing. The untimely demise of Madame de R, my dearest niece and longtime companion has not unnaturally left me sorely bereft. Notwithstanding the bereavement from which I suffer and which I daily offer up to Our Lord, I am happy to be able to confirm that I am comfortably settled at St Pancras where I have many acquaintances among the exiled priests who, like myself, refused to bow to the Corsican's despotism.

In addition I have the blessing of knowing that I am among friends such as yourselves and the Lady J at whose daughter's wedding I was last week invited to officiate, Her Ladyship most kindly describing my discourse on that occasion as both moving and eloquent, for which encomium I was most gratified. The couple departed in a chaise and four and we who remained ate chocolate cake.

My dear Charles, it is with the greatest of pleasure that I now look forward to visiting you at Ditchford and with the greatest satisfaction that I reflect on my brother's good fortune in having married a wealthy wife, heiress to so fine a property. When I recall the troubled impecunious years of your youth, I am more especially gratified that Providence has seen fit to endow you with the inheritance of that property.

Much have I been plagued by those who decried my recognition of Protestant marriage and indeed of Protestant Holy Orders whilst you, my beloved nephew, have fully embraced the Protestant faith with a view to inheriting your dear mother's great wealth which you will in turn be able to pass on to your heirs. As the beneficiary of your constant generosity without which I would be considerably embarrassed, and for which I am most grateful, I am in no position to censure you. Thus I daily pray that the Blessing of the Lord may be upon you and your dear wife.

May the Lord bless and keep you,

Yr ever affectionate uncle,

A.D.

My dear nephew,

I write this in the hope that it finds you and my dear niece, your wife, fully recovered from the ill health that affected you when last you so kindly received me at Ditchford. No doubt this winter's inclement climate was responsible for your malaise thus I trust that you are keeping the fires stoked and yourselves well protected from the icy winds that blow.

It was indeed a very great pleasure for me to spend so long a sojourn in what must be one of the finest houses in the land of which you are privileged to be the guardian. It is with aforethought that I use the word guardian since in this world through which we pass so swiftly, nothing belongs to any of us though some may be blessed for their lifetime, or part thereof, with the guardianship of great possessions.

At Ditchford I am much reminded of my late beloved niece's property in Picardy at which I was so fortunate to pass many a happy month, indeed many a happy year should the sum of all those months be calculated. That property which you yourself well remember I loved as if it were mine own and during the long, dark colourless weeks here in London, a town in which I never thought to end my days, I am often inclined to think of it with a sweet melancholy.

The news they bring from France of the Corsican's *Sacre* is especially distressing to one who was an intimate of the good King Louis XV and of the Daughters of France, one so well regarded at court as I.

195

Here at St Pancras I said a Mass for the good people of Hautefontaine which was well attended by many of the priests who, like myself, were forced by the disgrace of the Civil Constitution of the Clergy to leave their native land. Napoleon's Concordat I fear did little to rectify that situation thus I follow events across the Channel with trepidation, fearing for the future and doubtful of ever returning to that dear country.

I shall grow old and die in this benighted land, but tonight I dine with the Prince of Wales.
May the Lord bless and keep you,
Yr affectionate uncle
A.D.

The Bishop, alone in Annie's gloomy *salon* with his regular evening drink of a thimbleful of *porto* balanced precariously on the arm of the Louis XV *fauteuil* in which he was sitting, let the Archbishop's letters fall and slide slowly from his knee to the parquet floor. He pulled his half-moon spectacles down his aquiline nose, closed his eyes, rubbed his forehead with the tips of his fingers and sighed. This, he thought, is the man – an excellent subject for biography no doubt – whose candidacy for canonisation some people wished him to promote. Mathilde, he decided, would do just as well to pray to Lily of the Mohicans, one of the saints His Holiness the Pope had most recently seen fit to canonise, whose characteristics were to put burning coals between her toes and to refuse nourishment. 'Dear God!' He uttered a silent prayer for the sanity of the Church.

XLIII

Anxiety about his unexpected guest and how best to help him caused the old verger to wake early. He dressed and shaved and prayed, then as he wandered for a while in his small garden, checking the condition of his precious collection of conifers – one blue, one gold, one vivid green – his mind turned back to Fafa. The drought that might have killed the conifers was comparable, he felt, to the spiritual drought from which the young priest was suffering.

Fortunately a different verger was in charge of the cathedral today thus Duval would have time to talk to Fafa, to try to help him to see a way out of his difficulties and perhaps even persuade him to return from whence he came since ultimately there was no reasonable alternative but for him to do so and thus to face up to the consequences of his actions, however disagreeable they might be. But the old man wanted to make the whole process as painless as he could for the younger man.

After breakfast at which Duval had talked so much about this and that, the verger rose to clear the table and, with his back turned to Fafa, casually asked him if he wished to say Mass.

Fafa had neither said Mass nor assisted at it for several days. Unsure of what he wanted to do, unsure of what was going to happen next, of where he was to go or how he was to go there, he didn't answer.

Duval knew that although it was not compulsory, it was advisable for a priest to say Mass every day, but he also knew that no priest should say Mass entirely on his own, thus after a lengthy, heavy silence he suggested that Fafa might like to say a Mass *sine popolo* at which he, Duval, would be present, to serve. Fafa, he felt, could only benefit from prayer which would help to strengthen his resolve. Not that he appeared to have any resolve at the moment.

Not wishing to say Mass under such conditions, Fafa decided to retire to his room – to pray, he both claimed and hoped.

'I do not have to be at the cathedral today,' Duval said, 'so when you are ready I suggest that we go for an outing. I know of a place not far from here which it might interest you to visit. It is very peaceful there so we will take a walk and you will be able to think things through. You are very welcome to stay here another night but after that I fear you will have to make up your mind as to what you intend to do.'

Fafa was halfway out of the room by the time Duval finished speaking but as he closed his bedroom door, he heard the old man call, 'I will prepare a little *sahndweetch* for us both.'

'Do you know the forest?' Duval asked as he and Fafa climbed into the *deux-chevaux*.

Of course not. Fafa had never before been in that part of France but something about the Forêt de Compiègne rang a bell in his head. *Bon Dieu!* Was it not there that the evil creature suspected of having abducted Isabelle had recently killed a girl?

'It is a very beautiful place,' Duval insisted. 'I go there frequently to walk. On such a day as this in late summer with the sun filtering through the foliage, it will be at its best. The trees there are very old – it was a great hunting ground in the days of the *Ancien Régime* you know…'

But – there had recently been this murder – this horrible murder of an innocent young girl…

Despite the fact that Fafa had poured his soul out to Duval the night before, he had never made it clear that the girl to whom he had lost his heart was one and the same as the missing English girl for whom the police had been so anxiously searching during the last few weeks – indeed he had never mentioned her name. He never said that Isabelle had been abducted, merely that she had run away.

Duval assured Fafa that the forest was very large and they would not be walking anywhere near where that terrible event had taken place. An unpleasant atmosphere had always hung over that part of the wood, not least because of the fact

198

that way back in the eighteenth century a laundress's child – a young girl of about sixteen – had been found strangled in the very same place where the body had been found the other day. As an amateur of local history, Duval knew the whole story; how the girl's lover had been arrested on his way back to England from whence he came.

'He was hunt servant,' said Duval, 'to a pleasure-loving old archbishop who kept a pack of hounds to rival the King's.'

So stricken was he by the extraordinary coincidence that was bringing him to within a few kilometres of where Isabelle had been only recently, that Fafa was no more than half listening. He was beginning to think that God had surely guided his footsteps, brought him intentionally to this very place so that here he might find some clue, something overlooked by the police that would lead to the discovery of his loved one. It did not occur to him that the Lord might not presently be of a mind to answer his prayers, but he did think that were he to be instrumental in finding Isabelle, he would, with renewed faith, thank God on bended knee every day for the rest of his life. He wished that, like some medieval potentate, he could be in a position to promise the Almighty that he would build a vast church to His greater glory, if only he could be the agent whereby Isabelle was found alive.

For a while they drove on slowly saying nothing with Duval barely accelerating even on the straight empty road until they finally reached the edge of the forest, where the verger carefully parked his car under the shade of a huge beech tree.

As they walked beneath the ancient forest trees with their heavy canopy of late summer leaves, Duval began to talk quietly and, as he hoped, persuasively, urging Fafa who seemed just now to have retreated into himself, to make up his mind. He might perhaps like to seek the advice of a local priest who could in some way ease his passage home.

Fafa no longer knew where home was or even what the word meant. Since his ordination – and even before – he had thought of the Church as his home but now that he had let the Church down would it, he wondered – could it – welcome him back as a prodigal son?

Eventually Duval fell silent, waiting for Fafa to speak; he sensed the younger man's inner turmoil but could not fully understand why he was unable to make up his mind to do the only sensible thing. It seemed as though he was in some way possessed – clearly the balance of his mind was disturbed and he needed more help than Duval could or should offer. He didn't appear to have committed any very grave sin and the verger was in no doubt that, if only it were given the chance, the Church would come to the rescue of its own and look after Fafa so that within a short time he would probably be relocated to a new parish and the whole sorry episode would be forgotten.

But for the crackling of twigs beneath their feet, the occasional *rendez-moi mes deux sous crou-crou* call of a dove or the sound of a bird fluttering its wings among the branches above them, they had been walking for about half an hour in silence when Fafa suddenly seemed to come out of his trance.

'You spoke of an eighteenth-century archbishop who hunted in this forest,' he suddenly said.

Duval was surprised. Surely the young man had better things to worry about than a rapscallion of a long-dead cleric.

'Indeed I did. He lived not far from here in a château where he entertained the rich and powerful of the day...he was a great figure – the last Archbishop of Narbonne before Napoleon saw fit to abolish that see. He's well known around here and, despite his worldly reputation the locals are quite proud of him. Why do you ask?'

Fafa knew a good deal about the Archbishop to whom Mathilde – dear good Mathilde – had been so ardently praying, in the first place about her health and then of course about Isabelle. She had indeed urged him to beg the Archbishop for his intercession. Perhaps in a more faithful moment he had even done so.

'Truly God does work in mysterious ways,' he announced flatly. Of course he knew that the old prelate's body had been brought back to his former see and reburied in the cathedral there but he never knew of his connection to this part of the country. Even when Duval first mentioned him, it didn't enter his head that the hunting cleric and Mathilde's patron were one and the same man. Mulling things over as they walked, the realisation had suddenly come to him.

Yes, yes, of course Duval had read of the re-interment. It had been reported in all the local papers here; but why was the Archbishop of such importance to Fafa?

Fafa felt himself falling over his words, making little sense as he tried to explain how Mathilde and Isabelle and the Archbishop were somehow all connected with him and with his problem and with his loss of faith, whilst all the time mysteriously wishing to be taken to where the Archbishop had lived in order to pray in the church there. A miracle could occur…the Archbishop might really be a saint. What about Saint Hubert, the patron saint of hunting. How could there be a patron saint of hunting if hunting were a sinful activity?

No one, as far as Duval knew, had claimed that hunting was sinful, although there were some these days who declared it to be cruel and therefore wrong. But, 'Let us go back,' he said. He looked at his watch, 'We will eat our *sahndweetch* in the car and then proceed to Hautefontaine. He was greatly relieved to learn that it was Fafa's intention at last to pray. Tomorrow he felt he would be able confidently to send the young man on his way.

XLIV

Things were going along just as well as Etienne could have wished. He had managed to dump the tractor and trailer about fifty metres away from a petrol station on the edge of a small town just after midday when everyone was indoors having lunch. The only person who might have seen him was a bent old man mumbling to himself and staring at the ground as he shuffled up the street leaning on a stick. It was a risky business but it was his only option and in his present omnipotent mood Etienne was sure that he would succeed.

He ordered Isabelle out of the trailer and with the shotgun under his arm dragged her across the road to the empty forecourt of the garage which he was glad to see hadn't closed for lunch then, looking quickly around, pulled her with him behind a low wall which would hide them from any passers-by.

'Get down,' he said. 'We'll have to wait here for a chance.'

And wait they did, crouching uncomfortably behind the wall.

Isabelle tried to ask what they were doing, where they were going. She tried to tell Etienne that she was frightened. She even tried to tell him that she loved him and that she would never ever give him away if only he would let her go, let her go home to her family. And she did love him when he looked at her with those dark eyes of his, even when he was angry or threatening, even when she was afraid. There was something hypnotic about him. She felt she could never betray him. Never. He was quite unlike anyone she had ever known or imagined. He was as he was and nothing, she supposed, either would or could change him.

She had asked him repeatedly to tell her about his family, his childhood, but all he ever wanted to talk about was philosophy. He talked, she thought, so brilliantly that she could rarely follow the arching tortuous workings of his mind.

As they squatted behind the wall with Isabelle completely in the dark as to what lay ahead, Etienne began to talk and to talk, refusing to answer any of her questions.

He talked about his hero, Sartre's Roquentin, and about how he, Etienne, shared that character's feelings of nausea – how everything he looked at caused him to feel sick, how nothing was real, nothing related to anything else and about how he and Isabelle and the garage were all equally contingent.

Isabelle had no idea what he was talking about but understood that to interrupt him would be to provoke him and so long as he wasn't angry with her she could tell herself that she was happy.

'Our only existence is through our actions,' Etienne was saying, 'and so ingenious and so beautiful is what I plan to do that I will at last be free of this contingency and this nausea…I will exist at last…be seen to be what I am…' He went on and on, only occasionally popping his head briefly over the wall and saying each time 'Not yet.'

The garage was not doing very much business that afternoon. Twice a car drew up for petrol and from behind the wall Etienne watched as the driver disappeared into the office to pay. Then, after they had been waiting for some two or three hours an ordinary battered little Citroën stopped and a woman got out. She put fuel in the car and then, leaving the driver's door open, walked towards the garage.

'Now's our chance – get up.' Etienne pulled Isabelle to her feet and, still clutching the gun, ran with her towards the Citroën. In no time they were in the car, Etienne had started the ignition and they were away.

Isabelle was never able to understand by what peculiar osmosis, what extraordinary intuition or animal instinct,

Etienne had known that that woman had left her key in the ignition.

He laughed as they drove away. 'But,' he said, 'we have to be careful, it won't take the police very long to find us.'

'Where are we going?' she asked.

He laughed again.

He drove with his foot flat down on the accelerator, forcing the little car forward at a speed with which it appeared to be quite unfamiliar. 'The police will be after us in no time,' he said, taking his hand off the wheel to grab Isabelle fiercely and excitedly by the knee.

She looked over her shoulder. The road behind was as empty as the road in front – but where – where were they going?

After a while they reached the edge of the great forest and turned into a ride running through it along which they continued for a kilometre or two before Etienne veered off the track into the undergrowth and drove bumpily, deeper into the wood, weaving between the tree trunks like a crazy pony in a bending race.

Clutching at her seat desperately with both hands until her knuckles turned white, Isabelle said nothing. She dared not speak.

Suddenly, with a horrible jolt, Etienne brought the car to a halt.

'Get out!' he commanded. 'They'll take a while to find the car here – it can't be seen from a helicopter.' He took the gun under one arm and with the other hand clasped Isabelle by the wrist. 'And run,' he shouted with his face pushed right into hers, black eyes flashing.

They ran and ran through the forest, Isabelle weak with exhaustion, hunger and fear being dragged mercilessly in his wake; Etienne fired with the strange energy of a man possessed.

Towards the middle of the afternoon they found themselves coming out of the forest into what appeared to be a small village. Etienne had no idea where they were but seeing the peaceful old-fashioned little hamlet which might have been a set for a film with the spire of the grey stone church dominating a small square, he suddenly felt as though he had reached his final destination. A destination not in the depths of the forest, as he had formerly imagined it would be.

There was no one about. *Pas un chat.* How glorious in his twisted imagination were these dead little hamlets which gave him such an overwhelming feeling of omniscience. As if he were God looking down on his own creation.

They had walked down a track towards the village that lay in a dip wrapped in a cocoon of gently sloping wooded hills until they came out into the square with the church facing them. *Pas un chat,* only an old yellow *deux-chevaux* parked in front of the church and a brown and white mongrel that crossed the square and trotted off down a street of low, grey stone, grey-shuttered houses leading away to the left.

As they looked, the church door opened and an old man stepped out, with behind him another figure just discernable in the shadows. Etienne still holding tight to Isabelle's wrist whipped instantly round and began to pull the wretched girl back up the track towards some ruins they had passed on their way down.

Seeing the two people stepping out of the church, Isabelle glimpsed a chance – a chance of escape – but what then would become of Etienne? She opened her mouth to scream, to cry out for help. But no sound came.

'Bitch,' said Etienne between his teeth as he pulled her back up the hill. He had seen her open her mouth and although she made no sound he slapped his hand across her face, dropping the gun from under his arm as he did so.

'*Merde!*' He stooped to pick it up.

Despite the blow Isabelle once more opened her mouth only to discover that again she had no voice.

This time Etienne didn't notice as he strode purposefully forward, dragging her brutally behind him. Ever careful not to lose it, he still had tied around his waist a length of white nylon rope with a blue thread running through it.

To their right they passed a small old, turreted building whose steps with their elegant wrought-iron balustrade led sideways up to the door. It was clearly empty and, Etienne thought, as he glanced at it, struck by its simple beauty, it would have been a fine place for his grand finale. Only it would be difficult to break in, and then he saw a discreet notice announcing that this was the *Mairie*. He pressed on up the uneven track with Isabelle stumbling at every step behind him.

Etienne had long since realised that he would only be able to kill Isabelle, which was what he had to do, if he raped her first. He loved her for her beauty, as if she were a perfect ornament, so that initially he had had no intention whatsoever of molesting her in any way. She was the ideal woman – Petrarch's Laura, Dante's Beatrice – the one he had been seeking all his life and for her to have sexual contact of any kind with anybody, even himself, was for her to be sullied, degraded, ruined and only if she were sullied, degraded and ruined would he be able to kill her. It was a shame but it had to be.

But the rape, the murder, had both to take place somewhere special because Isabelle was so special. At first he had planned for it to happen in the forest but as they ran beneath the beech trees he had been reminded of the little redhead he had strangled there not so long ago and been disgusted by the thought of Isabelle, the lovely Isabelle, his great love, being treated in the same way as that silly girl. She deserved something better.

As they reached higher ground Etienne's pace slackened. Off to the left a grassy path led between the high half-ruined walls of what must once have been a great house. The roof had fallen in, there was no glass in the remaining windows and the stones were charred and blackened, making it seem that at some time there had been a fire. They walked on through an open space and out through a *porte cochère* that was still in relatively good condition, to find themselves in a surprisingly well-tended garden. Etienne looked round nervously for signs of a human presence but the place seemed to be entirely deserted. He turned back under the *porte cochère* into what had most likely been the stable yard in which he had noticed steps leading down presumably into a cellar of some kind. Here, he thought, no gardener will come.

At the bottom of the broken, moss-encrusted steps Etienne found a rotten-looking old door protected only by a few remaining streaks of blistered grey paint and held shut by a rusty padlock holding an equally rusty chain to a hook driven into the jamb. With one heave of his shoulder against the door, the hook came away from the jamb and Etienne was able to lead Isabelle into the chill dank, vermin-infested cellar that was to be the last place she would know on this earth.

Smelling of mould in the corner of the cellar there lay a heap of rotting hay. Seeing it, Isabelle looked up at Etienne and asked him faintly if she might sit down. He looked back at her with those extraordinary black eyes of his and her head swam as she stumbled across the floor, sank on to the hay and instantly passed out.

Etienne followed her and looking down on her as she lay there, pale, exhausted, sick, hungry, terrified and for the moment unconscious, he leant the gun against the wall and began to untie the rope around his waist.

'You are very beautiful,' he murmured.

XLV

As he came out of the dark little church into the bright sunlight, Fafa blinked. He felt refreshed and more settled than he had since leaving his parish which, he was sure, resulted from the fact that he had at last been able to pray. Something about being in the Archbishop's own church made him feel that he was not only once more in contact with his Maker and with the Archbishop himself, but that he could think calmly about Mathilde and thus consider the reality of his own problems.

He had prayed long and fervently, for himself, for Mathilde, for his parishioners and of course that Isabelle might be safely found. As he prayed he had convinced himself that the Archbishop, for whose intercession he pleaded, could hear him and help him. He felt inspired by Mathilde's faith and her firmly held belief in the sanctity of the old man.

'Thank you for bringing me here,' he said to Duval as still blinking in the sunlight he glanced around him. There appeared to be no one, only a stray dog. Then looking across the square he suddenly saw two figures – a man and a woman, their backs turned, walking away along the track that led uphill out of the village.

There was something profoundly unsettling about the sight of the couple who, as he rubbed his eyes and blinked again in the bright sunlight, disappeared. It was as if he had seen a vision. He kept on blinking. The couple had vanished, there was no longer anyone on the track which continued gently on with, as far as Fafa could see, no turning off to right or to left.

'What's the matter?' Duval wanted to know.

'Did you see two people walking up there?' Fafa pointed across the square.

Duval had seen nothing.

'I must have imagined it then.' But the couple had reminded Fafa horribly of two people he had seen walking away from him along the canal path on the day Isabelle disappeared. He was feeling frail and emotional and his imagination was playing him false. 'Thank you,' he said again, and then, attempting to collect himself, 'it has been a great help.'

Sensing that, after so long on his knees in the church, Fafa had found comfort in prayer, Duval decided that before driving home it would be a good idea to show him round the village. Filling him in on the history of the Archbishop who had had his private reading room in there, he indicated the old building to the right of them on the other side of the square. 'It's the *Mairie* now,' he said, 'but the Archbishop used it as a refuge from the high life of the château where he entertained not only the powerful of the day, but endless impoverished Irish relations who battened on his generosity. He was a very rich man, though both profligate and generous. When he left France at the time of the Revolution, his debts were enormous.

Puzzled by everything he heard about old prelate, the contemplation of whom consoled him so greatly, Fafa asked about the château. How far away was it? Could they see it?

'I'm afraid that only the ruins remain,' said Duval. 'It was burnt down during the Revolution, but it was just up there. We can take a look if you like.'

They walked slowly towards the track up which Fafa had seen the two people disappearing. Suddenly he felt his heart pounding so hard in his chest that he imagined Duval must have heard it. But why? He had an inexplicable sense of foreboding and an urgent need to hasten his step.

Leaving Duval well behind, he reached the grassy path that led to the left between the château's crumbling walls, turned and broke into a sudden run. He stopped to look around him but could see nothing untoward; there was no one about and all he could hear was a cock crowing in the distance, then Duval's measured steps as the old man followed him on to the path and into the old stable yard.

Was he mad? Fafa ran forward through an arch only to be surprised by finding himself in a well-ordered garden, but still there was no one about and still that cock was crowing – ominously, he thought, at this time of day.

He went back to find Duval who was standing looking down some old stone steps that must have led to a cellar.

'Look at that,' said Duval, pointing, as Fafa approached, to the door at the bottom of the steps. 'Someone must have broken in there. It looks as though it's only recently been done. Some *voyou* I suppose…'

Then they both froze.

'There's someone in there,' Fafa whispered. But why – why the fear? Ought they just to go away? Perhaps whoever it was had every right to be there. Perhaps it was only an animal that they heard moving about.

But Fafa, believing he knew not what, yet obsessed by the vision of the couple walking away from him up the hill in the sunshine, was unable to go; instead he was at that moment empowered as never before to shout.

'Isabelle!' he cried. 'Are you there? Isabelle!'

Duval looked round in amazement at Fafa who appeared to have taken leave of his senses.

Then there came again the noise of someone moving around in the cellar.

'*J'arrive*,' Fafa called as with the confidence of one who believes himself to embody the entire French police force. He began to descend the steps, but he came to a sudden halt, paralysed by a voice from behind the rotten door calling out, 'I'm armed. If you move I'll shoot her.'

Turning and looking helplessly at Duval standing above him, Fafa leant slowly back on his heels, holding his arms out on either side of him with his palms facing forward as if to welcome an old friend. 'What,' he whispered, 'what do we do?'

In the drama of the moment, it seemed entirely normal that he, Fafa, should at last have found Isabelle; the extraordinary coincidence of their both being in the same place at this crucial moment meant nothing to him because it was abundantly clear that the saintly Archbishop to whom he and more importantly Mathilde had prayed so earnestly had, with the blessing of the Almighty, guided his footsteps in the right direction. Yet now, at the eleventh hour, they were in very deep trouble. Had the Lord brought him here only that he might be punished by being the ultimate agent of Isabelle's murder?

'We have to call the police,' Duval spoke in a low tone as he pulled his mobile out of his pocket and scrutinised its screen. Then, with a terrible sigh, 'No signal,' he moaned.

'Call the police and I shoot,' came the inevitable threat from the cellar.

Fafa walked slowly backwards up the steps.

'What do you want?' he called down. 'We won't hurt you if you let Isabelle free...'

Etienne cackled. An ugly manic cackle. 'Who are you anyway? And what do you know about Isabelle? She is here with me – she is mine to dispose of as I please – I have a loaded gun pointed at her head. If you don't leave at once, I will have no alternative but to pull the trigger...' Crazy and hysterical he laughed again, and laughed again.

'We'll go,' Duval said calmly, taking Fafa by the arm and leading him away from the steps. 'We must pretend to leave,' he whispered, 'but one of us will stay while the other goes for help...'

Fafa wanted neither to stay nor to go; he dithered, thinking that he could probably run faster than Duval but then Duval would be better able to describe exactly where they were, to direct the police…

Afraid of being responsible for the young man's death Duval pressed Fafa to go – to run – to hurry *pour l'amour de Dieu*. If that lunatic came out of the cellar, thinking that there was no one there to witness his escape, only to find Fafa, he would surely shoot. As it was, a continuous din came from below as Etienne alternately laughed and threatened or boasted fantastically of his own singular powers.

Then as the little priest made up his mind to turn and run to the village, there came a yelping and a yapping as of hounds excitedly picking up a scent and suddenly there appeared round the corner of the half-ruined walls of the old château two huge German Shepherds, both straining at the leash and dragging behind them a pair of burly policemen one of which kept shouting, 'Police, police!'

'Out the light,' the other yelled as he pushed Duval rudely aside and the yelping of the dogs rose to a crescendo that almost drowned the sound of a vehicle and the screech of tyres on the track beyond the walls. There was a banging of car doors and then, as if instructed by some superhuman choreographer, a posse of policemen, pistols at the ready, burst between the walls into the old stable yard.

The dogs continued to whimper and yelp as they attempted to drag their minders down the steps to the cellar.

'He's armed,' Duval said quietly to no one in particular as he stood there, surrounded by the swirling mass of policemen, and then Etienne's voice, reaching fever pitch was heard to cry, 'It is finished!' and as he spoke a gunshot blasted the air. For a moment there was silence. Even the dogs were quiet. Then came the second shot.

XLVI

When Christiane heard the news she began to shake; after all this time of waiting, hoping, dreading, it was almost impossible to take in, to realise that it was all over. Up to a point.

'I have to sit down,' she said turning to Claud and holding out a trembling hand which he, with tears streaming down his cheeks, silently squeezed.

It had all happened so quickly that there had not been time to warn Claud and Christiane that the police were at last closing in on Etienne. After a dazed farmer had been discovered looking for a lost tractor it hadn't taken them long to find the stolen car abandoned in the forest and with the help of the dogs they had then traced him and Isabelle to Hautefontaine where to their amazement and annoyance they had found the priest accompanied by an old man. They had as yet to discover exactly how those two chanced to be where they were.

Before they had begun to comprehend what had happened – or indeed what had been happening throughout Isabelle's absence – they found themselves, with Agnès, bundled into Fayard's car and taken to Toulouse to catch a flight to Paris. Isabelle had been taken there to be questioned and looked after. She needed to see a doctor and a psychologist before she could even see her family. They had the little priest there for questioning as well.

The reunion took place in a faceless room in a faceless building where the family were kept waiting for what seemed like a year until at last the door opened and Isabelle appeared limping, accompanied by a woman police officer. She looked pale and thin and dazed.

Agnès was the first to reach her and the two girls fell into each other's arms only to cling together weeping as their wretched parents tried to join in.

It had been a narrow escape and yet, even when the family finally reached home in England and attempted to carry on with life as if nothing had happened, Isabelle continued to defend Etienne. She had left with him willingly, as she remembered it, and he had never touched her. He had loved her and cared for her and she loved him. She never knew that he was a killer – and as a matter of fact she chose to doubt it. It was not until the end that he frightened her and that, she insisted, was only because he was frightened himself. But, she pleaded, he couldn't help what he had done. He was as he was. She felt that she and she alone understood him so that even though she was terrified when he tied her up in that cellar and told her that he was about to rape her, she could see why. He thought, she convinced herself, that if he raped her he would be able to spare her life.

'He was going to kill you,' Christiane kept saying in the hope that her daughter would begin to come to terms with how things really were.

'In the end he thought he had,' Isabelle said. He'd taken off his clothes and was pounding up and down that cellar in a dreadful state of excitement and when he heard the police outside with all their dogs he fired straight at her. She'd felt the shot whistling past her ear and had lain still as he turned away from her, shouted some last words, she couldn't remember what, placed the barrel of the gun under his chin and fired the second shot. He must have pulled the trigger with his toe.

She went over and over the story, time and time again which was perhaps a good thing, always, whatever anyone said, defending Etienne. He was as he was she kept repeating. 'Just as we all are. Ellen's a spiteful cow, Jake's decent, Maddy's wet, Dad's kind. None of them can help it…Dad doesn't want to abduct and imprison girls,' she added, 'so it's not especially nice of him not to do it. Some people don't want to write boring old theses about dead writers.'

214

Christiane sighed, put an arm round her daughter's shoulder and kissed her gently. 'As long as you are all right,' she said. But who knew what permanent damage the trauma of the last few weeks might have done? At the moment Isabelle was so volatile, so nervy, waking screaming in the night, that she hadn't yet gone back to school. Besides, she might have felt the shot whistling past her head but her leg was badly wounded and would take some time to heal. People, Christiane supposed, couldn't help falling in love with their captors however badly they were treated, but she said nothing, only worried about how long Isabelle's deluded passion would last.

'You know, don't you,' she went on, 'that Mathilde is now more than ever convinced of the Archbishop's sanctity and is furious with Oncle Hervé for telling her that the fact of you having been found in time by Fafa is not something about which he can trouble Rome.' She paused. 'Sometimes I feel that Mathilde has a point.'

'Oh – Mum…' Isabelle groaned. 'That old rogue – you should know better.'

'Well,' Christiane said, 'in the eyes of the Church he should be in the clear. He made a very good death. I've just been reading about it. He confessed his sins and died like a saint. His last words were, "May God's will be done."'

'We all believe what it suits us to believe,' said Isabelle. 'Even Oncle Hervé – bishop or no bishop…suppose it was just a coincidence.'

The door suddenly burst open and Agnès appeared. They were in the kitchen as usual, not the bright, sunny French kitchen but a darker more cluttered one, the central point of the tall Victorian town house in which they mostly lived.

Agnès chucked a bag of school books on to the kitchen table and dropped her coat on the floor.

'It's pouring with rain?' she said. Then, 'Do you know, I've been thinking, one of the best things about what happened this summer is that *Monsieur l'Abbé* won't be hanging around next year.'

Her mother reprimanded her. 'Pick your things up and don't be so unpleasant.' Poor Fafa, strengthened by his renewed faith, he had been sent away to nurse the memory of his love and ponder over miracles in a *maison de repos* for sick priests somewhere in the Jura.

La fin

ACKNOWLEDGEMENTS

My apologies to Arthur-Richard Dillon (1721-1806) Archbishop of Narbonne for the invention of his diaries and for other liberties I may have taken with his life.

I would like to thank my editor, Gavin James Bower, for his enthusiasm, Nathalie Muller for ensuring a lack of solecisms in the French and Richard for his unending support and encouragement.